# A Game of Crones
## PAUL MAGRS

Proudly published by Snowbooks Ltd
ISBN 978-1-913525-12-5
Cover art by Matthew Bright
Typeset by Emma Barnes in LaTeX
British Library Cataloguing in Publication Data.
A catalogue record for this book is available from the British Library.

Read the whole Brenda and Effie Series:
    978-1-911390-61-9 Never the Bride (1)
    978-1-911390-75-6 Something Borrowed (2)
    978-1-911390-76-3 Conjugal Rites (3)
    978-1-913525-05-7 Hell's Belles! (4)
    978-1-913525-07-1 The Bride that Time Forgot (5)
    978-1-913525-10-1 Brenda and Effie Forever! (6)
    978-1-913525-12-5 A Game of Crones (7)

In this new volume of adventures for Brenda and Effie we do battle with vampires and mummies and haunted cats! We uncover the mystery of both Elephant Men and meet Tolstoy the Long-Eared Bat out of Hell! Brenda also gets to go back to her roots with Baron Frankenstein, and we even share an investigation at the Christmas Hotel with the famous Sherlock Holmes.

Whitby has never felt so hectic, and everyone here is very glad to welcome you back..!

# A Game of Crones
## Further Adventures with Brenda and Effie

PAUL MAGRS

snowbooks

# The Days of Brenda and Effie

You have to wait for the right moment to bring characters back to life.

I really believe this.

Sometimes they haunt your subconscious and flicker about at the edge of your vision. Other times they're jumping up and down trying to catch your attention.

But you can't fully do justice to them until the moment is right.

I guess this sounds a bit crazy, doesn't it?

Like the old clichéd idea of a writer's head being filled with all his or her characters dashing about inside. As a child I used to love that portrait of Dickens in his study – have you seen the one? – and there are little puffs of smoke all around him, and characters from his novels can be seen floating around in each one. I thought it was a beautiful image of how writers carry all these people around with them, all the time.

Readers, too. We absorb characters, I think. When they've made a big impact upon us characters get incorporated by their readers and we never forget them. Readers are haunted just as palpably as writers are.

Anyhow, I was going to tell you about being haunted by Brenda and Effie.

These two characters are the mysterious sleuths in my series of six novels set in Whitby, beginning with 'Never the Bride', which I published in 2006 and wrote during the previous year.

But those characters and their town and the things they got up to had been in my head for quite a few years before that.

They'd been there since at least 1998.

Back then I was working at the University of East Anglia, and I was commissioned by Radio 4 to contribute an afternoon Short Story for their famous weekday slot. That week's collection of stories was to be themed around the idea of writers bringing new life to a nineteenth century novel by focusing on a lesser-known background character. I was told that, for example, the marvellous Shena Mackay was writing a tale from the viewpoint of Long John Silver's parrot.

For this, my first radio commission I was a last minute replacement, and I had less than twenty four hours to produce my 2,200 word story (precisely fifteen minutes when performed aloud). So, after a long day on campus I raced home on the bus and practically skipped all the way back to my rented house. I was so excited by the idea. Not least because I knew exactly who I was going to write about.

The Bride of Frankenstein.

Who'd ever done justice to her afterlife before? I meant, the version we read about in the original Mary Shelley novel. She gets constructed in a makeshift lab on a remote Scottish island. The great surgeon Frankenstein is bullied by his first-born monster to make him a mate but, upon seeing what he has done and, horrified at the thought of the possible offspring, Herr Doctor Frankenstein destroys his handiwork at once. He flees into the night, pursued by his monster, and the two leave the poor discombobulated lady behind.

I wanted to tell the tale – in my fifteen minute monologue – of what life had been like for the Bride in the ensuing two hundred years. Like many badly-treated women, she tells us, she had to pick herself up, put herself back together, and simply carry on.

Rushing home that Friday night, on the bus, down the street, letting myself through the front door, I could hear that voice. Homely, pungent, mysterious. I could actually hear her! I knew what Brenda the Bride of Frankenstein actually sounded like.

Actually, at that stage, she wasn't called Brenda. Her name in that first story was Bessie.

Her monologue was written in bursts of text throughout that night, on different bits of paper. I scratched away in pen and ink at the dining room table, sitting up all night with pots of tea turning darker and murkier as the hours passed.

I experimented. I free-associated. I sent myself into a trance. I took all the bits of writing so far and cut them all up into pieces and rearranged the order of paragraphs, sentences and each and every word. I tried to think how Brenda thought – this perplexing, scrambled, stitched-together woman. This creature of shreds and patches. What was her mind like? How did her thought processes flow? How did she reveal her secrets to her audience? How would she yield herself up? Would she tell all? Would she tease us? Would she hold everything back and just drop hints about her incredible, long ago past?

Dawn came up and the story was done.

And she was alive..!

I was very happy with the result, and I think my producer and the BBC were, too.

I remember listening with my partner Jeremy, in our new house, several months later. We had bought our house on Onley Street and were filling it with all our stuff. We had men in doing plastering in the living room on the very day my story was broadcast. They took a break while 'Never the Bride' came on and we all listened – hearing the wonderful tones of actress Joanna Tope reverberating off the empty walls and the bare boards.

So that was Brenda in 1998.

Of course at the time I wondered whether I would tell more stories about Brenda. I'd brought her to life, and her snooty friend, Effie, and plopped them into the spooky town of Whitby. Were they really living in quiet retirement, though? Was this glimpse of Brenda really the first and last we'd see of her – right at the end of all the excitement of her life?

But other stories and other characters came my way instead.

Years went by. I wrote other stuff. I left one job, and left the city. Moved to another and started another job.

Still no Brenda.

Had I forgotten her?

Then in 2005 all of a sudden... I don't know what it was that provoked it.

It was the summer vacation starting. It was our first summer in this house in South Manchester. The lawn at the back was overgrown. I had a deck chair under the magnolia tree. I was sitting out there with a great thick pad of paper and I was writing in chunky black felt tip.

What was I meant to be writing?

My agent at the time had given me a very earnest talk about how I had to think very seriously about what I wrote next. I had to approach it very carefully and check out every stage with her. I had to do something we could all be confident about. Something that would 'break through' this time. Nothing daft. Nothing 'cultish'. Something more mainstream.

Oh dear.

She was clear that I had to ratify my next fictional project with her first. We had to check and double check that it had *legs*. That it was viable. And that it was right for me.

Right. Okay.

I would do that.

Too often in the past, I thought, I had made the silly mistake of writing just what I wanted to. I had followed my own stupid, idiosyncratic nose. I had blundered into writing some of the least commercial or successful novels the world had ever known. Yes, I needed saving from myself and my ridiculous instincts.

Ok.

So what did I do?

I went out into the sun – it was late in May, 2005, and it was the beginning of a lovely long summer in Manchester. I flung myself down into the deck chair under the shade of that tree and I wrote and wrote like a demon. I wrote an entire book synopsis that afternoon in black felt tip. I wrote something like eight thousand words of outline for a novel called 'Never the Bride.'

Somehow, as soon as I was installed in that deck chair, my old ladies of Whitby came back to me. My spooky investigators were going into business!

And it felt supremely naughty, too. I was suddenly writing exactly what I wanted. And it was a very wayward, silly, eccentric novel I had in mind. Not at all the kind of thing my then-agent would have wanted.

But I just couldn't stop myself.

Not from writing that one, or the sequels that followed every year afterwards.

My then-agent despaired, I think.

But at least I was sure. At least I knew what I was doing.

But really, there was no choice in the matter.

I mean it. Even though it sounds crazy.

If you've got the knack of creating great characters – beware.

They will ambush you. Any time, any place. If you ignore them they won't go away. They'll wait years. Even when your agent that wants you to write about something sensible and different... that could well be the moment that your characters decide to... POUNCE!

§

The Brenda and Effie days were very happy ones.

When I think about publishing each of those books, I think about the people that I met as a result of Brenda and Effie. Sometimes people would dress up in fancy costumes for the occasion – especially when there was a signing at the splendid Whitby Bookshop during Goth Weekend at Beltane or Hallowe'en. Year after year we had these launches for the books, and sometimes the shop was so busy people couldn't even get in through the doors...

Brenda fans are very loyal.

Sometimes I'd meet people who'd say: 'I'd never read fantasy, or horror, or science fiction. But I read these books because I love Brenda...'

They'd follow Brenda into any genre, is what I was discovering. And Brenda led them a merry old dance through those novels. She time-travelled, she went into alternate dimensions... once she even fell into the making-of DVD extras of a Cult horror movie. And everywhere she went in Whitby she uncovered nefarious goings-on and very spooky mysteries.

I can't stress enough how much I loved writing these books, and how chuffed I was to discover they had readers who loved them.

My publisher at the time never really understood what the books were about, or why anyone would love them, or who those people would be. They certainly didn't know how to market them. They always seemed mystified and a bit embarrassed by poor old Brenda and Effie and me. I was told by publishing people I was working with that, really, I ought to be writing darker and edgier supernatural fiction. My heroines should be younger and more feisty...

My heroines should, in short, be more kickass than bus pass...

But I carried on writing Brenda's adventures in exactly the way I wanted to. Eventually my then-publisher pulled the plug, and the wonderful Snowbooks published the sixth and ostensibly final volume in the series. There have been side steps and related novels, of course – '666 Charing Cross Road' features the adventures of Brenda's slightly rougher sister, and 'Fellowship of Ink' takes us back into the 1930s for some mysterious goings-on investigated by Henry Cleavis, Reginald Tyler, and Tyler's housemaid – who turns out to be a slightly younger Brenda.

One feature of many of my books is that they interconnect in many subtle – and some not-so-subtle – ways. I love it when readers chase up these links and see the bigger story...

I once had a literary agent (not for very long) who told me that I had to abandon Brenda and Effie. 'They're dead in the water! Those books are dead! A flop! They were a commercial failure! You've got to do something else! Something more sensible!'

A commercial failure perhaps, in this world of disposable stuff that people pick up and swiftly chuck away: all those cookie-cutter books with feisty kickass heroines. But Brenda and Effie somehow endure, and I hope they'll go on enduring and finding a wider and wider readership who take them to their heart in the way the loyal hardcore has done, so far.

The current volume features a bunch of inter-related stories for our heroines. Some of them have been produced as audio dramas by Bafflegab Productions in recent years, with Anne Reid performing all the female roles. She was wonderful, of course, but the real voice of Brenda for me will always be Joanna Tope, who read the first six books as unabridged audios for what used to be AudioGo (or AudioWent, as we now call it). Jo will always be the real Brenda to me.

So here we are, with the ladies of Whitby again. Time for another trot down to the harbour at twilight, and maybe a drink or two at the Christmas Hotel. Even writing those words makes me feel nostalgic. They get me hankering for those days between 2005 and 2012 when I was writing these stories and thinking about these adventures all the time. They really were happy times with those two old dames... and maybe those days aren't over yet.

Paul Magrs
Manchester, November 2019

# 1

# The Woman in a Black Beehive

My name is Brenda.

This is the tale of how I came to live in this new town of mine.

I arrived here by the coast in the early spring. I fell in love with the vastness of the grey sea and the brightness of the light. You see, I'd been hiding away for far too long in the shadows. Now I wanted to be out in the open air. Feeling that salty breeze on my cracked and ancient skin. I've been well nigh cloistered. Out in the daylight I was feeling positively macabre.

Such a long, long life I've had. And I don't remember the half of it. When I say that, you must believe me. It's like there is some kind of fault line in my head and many of my lifetime's memories have drained away. Sometimes I think the human brain has capacity enough for only one average lifetime. And I have had much more than that. I am very old, you see.

But this is my new life. A quiet life beside the sea in this town of Whitby, which has protected itself well against the oncoming crassness of the ages. In the twenty-first century it still feels like a Victorian holiday town, with its higgledy-piggledy rooftops and stovepipes and labyrinthine streets. This pleases me for I am, at heart, somewhere deep inside my bosom, an old-fashioned girl. This place – with its busy harbour and hulking, rocky headland and gloomy ruins – suits me quite well.

It is here that I have decided to sink all of my savings into a Guest House, bang on the harbour. Here I will live as just one more landlady in a town overrun by that fussy, capable brood. And no one here will ever know my secrets, or anything about the many complicated lives I have left behind me. Here I will simply be Brenda. A little tall, perhaps, and heavyset. Slathered in too much make-up, covering scars that only I know about. Brenda with her towering black beehive. As I sit writing my journal by candlelight, here in my attic sitting room, my wig sits on its stand beside me. A fluffed up and neatly-coiffed sentinel in the moonlight.

I gaze past my wig through the circular attic window at the sea mist that slinks up from the harbour and at the stars above Whitby Abbey and I think over events during my first few days in this place. Already a great deal has gone on, despite the fact that the last thing I was looking for was any kind of mystery or adventure...

§

I suppose you might say it all kicks off when I meet the woman from next door. The very day after I take possession of my B&B. I've only just put up the sign that says 'vacancies' and I am anticipating a few days' solid work – cleaning and stripping and painting and varnishing and buffing everything up until it is just so. The place needs a thorough going-over before I can invite anyone in over the threshold to be my first paying customers. So I am bustling out of the door in my side passage, on my way to buy all the necessary cleaning supplies when there comes this rather shrill call.

'Yoo hoo,' it goes and I turn round to see a skinny, oldish woman with her hair in a bun and a sucked lemon face. She's done up rather smartly in a worsted two-piece, clutching a shopping bag somewhat aggressively. She glares at me, asking, 'You're the new lady, aren't you?'

I have to admit that yes, I am the new owner of this particular B&B. She stares at my sign, which says, 'Brenda's B&B' and seems unimpressed.

'Plain old Bed and Breakfast won't do these days, you know. You have to have an interesting gimmick. A unique selling point. You have to add value. This couple I know in Scarborough, they went in for a Medieval theme.'

'Oh yes?' I say, trying to be polite.

'It wasn't very nice. The hygiene in their dungeon was shocking and that ought to be paramount, oughtn't it? I'm Effie Jacobs, by the way. I live next door to you. That's my Antiques Emporium.'

Well, I've already taken note of the dusty windows of the tatty junkshop next door. Now here's the owner, puffing it up into something far fancier than it looks from outside.

'Curios and trinkets, some furniture and antique costume wear. All very select.' She extends a skinny hand. 'I take it you're Brenda?'

'I am,' I shake her hand. She flinches at my grip.

'You'll be wanting someone to show you around the place,' she says.

'Not especially,' say I, preparing to go.

'Oh, you will,' she says. 'It can be a funny old place, can Whitby. Hard to get the hang of.'

I tell her – a tad brusquely – that I'm sure I will manage. Then I leave her gawping after me and I hurry in the direction of the shops.

§

So I'm setting about my cleaning regime; making my Guest House spick and span. Now that I'm going into business I feel very determined about it all. I am intent on having the finest establishment in Whitby.

As I go about my business in these early days, however, I keep seeing Effie from next door wherever I go. I'll be carrying my shopping bags home and she'll come dashing up. I'll be supping a restorative cuppa in a little café and she'll come hurtling in, trying to engage me in idle conversation. And then one day we arrive at our front doors simultaneously. I am returning from the green grocer's and Effie is manhandling what is obviously a large picture in a frame through the doorway of her antiques emporium.

She notices me pausing to watch and she calls out: 'You couldn't lend a hand, could you, Brenda? I've carried this thing across town and I'm out of puff. You've got the muscles for it more than I have.'

I don't say anything. I simply put my bags down beside my front door and go to help the gawky old mare. I do most of the work getting the thing through the door and into the cavernous, cluttered shop. The frame is surprisingly heavy and I wonder how she even got it this far.

'It's from the auction rooms across the other side of the harbour,' she explains. 'Soon as I saw this, I knew I had to have it. Here, pop it on the floor. Marvellous, Brenda. You're as strong as an ox, aren't you, ducky? Come on through to the kitchen and I'll make you a frothy coffee.'

Next thing I know I'm on a stool beside a breakfast bar stacked with dirty crockery and littered with burned bits of toast. Effie is telling me all about her latest acquisition.

'You know, sometimes, when a piece just cries out to you, and you simply have to have it? Oh, not only pictures. Ornaments, gee-gaws and objets d'art of all kinds. I often hear them crying out to me and wanting me to take them home. I'm quite loathe to part company and that's why this place is overstocked.'

It certainly is. I've never been in such a cramped and uncomfortable shop. I count myself lucky at my relatively unencumbered life. I have very few wants and hardly any clutter to hold me down. Just a few treasured mementos that I've kept down the years. Nothing like this almighty treasure trove of Effie's. I'm assuming it *is* treasure, mind. It might simply be a load of old tat.

Next thing, Effie is passing me a mug of instant coffee with powdered milk and beckoning me to watch as she ceremonially rips the brown paper off her painting. I stand back to admire the masterpiece as she reveals it.

It takes a few moments to make sense to me and, when it does, I'm not sure whether I like it at all. It's a gloomy midnight scene, all swirling purples and greens. Silhouetted in the creamy moonlight is a man atop a giant stallion. There's a scantily clad lady looking distraught and clutching his shoulders. The foreground is worse. There's a creepy-faced child in a nightgown. A single tear rolls down its cheek. A malicious-looking cat stares out from behind the child's rickety legs. All in all, the painting is – I think – a monstrosity. I wouldn't give it house room lest it give me nightmares. However, there's no accounting for taste.

Effie is beaming at this sepulchral travesty and saying to me, 'Isn't it a marvel, Brenda? Now, would you mind helping me to lug it upstairs to my sitting room?'

§

By the time Effie's painting is up I'm worn ragged and regretting stopping in the street to talk to her. Every limb is shaking with over-exertion and my poor old heart is banging like billy-o. I make my excuses and go back to my home, where my groceries are still waiting in the side passage for me.

I pass the evening quietly alone, listening to the wireless and having a glass or two of sherry. Well, here I am – and my B&B is almost ready for business. I've a phone line and I'm having some little cards printed up. I've taken out a modest advert in the local paper, *The Willing Spirit* and now I am ready for the hordes to descend.

I have just four rooms, all en suite, and each of them furnished plainly but immaculately. There are three further bedrooms still unfinished and ready to convert at a later date. Already I feel like the queen of an almighty empire. I fall asleep in my sumptuous attic room feeling very pleased with myself. Though I have rather troubled dreams concerning handsome men astride stallions. Plus,

I find myself haunted by that whey-faced child and its raggedly-looking cat. Actually, I can even hear something like a cat's plaintive mewing. A horrible racket, like fraying strings on an ancient violin.

I awake cursing my next door neighbour and her painting as the source of my horrid dreams and I lie awake muzzily, realising that I can still hear that screechy music in the night. It is coming from above me, I am sure. My bedroom is at the very top of my building. There isn't even storage space between me and the dark sky. Just a skylight and hundreds of slate tiles. But still I can hear that shrill song. Now it even sounds as if it's taunting me:

La, la, la, la, lah…!

It is accompanied by little footfalls. I imagine velvety footpads dancing on cold slate and lead. The occasional scratching of sharp claws. Am I going out of my mind? Next thing I know I am standing on the blanket box, shoving open the skylight and poking my head and shoulders out into the night. It is the very early hours and, for a moment as I perch there, looking at all the rooftops, I can hear nothing at all. I am relieved and ready to dismiss the noise as just the dregs of my dream. But then it comes again:

La, la, la…

That high, haunting noise. In that same moment I see who is singing and tip-tapping on my rooftop.

It is a cat. More or less like the one in my dream. It is padding expertly over the apex of my roof on its hind legs and gazing at me speculatively. The queerest thing of all about this cat is that it is glowing. This isn't some trick of the moonlight. The cat is glowing like it has gone radioactive. It's like a willow-the-wisp, blinking its green eyes at me and they are like fog lamps, beaming at me as it brings its song to a ghastly climax. Then it gives a nimble hop, skip and a jump and it is gone. Scampering off down the drainpipes and fire escapes to who knows where.

I clamber awkwardly back into my bedroom and shut the skylight firmly behind me. I don't want that tone-deaf beastie landing on me claws-first during what remains of the night.

I lie awake mulling it over. Of course, in my long life, I have had far worse supernatural visitations. This one has unnerved me, not because I'm not used to such things, but because I thought I'd seen the last of such mysterious, netherworld creatures. Well, hard cheese, Brenda. Now you're being haunted by a singing cat.

§

The next day – and I really want to wriggle out of this – Effie announces her intention to thank me for my help with her ugly painting by taking me out to lunch. I try to tell her it's quite unnecessary but the spiky old lady won't listen. I don't want to hurt her feelings so I go with her to *Cod Almighty*, a fish and chip restaurant on the other side of the harbour, in the older part of town.

Actually, I'm rather partial to battered cod. Effie is scandalised to hear I haven't yet indulged myself in one of the town's most famous specialities. She announces to all the waitresses that I am a fish supper virgin.

It is all – I must admit – sizzlingly delectable. The fish itself is melt-in-your-mouth good. We follow it down with Effie's suggestion of a crème-de-menthe knickerbocker glory each. It's while I'm spooning up acid green ice cream that I tell her about last night's spooky visitation. Somehow I can't help letting the luminous cat out of the bag.

I didn't reckon on such a dramatic reaction. Her spoon clinks down on the melamine table and she stares at me.

'The Crispy Cat!' gasps Effie. She's turned white as the flaky cod.

'You what?' I ask.

'It's a legend in these parts,' she says. 'A ghostly moggy that patrols the rooftops and alleyways of Whitby by night.' Suddenly she looks horribly alarmed. 'Did you read about the mauling that happened last night?'

'A mauling?'

'An old dear who works in the woolshop. Audrey Beardsley. She was going home very late from Bingo Night at the Christmas Hotel. She was attacked in a gloomy ginnel and was found with a mauled leg. Some beast had chewed right through her support stocking before she managed to beat him off. I assumed it was just some maniac... But now...!'

I hold up a hand to stop her flow of chatter. 'What do you mean – mauled?'

'She was chewed almost to bits. Last night. Don't you listen to the local news?' Effie sniffily picks up her long-handled spoon. The grisliness of her tale hasn't put her off dessert.

'This cat I saw last night... It was singing and glowing...'

'The Crispy Cat,' she says. 'First time in years it's been seen. Nasty, spectral, vicious thing. But it all makes sense, you see. It's come back to plague the town – and it wasn't just a random pervert biting Audrey from the wool shop after all.'

Effie pays up and asks if I'd like to take a stroll through the old town. We can go as far as the 199 steps that lead up to the church and the abbey at the top of the town if we like, in order to walk off our calorific excesses. If I feel up to it we could have a look at the view from St Mary's churchyard. Well, that's a vista I haven't experienced yet and so I agree readily, quite determined to make it up the winding stone steps less out of puff than my shrewish companion.

Soon we're at the top and both short of breath. The view of the harbour is well worth it, however. We sit on a bench between the slanting gravestones and Effie points out various landmarks, such as the hotels on the Western Cliff and the location of our very own street, near the harbour front. I can even see my own roof and attic skylight, from which I watched that singing cat.

Then Effie is saying, 'I couldn't tell you the full legend while we were still ensconced on our banquette. I had to get us away from *Cod Almighty* before I could tell you the tale of the Crispy Cat.'

'Oh yes?' I say, wondering how much I could ever believe of this gossiping besom's stories.

'It's over eighty years ago, but back then there were only two fish shops in Whitby and they were deadly rivals, vying for supremacy. *Cod Almighty* and its opposite number across the bay, *Assault and Battery*. Now, things escalated nastily one long, hot summer. There were dirty tricks played by both sides in the war of the fish suppers. They were both owned at the time by unscrupulous ne'er-do-wells – both, thank goodness, long gone. And what they used to do, you see, Brenda, is try to sabotage each other's business. They'd put about evil rumours concerning the freshness of the other's supplies – and their provenance. It all became rather nefarious.

'And now I come to the worst part of the story,' says Effie. 'Legend has it that the owner of *Cod Almighty* paid some heavies to march into *Assault and Battery* one evening during its busiest time. They barged to the front of the takeaway queue and took a dead cat out of a bin bag. Then they dropped it into the deep fat fryer. Contaminating the oil, you see. Contaminating everything. It certainly put everyone off visiting *Assault and Battery* ever again – even after it closed for a week's fumigating. The place never quite recovered from this awful sabotage and since then *Cod Almighty* has reigned supreme over the bay. Well, what do you think of that then?'

'It's a horrible story,' I tell her. 'Is it just a local legend or is it true?'

'Every word is true,' she says proudly. 'And I'll tell you something else. My Aunt Maud was there in that queue, and she was put right off her supper by what she saw that night. She couldn't face anything battered for months after that. Not a sausage.'

I try to steer her back to the point. 'And what about the singing cat on my roof?'

She lowers her voice, though there's no one in the graveyard to hear her. 'Word has it that the batter-covered, glowing ghost of that poor luckless feline is doomed to wander Whitby forever. Attacking folk and mauling them to death when it gets the chance. No one has heard it or caught sight of it or been savaged by it for years. You've been fortunate to clap eyes on the monster and get away unscathed...'

§

That night the glowing cat appears to me again. I wake with a start just after two a.m. and I can hear that ululating pussy once more.

La, la, la, la...!

I shake myself awake and reach for my wig. I don't even have to switch on my reading light. I look at the window and there's the cat. Its phosphorescent paws are pressed up against the glass.

It doesn't look like it's covered in fish batter. But it does look very much like a cat who's come back from the dead.

Curiously, I'm not at all scared. Even though Effie swears blind the beast is deadly. There is a sadness about its green eyes. I'm mesmerised. Next thing I know, I'm across the room and throwing open the sash window. He hops lightly off the sill into my bedroom. He perches heavily at the end of my continental quilt.

'You'd better get back into bed. It's a chilly night and I've a tale to tell...'

Funny that I don't baulk for a moment at the way it addresses me. He has a high, quavering tone, much like his singing voice. I clamber back beneath my duvet, feeling his considerable weight on top of my shins. Some phantom!

'It's a tale about how I lost my ninth life, here in this very street. Harbour Street. So many years ago. We're talking about the 1930s now. And back in those days I was called Harold. I was the only male personage allowed to spend any time at all in that tall house where Effie's aunties used to live.'

'Oh! You belonged to Effie's family?'

'Her witchy brood. Her wicked gaggle of female cousins. The eldest, Maud, with her rock hard bosom and her twitchy fingers. And the beautiful Natasha, clever Eliza, brave Beryl and the youngest and most beguiling, Angela.'

'Were they really witches?'

'I was their familiar! Oh yes. I saw everything that went on behind the respectable façade of their herbalist and green grocer's shop. I saw their rituals and potion-brewing and the setting of their hexes. I saw them dance naked at midnight around the ruins of the Abbey. They said they were warding off nasty spirits and the Nazis, but I reckon they were doing it for kicks. They were naughty girls.'

'I see. Erm, why are you telling me all of this, Harold?'

'I have come back to this decrepit town because I have been sent on a mission. It's all to do with Effie. Your new best friend.'

'Oh, now. She's not my best friend. I barely know the woman and, I must confess, I find her abrasive and peculiar.' Maybe dangerous, too, I think to myself, if she really does come from a line of Whitby witches. It's all this supernatural gubbins that I'm trying to avoid these days. Just remember that, Brenda!

'Nevertheless. I am a long-lived and clever old cat and I can see a little way into the future. I can see into the reasons for things and I happen to know that you and Effie are going to be very important figures in each other's lives. Why, I would say that it is destined to be.'

I pull a face and let this pass. Since I don't want to sit up all night with a flaming cat I tell him to go on with his story.

'As I said, Angela was the youngest and most beguiling witch in that house. She had all this scarlet hair and emerald eyes. No wonder she attracted the attention of the dark demon lord when he came riding by one day, across the cliff tops on his stallion...'

'Hold it. Demon lord?'

'That is how he styled himself. What can I say? He claimed – very earnestly – to come from the Land of Faerie, in the far north. He was the Erl King.'

'Goodness!'

'He came riding up to the sisters and he cut a very impressive figure indeed. His eyes and those of his mount blazed a hungry scarlet. And the witchy sisters were dressed in their raggiest garments, carrying panniers of herbs and wildflowers they'd spent the day gathering in the meadows above Robin Hood's Bay. They were stopped in their tracks by this demon rider and he peered into each of their faces. He decided Angela was the one he wanted.'

'Just like that? Like he was shopping? Or picking flowers and herbs for himself?'

'So it goes for Demon Kings. He was known far and wide for simply making off with those young'uns who caught his eye.'

The Erl King, eh? I wonder. I have heard of this mythical figure, of course. But why on Earth would he come looking for possible romantic interest in an obscure seaside town such as this? Does Harold the luminous cat truly expect me to believe his tale? He pauses to brush his moustache and round one ear with a languid paw.

'She refused him, naturally. She was terrified. Her sisters took her home and shielded her inside the tall, dark house. The eldest, Maud, took charge. They barricaded their doors against the Demon Lord. Time went by and it was Christmas and snowy and each morning brought new gifts which he laid on their doorstep.'

'Peppermints, lilies, a music box – and fish pulled from the deepest reaches of the seas. (Nasty-looking fish that were soon tossed my way. I wasn't complaining.) He even brought her a walking, talking, mechanical doll dressed in ermine and called Mrs Claus. She sang Angela songs about how much the Erl King loved her. And, of course, before that festive season was over, Angela found herself enchanted. Ah, isn't it always so? She succumbed to his blandishments and his fancy goods.'

'She didn't?'

'She did. And her sisters were absolutely wild with fury.'

'I bet they were.'

'This is where my story turns tragic. For me, at least.'

'Go on.'

'The witchy sisters defied the Demon King. They stayed locked indoors with his beloved. On Boxing Day, when a snow storm was looming over the horizon he came thundering up to their front doorstep. He proclaimed he was going to steal their youngest sister away. He knew that she loved him as much as he did her and their destiny lay in his faraway Faerie Realm, the portal to which lay somewhere north of Newcastle on a windswept Roman road. Maud and the others all stood firm. He will not take her! Over their dead bodies!

'But then – something odd. The witches held their breath, horrified, as Angela went to him, pliantly, wearing an ermine cloak that had arrived as that morning's present. An exact copy of the cloak worn by the living doll. She clutched to her all the gifts he had given her: almost too many to hold.

'There was nothing her sisters could so as they watched Angela being swept up into the saddle with that bad man. And here comes the tragic part, Brenda. I could see my favourite of those sisters being taken away and all I could think was that there'd be no more fishy tributes from deep beneath the sea. And so I found myself springing and hissing at the Erl King.

'I shot through the air making a hullaballoo, just as he was about to turn and gallop away. He fetched out his great flaming sword and he ran me through. Right there and then, at the front of our house.

'The witches froze with shock. On the instant I lost my ninth life, sliding off his hot sword like melting butter onto the cold cobbles.

'The blizzard was just beginning as he spurred his stallion and they thundered away up the hill of Harbour Street, and out of town. There I lay, curled up, quite still – and glowing slightly from his fiery blade. And this is how – all that time ago – I became a ghostly puss.'

He goes quiet at this point, mulling over his final demise. I'm not quite sure what to say. In my previous meetings with supernatural beings, I've found it's best to keep mum and let them tell you things at their own pace. Otherwise, if you get peremptory, you can scare them off. Or they can get the hump. At last I ask:

'You said you have a mission, Harold?'

'I do! I do! And you can help, Brenda. Now that you are here in Whitby, you can help me! You will, won't you? You'll do what you can to help me?'

'I'm not sure. Tell me first, what it is you want me to do.'

Suddenly he's full of energy and glowing even brighter. For a moment I'm scared he's going to set light to my new sheets.

'You will know what to do when the right moment comes! I'm sure you will know exactly what to do! Good Brenda! Clever Brenda! Lovely Brenda!'

And then he is bounding towards the window again.

'Wait! What about the rival fish shops and the vat of hot oil? Where does that fit into your story?'

For a moment he pauses.

'I don't know what you're talking about!'

'But... you're the Crispy Cat, aren't you? The feline scourge of Whitby's back allies? Mauler of old ladies?'

'I am nothing of the sort! Who told you this?'

He whirls about haughtily and then he's gone. Out of the window and down the fire escape. I can hear his light scamper as it fades across the rooftops and then I can hear a snatch of his ludicrous song...

La, la, la, lah...!

Before I return to sleep I believe I hear his voice floating back into my attic...

A new life, Brenda. I've been promised the chance to live again! As a real cat of flesh and blood and fur! If only I can succeed in this little mission of mine..!

§

I am lying on a very hard bed. It's made out of stone, I think. The whole room is freezing.

I've woken up in the middle of an operation.

An operation someone is performing on *me*.

Lightning roars. Thunder crashes. Ooh, the ceiling of the operating theatre is open to the elements. Rain lashes in as I lie there. There's nothing I can do. I can't pull myself together. Am I drugged? I can't feel my limbs...

Herr Docktor... the brilliant surgeon... he's leaning over me. His breath smells rank. He's drinking Schnapps as he works. He mutters to himself... feverishly. He sews like a champion seamstress. Black cat gut. Pulling the sutures taut. Making soft skin pucker. He runs his dirty fingers over my fresh scars. His work is hasty and careless.

He isn't making a masterpiece this time.

He swears and shouts and protests. He is working under duress. In terrible conditions. Ghastly lamplight. Dirty implements. I wake in the middle of the operation into a world of pain and my screams are just horrible to hear...

And up at the window – watching these proceedings with glee – is the hideous face of the creature. The monster. He's watching my birth. His awful face is full of eagerness, excitement...

I twitch... I tremble... my senses are stirring...

I awake with a screech of sheer horror.

Oh.

Just that nightmare again.

The recurring dream.

The one I've had for two hundred years.

It always comes back with redoubled strength, whenever I move to a new place. It's as if it's telling me – you can't simply start again. You can't leave your heritage behind. You might have forgotten huge swathes of your life and times – but you can't forget who you really are. You can't forget your roots, Brenda.

I push all the nightmares aside and throw myself into work. It's the only way.

§

The following afternoon sees me out with Effie as she introduces me to the splendours of the Christmas Hotel. It is a once-grand edifice on the West Cliff where, according to Effie, it is Christmas Eve every single day of the year. There they are, busloads of pensioners brought in each week, to enjoy festive revels of the most shameless kind. There are trimmed trees and swags of glittering tinsel everywhere. We take high tea in the conservatory, with a beautiful view of the ruined Abbey, and even there we are beset by Christmas Carols coming through the loudspeakers.

We are tended to by a mardy-faced waitress called Jessie, who brings us egg and cress sandwiches and miniature tartlets. Effie takes little bird mouthfuls, trying all the while to enlist me into traipsing the streets with her in the middle of the night.

'Think of it as your civic duty, Brenda,' she says.

'I've only just arrived,' I tell her.

'But I need your help, Brenda. I can't face that vicious creature alone.'

I wonder why she doesn't alert the proper authorities. I mean, if there's a dangerous beast on the prowl, is it usual to let two elderly ladies go out to fettle it?

'What about the RSPCA?' I wonder aloud. 'Or the Cats' Protection League?'

Effie tuts and crams a sponge finger past her pursed lips. 'They don't deal with paranormal creatures. Believe me. I've tried before.'

'Erm, Effie,' I say. 'You get mixed up in magical and spooky affairs like this quite a lot then, do you?'

She nods, almost proudly. 'Oh, yes. It's in my blood, you see. I feel like something of a custodian to this town.'

'Do you, now?'

'I do. And that's because I belong to a very honourable matriarchy, you see. Witches, Brenda. All my relatives were witches.'

I nod. 'I do know.'

Her eyes widen. 'Because it takes one to know one?'

'I'm no witch,' I tell her harshly, and the fruit scone I'm buttering crumbles into bits. 'But I do know the type.

And you've got magic running through your veins like the name of this town through a stick of pink rock.'

She shrugs modestly. 'I'm not such a dab hand with the spells and the hexes, mind. All my aunties are long gone, leaving me alone in this world, with nothing to show for my heritage but a houseful of old grimoires and cupboardfuls of arcane objects.'

'Really?' I say. 'I must have a gander some time.'

'You'd be welcome, Brenda. I can't make head nor tale of most of the spooky stuff that's been passed down to me. You say that you've got some experience of the... you know, the uncommon and unearthly?'

'Oh yes,' I tell her. 'But all that's behind me now.'

She shakes her head. 'Not when there's something amiss, ducky. When there's magical shenanigans going on, then it's up to us with the knowhow to be up and at 'em. So – will you join me tonight on my hunt for this killer moggy?'

I realise that I've no choice but to be Effie's back-up. After I promise and we finish up our pot of Assam, plus the last of the dainties, we head home across town. Effie has a spring in her step at the prospect of company during tonight's macabre safari.

§

I dress in an old fisherman's gansey, a fleecy anorak, a heavy scarf and stout shoes. I draw the line at pulling a balaclava over my newly-set wig, however. When I pop round Effie's Antiques Emporium I'm amazed to find her glammed up to the nines in a wine red frock and covered in theatrical jewellery.

'Just because we're on a mission tonight, doesn't mean we can go all frumpy,' she says, eyeing me up and down.

A mission. I can hear my spectral pussy using just the same term. I wonder to myself why I haven't confided in Effie yet about that curious nocturnal encounter. Could it be that I don't completely trust my neighbour yet?

She's rabbiting on about some form of magical defence that she's whipped up for us, but I'm not really listening. We're in her sitting room at this point and my whole attention is caught up by the monstrous painting I helped to put up on her wall.

It has *changed*.

Now, don't think me crackers. That's what I think at first, too. That perhaps something in the sea air has turned me doo-lally or maybe the cream in my sticky buns this afternoon was on the turn. Yet I must conclude that the picture is quite altered. It's even darker and more sepulchral. The man on the stallion is riding off into the far distance and can hardly be seen. I peer closer to make him out. In the foreground the cat has completely disappeared and the creepy child is sitting down, looking even more miserable now, wearing an even dowdier frock.

Her lank hair is longer and I realise the child has aged a little.

I cry out, startling Effie.

'Whatever's the matter with you?'

'Look!' I gasp. 'Can't you see?'

I stand aghast before the painting, quite sure that she will see at once what is amiss. But Effie simply stares at me. At the picture, and then at me again. It's obvious that she doesn't have a clue what I'm on about.

'You've had a schooner or two of sherry before coming out tonight, Brenda. Dutch courage, eh?'

I can't believe what I'm hearing. 'Your blummin' painting is possessed! It's different!'

She creeps closer to the blistered surface of the paint, thrusting her beaky old nose right in there. 'It's in exactly the same condition as it was when I won it earlier this week at Danby's Auction Houses. I swear to you.'

She looked so sane and convinced I just have to give in. It's me who's cracked, I'm thinking. I'm the one, after all, with the troublesome gaps in my recollections.

Effie starts showing me the little magic efforts she's made this afternoon, following our discussion in the conservatory of the Christmas Hotel.

'You made me feel I should make more of my latent gift for enchantment,' she tells me, and then brings out – with great ceremony – an old plastic tea tray. On it lie the curled up corpses of five mice. They are desiccated, she says, because she found them underneath her boiler. She has stuffed them with magic spell stuff – cobwebs and glitter, dried scabs and herbs – and she hexed them until she was blue in the face. We are to use them as bait, she says. For luring savage cats into the open.

Looking at her horrid offering I can feel my gorge rising. Effie urges me to stow them away in our handbags, but I'm beggared if they're going in mine.

So – then we're off on our first supernatural investigation together. Our very first evening traipsing the chilly ginnels and vennels together as a duo. And I get a queasy feeling in my water, as if it's to be the first of many.

We clatter across cobbles and totter on paving stones slimed with sea water and lichen. We find winding staircases cut into the rock, passing old cottages clinging precariously to the cliff face. We disturb courting couples, a treeful of noisy starlings, several hundred squealing bats, an old tramp and hordes of rats that scatter down by the docks. We come face to face with several cats, but some hours pass before we meet with one that glows.

It comes about when we are in the oldest part of town, rattling about in the empty lanes near the 199 steps. We have split up for a few moments when I wander off alone to take in the magnificent view of the harbour mouth. Here you can see the two curving piers closing in like pincers and the lighthouse feebly glowing in the pitch dark night. I'm having a lovely peaceful moment when I suddenly hear Effie shrieking her head off.

I find her near the famous kipper smoking shop and she has cornered a poor cat up a dark dead end. She has flung every single one of her enchanted mice at it.

Now the cat is gulping them down greedily. Grinning at her.

'Oh, look at it, Brenda!' she cries, clutching my arm. 'Look at how the nasty thing glows! It's the Crispy Cat! So the legend is true!'

But I have recognised that cat at once. 'It isn't what you think, Effie,' I bellow, elbowing her out of the way. 'His name is Harold, and he happens to be a friend of mine.'

I am too late to prevent him gobbling up the magicked mice. I try to warn him, but suddenly he's lying there, flat out. Dead to the world with his glow dimmed somewhat.

'Harold?' says Effie. 'Brenda, what are you talking about?'

'Quick. Help me carry him home. You'd better be able to reverse that silly spell of yours. Can you?'

'Why, of course.'

'Come on, then. Help me with him. He isn't the creature we're hunting. He wouldn't do anyone harm.'

Effie moves to help me, perplexed as anything.

Harold fits snugly into my handbag and I fret about him as we hurry back across town. He hasn't done any harm, has he? All he's done is come back from the dead and spoken cryptically about being on a mission.

Effie hurries along beside me. 'Are you saying that there's a second glowing cat haunting the streets and you already knew about it?'

I nod grimly. 'I'll tell you everything I know.'

'I should cocoa,' she snaps. 'The thing is, if we're going to work together as supernatural investigators, then we have to pool our resources. And that means transparency and honesty.'

I can't be doing with her mithering right now. I point out that I'm not actually keen on investigating *anything*, supernatural or otherwise. This shuts her up for a few moments. As we cross the harbour bridge into our part of town I'm trying to work out how this whole thing fits together. Harold once belonged to Effie's aunties, didn't he? That's what he claimed. So, perhaps it's Effie's he's really come back to haunt, and not me, after all? Maybe his mission concerns Effie and he simply got the address wrong?

All of this I'll have to explain when we get back indoors. Though first she'll have to do something about reversing her spell with those mice. Maybe she's killed Harold? But can you really kill a ghost?

It's as we're taking a shortcut through a rather unpleasant alleyway at the back of an unsavoury pub that we become aware of the noise. An unsettling, deep-throated growl. The throbbing noise of a hungry predator. I check my handbag, but Harold is still senseless. Effie grabs my arm and I can feel her bony grip even through my anorak.

'Oh help,' she gasps.

For there, jumping down from a wall beside us, nimbly hopping over the razor wire, is a second phantom cat. One who could only be described as crispy. It bares its fangs at us and we both feel its red hot breath on our faces. Hot as bubbling oil. He hisses at us and it sounds like a deep fat frier.

Effie starts shrieking her head off. 'It's real! It's real! The flamin' thing is real!'

Then the golden battered beast springs at us. It lands claws-first on me and luckily I'm well-padded, though I won't be for long, the way the beast is thrashing away.

'Effie, get him off me..!' I cry, and she dithers about, looking for something to hit it with. But there is nothing. The cat is screeching in my face and I'm whirling like a panicking fool, thinking: is this what it all comes to? A life as long and full as mine, and I end up mauled to death by a wild and ghostly cat?

He's quite a size. As big as a puma, I'd say. I pummel him and shake him off, but he isn't budging an inch. Effie comes running with the wheelie bin, dragging it across the cobbles and sends it careering into us both. We're both knocked flying, which dislodges the cat. But then he's got his claws into my wig and he's yanking it off my head.

At this desperate moment my handbag bursts open. I flung it into the shadows when the beast first attacked, and maybe it was the jolt that woke up Harold. Or maybe Effie's mousey spell has worn off. Either way I'm most grateful, because he comes springing out into the alleyway, shining an extra vivid fiery orange, with sparks shooting out of his fur. He looks like a vengeful spirit returned to do battle with the forces of evil.

The Crispy Cat turns on him with a venomous hiss. Soon the two are locked in mortal combat. Effie seizes the now-tattered arm of my coat and pulls me away from the deadly fight. I can hardly hear what she's saying because of all the racket. I always hate to hear the noise of fighting cats. They don't know how to stop themselves once they've begun.

'Come on, Brenda! Let's leave them to it!'

Yet I can't. They are a blurry ball of teeth and fangs and fur flying all about the place.

Effie covers her face with her hands, but I can't. I watch until the bitter end, until both cats are battered and bleeding and exhausted. Then the Crispy Cat slinks away into the darkness, leaving Harold lying there, breathing hard.

I kneel beside him. 'I thought you were a ghost. How can you be hurt?'

Effie creeps closer, holding her breath, just in time to hear Harold's shaky reply.

'I'm not a ghost. I've been allowed to come back in bodily form. By my master the Demon Lord. I'm as solid and as real as you are, Brenda.'

One ear is badly torn and he has a nasty cut on his nose. There's a bloody wound in his side where the Crispy Cat slashed him. Those wounds are already filling up with some weird kind of crispiness.

'Will you die?' Effie asks him.

He looks at her with fiery eyes.

'I feel quite poorly. And I don't have any more lives left.'

'You should never have attacked that beast,' I tell him.

'It would have savaged you both. You wouldn't have stood a chance.'

Effie looks gloomy. 'And now it's still roaming about in the back streets.'

'I couldn't let it harm either one of you two. I'm here to protect you.'

'Are you?' I ask, surprised by this. He is trying painfully to sit up.

'Oh yes. Especially Effie.'

'Me?' Effie says. 'Why me?'

Harold is on his feet, wincing and looking impatient with her.

'Don't you recognise me, Effryggia, you silly girl?'

Effie stammers and flusters. 'I, er, well, I'm not sure...'

'I'm from your painting, aren't I? Surely even you can't have failed to realise that?'

Effie looks genuinely shocked and, I must admit, it is a bit unusual. A cat telling her he has escaped from an oil painting she's bought. But there are times for scepticism and searching questions and this isn't one of them. We have to get Harold indoors and see to his wounds.

'Oh, by the way. Well done on the enchanted mice, Effie. He'll be ever so glad that you're experimenting with magic again.'

'Will he?' she says. 'Who? Who do you mean?'

'Ah, wait and see.'

Then he succumbs to exhaustion. I pick him up gingerly and he falls asleep, half curled around my neck. I feel his warmth and his ragged purring all the way as we hurry through the last of our journey home to Harbour Street.

§

Once in Effie's sitting room I pick him gently from my neck and lay him on the settee. His wounds aren't bleeding and he seems to be glowing more brightly. Still doesn't look quite right though. His fight with the Crispy Cat has knocked the stuffing out of him.

Effie goes to make some tea and comes back with the brandy bottle.

'What a night,' she says. 'Can you believe any of this?'

She pours and we clink two large glasses together before downing them.

'Now Brenda,' she says. 'Tell me everything this cat has told you.'

I am just about to divulge what Harold said the other night when he was luminescing on my continental quilt, but at that very moment I happen to glance at Effie's painting. I give a strangulated yell.

'Effie, look! Surely you can't deny the evidence of your senses this time?'

She turns to see – almost reluctantly – and downs the rest of her brandy. Then she looks shame-faced. 'I know. You're quite right.'

The oil painting has changed yet again. Now the man has dismounted and he's holding the young lady in the ermine robe very close. The young girl in the foreground is young no more. She stares out of the gilt frame and her face is the face of Effryggia Jacobs herself..!

'I admit it, she looks very like me,' Effie sighs. 'When I was somewhat younger. I was never much of a looker, was I? Such a pale-looking specimen. I look back at her now and think, what an unfriendly girl. No wonder she never had many friends. Who would ever dare to talk to her? Who would waste their time? She looks acid-tongued and bitter.'

I try to say something complimentary, about how she has a nice figure, but Effie isn't having any of that. 'What did that matter? Whitby was even colder during my young womanhood than it is now. We went round ten months out of twelve wearing six layers of woollies, all bundled up like Eskimos.'

There comes a mewing and a moaning from the settee and I go to Harold, who stirs in his sleep. He's having troublesome cat dreams from one of his past lives, perhaps. His glowing paws knead the air.

'So you were at Danby's Auction Rooms,' I prompt Effie. 'And you happened upon this portrait of yourself...'

'When I first saw it, it was showing a child I barely recognised as myself. It spoke to me, this picture. I went up to it and that's when I saw the purple bruises under the child's eyes and the stringy white hair. That's when I knew it was supposed to be me – the young, orphaned Effryggia Jacobs. I thought to myself, 'But who on Earth would have painted a picture of me? Who would have bothered to capture me in oils? And who would have cared to frame it with gold?'

'Well, someone did,' I point out.

She shakes her head. 'This isn't a normal picture, done with brushes and paint. No artist's hand and eye ever worked on this. This is magic through and through. It only looks like a painting to the outside world.'

'Oh,' I say. 'Then what is it really?'

Effie shudders. 'I'm sorry I lied and denied it before, Brenda, when I said that you were wrong and that the painting hadn't changed. I was lying to myself as much as I was you.'

I nod and peer closer at the picture. I examine the very handsome man that Harold described as the Demon King. The Erl King. 'Who are these people?' I ask my friend. 'Do you know?'

'I don't recognise them at all,' she says.

I peer at the gentleman and his young lady friend as if I'm expecting them to spring into life at any moment. 'You know, when he came to me in the night, Harold told me a very interesting tale. About the women who once lived here in your house. Your aunts – this is well before you were born of course – and the youngest sister, Angela, who ran off with a man just like this.'

Effie pours more brandy out. 'The cat seems to know more about it than I do. My aunts were quite mysterious, and I never knew Angela at all. When I was little they seemed very old and slightly crazy. Though I was proud of them and thought they were marvellous. And yes, it's true, now I think on, Angela did run away from them. They never liked to talk about her much. When I was a girl I used to try to imagine her. I pictured her being more like me, and I could have talked to her and not been frightened and overawed by her, as I was by Aunt Maud and Natasha, and Eliza and Beryl.'

Harold is awake. He's lying stretched out but one eye is half-open, staring at us.

'She was your mother, Effie. That's what I've been sent back to tell you. I've been granted an extra, tenth, life in order that I could come back and show you her image in the painting. I can tell you how wonderful and gentle and beautiful she was. And how she loved you. But she had to go away and stay away from home. After you were born she sent you back here to be looked after by your aunts but she never, ever forgot you...'

Effie is staring in slack-jawed amazement at the glowing cat. His high, halting voice hangs in the air. He's still looking dreadful. His cuts and scratches give off a strange, sickly light. 'Can we see to your injuries?' I ask him. 'Maybe bandage you up?' He shakes his head.

Effie says to him, 'This handsome pair in the painting – they're really my parents?' She stands before them, as if they're able to look back at her out of the frame. 'But where does the painting come from? And why has it come to me?' There is a desperate tinge in her voice. 'After all this time. I'm nearly seventy. I've spent all my life wondering and not knowing and feeling alone in the world. I thought I'd never know anything about them. Certainly, never see their faces.'

'There they are. There they are, for you to see.'

'Yes, but why?' she demands. 'What's the point? What good is seeing their faces going to do me now?'

She seems about to burst into tears. I pat her on the shoulder. 'I think it's a lovely thing to have. Look at them! So old-fashioned, so beautiful, the pair of them!'

Effie shrugs. 'Huh.' She turns away from the picture. 'Well, I'm glad they were happy together. Riding off into the flamin' sunset. Leaving me behind to get on with things here.'

I want to tell her that, as far as I'm concerned, she's a lucky woman. I wish I had some evidence of loving parents of my own. And, even if she was abandoned, at least Effie had family to take her in. Her aunts may have been witchy and scary, but they still stood by her and put a roof over her head and fed her and protected her against the forces of darkness and the cold north wind. What the devil did I have? Nothing. Nothing and no one. And I never will.

Oh, but as that thought occurs to me I feel like a goose has just walked over my grave. A great galumphing grave. I do have a grave, you know. Several, in fact.

Now I am much too tired and I need my bed. I turn to leave. 'This evening has taken it out of me.'

'And,' Effie puts in, 'The Crispy Cat is still out there somewhere, causing havoc. I don't think we've actually accomplished much on our investigation tonight.'

I pat Harold good night and he seems to fall asleep again on the sofa, purring contentedly. 'He'll be all right there,' says Effie. 'Though I'm not sure what I'll feed him come the morning.'

'I'm sure he can look after himself,' I tell her and then I leave.

§

Then, I'm in the throes of making my first guests feel welcome. I make up beds and fry up breakfasts and I find I don't have to try very hard to be all smiling and cheery for them. I actually enjoy letting them into my home. I don't feel at all awkward or strange. It turns out I'm a natural-born landlady..!

There have been a couple of sightings of the Crispy Cat. A spectral feline was spotted on the cliff-tops and a blurred photo snapped by somebody's mobile appeared on page two of *The Willing Spirit*. A few savaged gulls have been found in the harbour and I heard a rumour from Jessie, the waitress at the Christmas Hotel, that her nephew Robert came across something alarming in the sand dunes after midnight last Wednesday. Though what he was doing hanging about on the beach at that time of night I don't know. You can see some very odd things here. Especially if you go looking for them.

Jessie passed me this tidbit when I returned to the Christmas Hotel for tea. I went with Effie, who looked drawn and tired as if she hadn't slept at all in the days since I'd last seen her.

'There's been no sign of Harold, then?' I ask, being mother and pouring.

'Oh yes, there has,' she says. 'He's quite definitely back in the painting. I've seen his little face peering out at me once or twice. Once he was even winking, in a reassuring sort of way.'

'Ah, bless him,' I say. 'I rather miss him, actually. Last night I lay awake, hoping I'd hear his singing on my rooftop again.'

Hollow-eyed Effie is looking at me across the tableful of fiddly sandwiches and cakes. 'I can't help myself, Brenda. There is something endlessly fascinating about that painting. It shows the same events over and over again and I feel drawn in by it...'

She goes on to tell me about afternoons and evenings and middles of the night with her watching developments in the murky oils. She has grown addicted to seeing the same old Romantic plot being played out repeatedly. Her father woos her mother and then snatches her up; the pair of them cantering away atop his flame-eyed steed. The sickly young girl keeps on being left at home. The marmalade cat keeps on having the burning sword thrust through his chest.

Effie watches this narrative unfold as if she suspects there is a key secreted somewhere inside it. Something that will make her whole life suddenly unlock and make sense. There has to be a reason for it all, she thinks.

She eats a squashy cake rather delicately as she tells me about this and I think, No. Not necessarily, lovey. What makes you think there has to be a reason behind everything? Behind anything at all? Why flatter yourself with thoughts like that? I know better than anyone that this life doesn't work like that. It is random and occasionally horrible or lovely and the thing that superstitious folk call destiny or fate is actually a spiteful thing. But I don't say anything aloud, of course. I wouldn't want to upset the old dear.

Our afternoon tea is a subdued affair. It's like Effie is only half there. The remainder of her is still at home, staring at the painting.

More days go by, and in my rooms the guests come and go, carpets get hoovered and delicious breakfasts are served and money changes hands and charming comments get left in my guestbook in the downstairs hall. I feel as if I am starting to fit in around here. A few people say hello in the street as I happen by. They are starting to recognise me, and it isn't to cross themselves, make the sign of the evil eye or ward me off with burning torches. I feel like I'm becoming one of the locals, just going about my everyday business.

I don't see anything of Effie for a few days and I must admit, I feel guiltily grateful not to be getting hourly updates on her spooky shenanigans. There have been no more feral attacks, so it seems the Crispy Cat has gone to ground for a while. Sometimes in the wee small hours I will hear a familiar catty song echoing around the chimney pots.

La, la, la, la, lah...!

I fondly imagine that Harold has escaped from the confines of the painting for a frolic about the town. He's having a night on the tiles again.

§

Then, on a Saturday afternoon I'm pulling my shopping-bag-on-wheels up the steepest alley in Whitby on my way to the butchers and I find myself walking alongside that miserable-looking Jessie from the Christmas Hotel. (You can tell she was bonny back in her day. She should have herself done up, somehow, I think. Make the best of herself.) Anyhow, have I heard the latest about Effie, she asks? I say, no, I haven't done, since I've been ever so caught up in my own business just lately and what's going on?

'It's just,' says Jessie, 'That your friend and mine, Effryggia Jacobs, has been seen in the company of a rather attractive man.'

'Well, if that's true, good luck to her,' I say. 'Some male attention might take her mind off her problems.'

'Has she got problems, then?' asks Jessie and I clam up at once. I know an incorrigible gossip when I meet one. I lead the way into the butcher and put in my extensive order for black pudding, streaky bacon and sausages. Jessie tells me a little more about how Effie was seen on the arm of this darkly handsome, Byronesque figure, walking along Church Street, the night before last. (Who uses words like Byronesque in the butchers, I wonder?) Jessie has heard tell they were going from one pub to another. Having fun and gallivanting.

Jessie says, sotto voce, 'I've known ladies who've had their heads turned completely all for the sake of some bloke.'

Oh, she is a miserable woman, I think. I'm not too upset to wave her goodbye on Silver Street.

I call round Effie's on my way back, There's no answer when I knock.

All at once I know that something isn't right.

I put my shoulder against the door and force it open.

Inside the whole place is murkier than ever.

'Effie..?'

I creep upstairs. All my hackles are up.

Where has she gone? All this talk of her walking about the town with some unknown gentleman. It's got me proper worried.

In her sitting room it's very gloomy. When I put the lights on I get a shock.

The picture is darker than ever, and it's hard to focus on the shapes of the figures. It's like night has fallen fully on the world of the painting.

'La, la, la. If you've come looking for her, you're too late.'

What? You..!

'Forgive me for springing out on you.'

'What are you talking about? Where's Effie?'

'Where she wants to be. With her dad.'

'What?'

'That's why he sent me back into your world. I came to fetch her.'

'Harold, you better tell me what's going on.'

'He came to claim his daughter. She's in there now. She's gone into the world of the painting.'

'I draw closer to the nasty thing and all that mucky darkness is swirling round... it's like an endless, bottomless lake...'

'It's where she wants to be, Brenda.'

'I'm going in after her.'

'What? You can't!'

'She's my friend. She doesn't want to be in there. She's been kidnapped!'

'She went willingly..!'

'He had her under a spell! He must have! He took her just like he took her mother. Effie wouldn't have gone willingly. She loves her life here, in Whitby, in her shop...'

'But... it was my mission... to lead her to him...'

'We're going to get her back. And you're going to help me.'

'I can't... he will kill me... he'll snuff out any remaining lives I have...'

'She's my friend, Harold. I'll not let that Demon fella take her.'

'I can't help you...'

'Please... Harold...!'

§

It's a golden doorway – a mystical threshold – far more than a simple frame for a painting. He gingerly leads the way and I step out of the dingy sitting room into an even dingier world of sickly yellows and purples and greens. A world of permanent dusk, quite different and much nastier than any fairyland I might have imagined.

'Stay close to me, Brenda. There are strange forces all around us...'

'Ooh, I can feel them.'

On and on we trudge. For hours, it seems. Through stinking field and bog. Harold seems to know the way. I stumble blindly, with no sense of direction...

Until, at last, under a limitless purple, thunderous sky, we see something ahead. On the soggy, wind-lashed moor... there is a table with a clean cloth, and two chairs.

Effie is sitting there alone, stirring the teapot with her

spoon. She looks up, surprised, to see me standing there with Harold the cat.

'Fancy seeing you here!'

She sounds so vague and spaced out. It's like she doesn't have a clue where she is.

'Effie – we've come to rescue you. That dreadful man, whoever he is, has dragged you into this horrible place...'

'And I helped him, I'm afraid to say. I am sorry, Effryggia. Brenda is correct. We are here to rescue you.'

Effie's eyes flash. 'Why would you think I need rescuing? I'm back with my father, in his home. He has brought me home. After all these years. Look at this place! Isn't it wonderful? He owns all of this.'

She gestures around, at the desolate wilderness. Harold and I exchange a glance.

Effie pours out the tea, and I realise that there is a cup for each of us, even Harold.

'The portrait didn't do him justice,' Effie says. 'He wore evening dress and a dark cloak. Funny, strong and tender in the way he talked to me – and young! He looked about thirty, and saw nothing incongruous in meeting his daughter and she turns out to be a broken-down ratbag like me.'

'He spent time with me, Brenda. Lovely time. Hours and hours talking to me. We went walking all around the town. I was so proud to be out with my handsome dad. He told me about his life and my mother and he told me he hadn't even known he had a daughter. Not till very recently. My mother had kept him in the dark. They split up a very long time ago, and she left his magic realm...'

'Is that why he was so young still?' I ask. 'Because he lives in this magic realm?'

She pays me no heed. 'He told me that he wanted me to come with him. Back through the picture. To this mysterious world he lives in. He says that here I can choose to be any age I want to be. I can live my life all over again. And I can make a better job of it this time.'

'What?' I gasp. 'How does he know what your life is like? What's wrong with it?'

Effie smiles sadly. 'It's a life of dust and rubbish, Brenda. I never lived it to its fullest. Even I wouldn't claim that. But here... here I get another chance. Look at me! Back in my prime! Transformed! Young again!'

She holds up her wrinkled hands and pats her face. She looks like she's in raptures.

To me she looks exactly the same as she always does. The poor old thing has lost her mind. He's robbed her of her wits.

'Oh, Effie. Can't you see? He's hoodwinked you?'

'You're still an old woman! Can't you even tell?'

'No!' cries Effie, standing up and scattering the tea things. Thunder rumbles overhead and there's a lightning flash. 'I'm not seventy-four! I can't be! He made me young again!'

I shake my head, 'But he hasn't! And anyway, what's so great about being young again? You don't have to be young to have a new start. Look at me!'

'Ssssh! He's coming! Listen...!'

More thunder. More lightning. Yes, there is a sudden chill. A marvellous scent of winter spices on the air. And then he is amongst us. The Erl King. The Demon Lord. Just as beautiful and vital as he was in the picture.

'Leave my daughter alone.'

'She's coming back with us. Back to Whitby.'

'Who are you to tell me what's going to happen? Who are you?'

'I'm Brenda and I'm her new friend. And I'm telling you – you can't just take her away. I don't care who you are.'

'Her mother tried to steal her away from me. All those years ago. She placed her in the care of those harpies in that rotten little town. I'm just reclaiming her.'

Effie looks round sharply at this. 'I'm not just a bag of old belongings!'

'You belong to me. Effryggia, you must tell this... person to return to the land of the living and forget all about you.'

Effie looks at me, all beseeching. 'Maybe it's for the best, ducky. My life there is over. I'm an old woman with nothing more to offer the world. At least here someone wants me...'

'But you lied to her, master! You said she'd be young again! You offered her the Earth.'

'Be silent! You have done your part.'

'Did you lie to me, too? Will you restore my lives?'

'Your reward is a good long rest. There will be no more lives for you.'

'He lies to everyone! He's a terrible person! Harold – you can come back with us.'

'I can't, Brenda. Without him I'm nothing. I can only live here... in this realm...'

'Let them go, Erl King – or whoever you are.'

'He doesn't really want a daughter. He just wants her magic. She's got powers... the likes of which she doesn't even understand yet. That's what he's after...'

'The Erl King becomes furious at Harold's words. The cat has gone too far. There's a flash of flame as Effie's dad flings out his hand... and Harold is suffused in a deadly glare...'

'Kill me! Go on! It would be a relief... after so long as your servant...!'

'Harold...! No!'

'He's dead. The foolish creature.'

'Is it true, father?' Effie asks him. 'What the cat said? You only want me... for my magic powers...?'

'Of course not. You have no powers. None at all. I simply wanted my daughter back.'

'I don't believe you,' says Effie. She's shouldering her handbag and fastening up her coat. 'I think you lied to me all along. So, I'm going home now. With Brenda. Back to my normal life.'

Good for you, Effie! I feel like shouting. But I am still staring aghast at the smouldering remains of poor Harold.

'Do you think I'll just let you walk out of my realm?'

'If you love me,' Effie says. 'If you ever loved me at all, then that's what you'll do.'

'Love? What would you know about love?'

'A sight more than you do, evidently,' she says, very sadly. 'After what you did to that poor cat, who never did anything but serve you. Now. I'll be off then. And you won't try to stop us, will you?'

'Effryggia... Effie... I've wanted to see you again for all these years... I know I've got it wrong. I know I've done everything wrong... But, please. Stay here... with your old dad.'

But Effie turns her back on the tall, dark man. She grits her teeth and starts walking away. 'I'll give your regards to mother, shall I? And my ghostly aunts? I'm sure they remember you. The man who ruined all our lives, all that time ago.'

'Nooo..! Don't leave me here!'

'Come along, Brenda,' she tells me. 'He won't stop us walking back out of the picture. He's just a silly, sad old man. Don't worry about him. Keep walking. And don't look back.'

'Effie! Stay with me! Please!'

I have no choice but to follow Effie. We leave the Erl King shouting like a mad man in the middle of the moor. He's impotent, robbed of the only thing that ever gave him power – the love and adoration of those around him.

He stands in the middle of that murky moor, with his dead cat at his feet. Shouting after his only daughter, who shrugs her shoulders and grits her teeth.

It's a long walk back across those desolate, phantom wastes.

The howling wind at our backs is still calling her name.

'Effie...! I will come for you... again!'

But he doesn't do anything to stop us reaching the golden frame. Beyond it we can see the glow of Effie's messy sitting room.

We step through, and we're home.

'What a terrible man,' she shudders. 'I'm such a fool for ever listening to him.'

I turn back to the painting and I'm not surprised to see that it's turned completely dark. There are no figures to be made out. There's nothing to be seen in all that gloom.

Effie sighs and starts taking off her hat and coat. 'Tea? Or something stronger, ducky?'

'Sherry,' I tell her.

Effie smiles. 'Thank you so much for coming to rescue me. I'd have been lost forever, without you.'

I shrug. 'My pleasure.'

Then she says, 'You know, Brenda... I have a feeling that this friendship of ours is to be a fateful one.'

'Oh no!' I laugh. 'Do you think we're going to encounter even stranger situations than tonight's?'

She shudders, but then smiles. 'Oh yes,' she says. 'I shouldn't be at all surprised.'

# 2

# Bat out of Hull

I'm up with the larks this morning, and doing my exercises. Running on the spot, touching my toes and doing star jumps. All the very exhausting things I have to do in order to keep this old body of mine in trim. I've put a nice couple from Todmorden in the Blue Room directly beneath me and I remember this too late. Goodness what they'll make of all this thumping about from the attic.

Next I'm clattering about making breakfasts. I like to fry up twenty eggs to utter perfection before the first of my guests emerge. Symmetrical golden yolks exactly centred, and then thirty crispy curls of bacon with a golden fringe of fat. I think I'm doing a good job here, looking after my guests as they pass through the doors of my B&B, wanting me to look after them.

There was a couple this morning, asking me for recommendations. What did I think they should see of the town? The Abbey or the Museum? Was it worth taking a trip along the coast to look at Robin Hood's Bay? And I thought – I've not even been here a season, and already I'm an expert. I know quite a lot about this town and what's nice to do. Of course, there are secret things about this town that I already know, though I wouldn't tell any of my guests about those, in case I inadvertently put the willies up them. I wouldn't want them fleeing from my establishment without paying.

Breakfast done, I wave my various guests (from the Blue, Purple and Orange Rooms) off on their separate days out and then I turn to the mammoth amount of dishes that need doing. I'm interrupted by a phone call from Effie, who only lives next door, of course, but who tends to have long lie-ins reading Romance novels with the telephone to hand. She tells me her most shameful secret is to eat fancy chocolates in the morning as she sits there in her bed. Though you'd never believe it. There's hardly a picking on the skinny old mare.

'Brenda's B&B?' I put on my grandest phone voice, to make her chuckle.

'Morning, Brenda,' she says. 'How are you feeling, ducky?'

'Actually, rather better than I've any right to,' I tell her. And I can tell from Effie's voice on the other end that she's feeling gruesome today. Last night was Cabaret Evening at the Christmas Hotel and we went along to see a popular local combo called Denise and Wheatley. They do numbers from the famous musicals. She sings and he accompanies her with his electronic organ and then they go into their exorcism routine, in which Denise has her demons cast out by her husband, who turns out to be a defrocked vicar. It's quite a good show, though alarming the first time you see it.

The disco was hits from the Seventies and it was Two-for-One on the spirits, so Effie and I got a bit unnecessary, having a bop and knocking it back like it was somebody's wedding. Of course, I never really get drunk, and so the effects on me aren't anything like what poor Effie has to endure as she lies there in bed with her bodice-rippers and her luxury truffles.

'Oh, I feel proper nauseous,' she moans. 'Why ever did we say we'd go out again tonight?'

Did we? I wonder. That's not something I would usually do. Not these days. Not two nights on the trot. It sounds like I'm slipping into a dissolute lifestyle, gallivanting on week nights. I'm not sure that's very appropriate for the respectable owner of a high-toned guest house.

'You remember, Brenda. We made a promise last night.'

I'm not sure I remember any such thing. All I recall is the usual festive hullaballoo of the Christmas hotel, and swarms of elderly fun-seekers in their party frocks, doing the conga and the Birdy dance. Oh, hang on – there's a thought.

'Don't you remember meeting Barry Lurcher, Brenda? TV's famous puppeteer from yesteryear? He took quite a shine to you last night. How could you have forgotten that?'

All of a sudden – in a queasy-making dazzle – I'm having a flashback to the night before.

§

Effie and I have just tottered off the dance floor following two back-to-back Barry Whites and a Donna Summer. We're glowing with exertion and hurrying to our table, where we left our coats and bags unattended. Effie elbows her way to the bar though I actually think we've had our fill.

At our table the two free chairs have been taken by a youngish woman who seems quite out of it, and a man with a vast belly and an impressively bushy beard.

'My dear, we have occupied more than half of your table. I hope that you'll forgive us.'

I say, 'Of course – so long as you haven't been through our pockets and bags.' He looks rather blankly at me and, though he doesn't appreciate my sense of humour and has a thick Hull accent, I still think he's quite a catch.

'Going through your things! I should think not!'

I just wish I wasn't sneezing so much all evening. I'm wearing a new batwing jumper I've knitted in spangly black mohair and it's playing havoc with my sinuses.

'I am Barry Lurcher and this is Abigail, my darling wife and some time assistant.'

'Oh,' I say. And just as I am about to ask what he needs assistance with, I see that they have someone or something else sitting with them. It is a giant bat with overlarge ears and wings made, like the rest of him, out of somewhat moth-eaten black felt and fun fur fabric. I remark on the bat and the creature swings round its head to glare at me. It has fearsome green eyes and a livid red mouth full of needle-like teeth. I give a jump and then I realize that it's only a puppet. The man's arm is wedged up the creature's backside.

'This is Tolstoy. The Long-Eared Bat. Star of stage and screen for more than forty years.'

'Goodness! What a sweet puppet!'

'Shush! Don't go calling him sweet!'

'Who's this mouldy old ratbag? She looks like a zombie drag queen!'

I draw in a sharp breath.

'I think Tolstoy likes you!'

Barry is beaming at me through his beard and then Effie joins us, bringing vodka and limes. She looks puzzled at first and then she claps eyes on the amusing bat.

'Oh my goodness! Tolstoy!' she squawks, thunking the drinks down on the table and spilling some.

'Christ! Here's another frazzled old floozy. What are you doing, Barry? Can't you get any younger ones?'

'There aren't any younger ones here, I'm afraid, Tolstoy old chum. Just a load of old women.'

'At least you could pick out some with big knockers. Look at these two! Pitiful!'

Well, I'm too shocked to speak. This puppet is saying terrible things. I mean, of course, this man is saying terrible things through his puppet. I'll say this much for Barry, though. You can't see his lips budge an inch when Tolstoy is talking. Abigail sits there, simpering into space, ignoring all of us. I turn to Effie and see a look of enchantment on her face. She cracks out laughing at every horrible word Tolstoy says.

'Oh, he's just the same!' she chortles. 'Still the same cheeky old bat!' Then she reaches out to tickle behind one of the puppet's ears. He doesn't look all that clean to me, as he wriggles about, enjoying Effie's attention.

'Look, Brenda,' she grins. 'Don't you remember Tolstoy? From Children's television all those years ago? He was so rude and naughty!'

'It wasn't that many years ago! Up yours, Missus!'

'I've never really been one for watching much telly,' I say. I don't mean to sound so stiff and disapproving. I've just never heard of this puppet before.

'We won't hold that against you, my dear.'

Effie pipes up, 'I've been one of your fans for decades, Mr Lurcher. But what are you doing in Whitby?'

So Barry Lurcher explains that he and Tolstoy are the new cabaret attraction here this month. Mrs Claus has splashed out on talent that's actually famous, it seems. Effie looks thrilled, but I can't say I'm impressed.

'Ooh, when's your first show?' Effie asks.

'Tomorrow evening! Tolstoy and I will make our Christmas Hotel debut at the Witching Hour! Will you two lovely ladies promise to be there?'

Effie claps her hands together. 'Oh, of course! Won't we, Brenda?'

'Your chunky friend in the nasty jumper doesn't look so sure!'

'Tolstoy! She's just well-built.'

I fix them both with a beady stare. 'You don't know the half of it, chum.' And it seems to me that the long-eared bat's eyes glint at me with extra malice.

'I shall look forward to seeing you then.'

So that's how we end up promising, though it's the last thing I feel like doing. Traipsing up the West Cliff for another raucous night out, all for the sake of a rude hand puppet.

'It's not about the puppet,' Effie guffaws down the phone. 'Don't you think the Puppet Master had his eye on one of us?'

I'm scandalised. 'He's married! His wife was sitting there at the table with us!'

Effie sighs. 'I read an article in a mag at the hairdresser's. All about how his is a loveless marriage in name only, according to insiders. Apparently the spark went out long ago and now she's just the assistant.'

Effie seems very well up on showbiz gossip. In the end I give in and finish off the phone call wondering what on earth I'm going to wear. I arrived here in Whitby with one bag of clothes so I'm not over-endowed with gladrags. Most of my things got left behind. In my last place. When I fled. But I'm not thinking about any of that now.

§

The day passes pleasantly enough and I'm in a kind of trance as I go round with my duster and the ewbank. There's something soothing about mundane tasks. I feel like I've been doing them for two hundred years or more, and that's a lot of dust and muck to dispose of, when you think about it.

It's a mild afternoon so I go out with a mug of tea and sit in my small patch of back garden. It's adorned with some daemonic statues and boxed in by hedges and here I can sit and listen to wood pigeons and watch squirrels.

I'm interrupted by my couple from Todmorden. Both ladies are wearing sun hats and carrying bagfuls of souvenirs from their day out. They join me for a cuppa in the sun and they tell me about the junk shops they've visited in Robin Hood's Bay. It's a quaint town, built on a very steep piece of shoreline, and the streets wind about each other in complicated tiers – rather like an Escher print, as the younger of the women points out. It turns out they're both called Mary.

They tell me that they found a terribly old-fashioned toyshop, tucked away in the most obscure corner of that town. It was perched on a bridge high above a trickling stream. The two Marys ventured inside and they went back into a world of clockwork clowns, tin robots, wooden masks and puppets made from lustrous fur. The shop smelled wonderfully of wood shavings and something else... Gingerbread, says the older Mary. Snow on Christmas morning, says the other and they both laugh. They have bagfuls of presents for nieces and neighbours and they found the shop owner to be a wonderful old eccentric who has worked there all his life.

I'm entranced by all of this. I've been to Robin Hood's Bay with Effie and though I think we trotted along every hidden passageway I don't recall a toyshop like this. Judging by the curios with which I've decorated the rooms of my B&B the two Marys believe I'd be delighted by Grenoble's Toys.

I make a mental note of the name and ask Effie about it later, when she's dragging indoors antiques she's been displaying outside her shop. A rail of cocktail dresses, a tailors' dummy draped in beads and feathers, and an old gramophone that's been playing crackly old tunes all afternoon.

'They must have got it wrong, those two Marys,' says Effie, pulling a face. 'If it's been there forever, I'd have known about it.' Then she eyes me speculatively and asks if I'm ready for the evening's entertainment. Then she's dragging me indoors to inspect a vintage frock – it's aubergine and covered in black embroidery. Even though it's the size of a tent, when I try it on in her bathroom it still pinches under my arms.

'It'll be fine, just so long as you don't do the actions to Agadoo on the dance floor. Go on, have it. It's yours.'

She won't take a penny payment off me. That's the thing about Effie. She might be shrewish sometimes but she's kind deep down.

Well, then I'm titivating myself. Bathing in scented oils and powdering myself like mad. I try not to look at the scarred battleground of my body as I stand in my bathroom. I blot all those markings away with talc. Then I tug on my dressing gown and sit at my mirror. It's time to slather on layers of concealer, foundation and every unguent I can make stick. I ply on my finest lashes and finally brush up my towering beehive, laminate it with hairspray and place it ceremonially upon my head.

Like a queen in Westminster Abbey taking delivery of her crown.

Then I slip into the voluminous party frock and some suitably dark shoes with heels as high as I dare go. Not having a full-length mirror I make do with the one in the hall, peering at myself at odd angles and do you know what? I'm not at all displeased with the effect.

'I knew you'd brush up well,' Effie tells me when I go round. She herself is in a crimson wraparound number with a daring amount of somewhat crepey cleavage on show. She's had something frizzy done to her hair. 'By the way, have you seen this?' She hands me the evening paper to look at while she goes round doing up her window locks. The headlines scream that the Crispy Cat has carried out its fifth murder of the year. One of the ladies from the Heritage gift shop at the Abbey has been found with her face chewed off.

'Oh dear,' I say.

'Quite,' says Effie, shouldering her clutch bag. 'We should have dealt with that monstrosity when we had the chance, in the last episode.'

Now we're heading out the door for another night out. With a wild beast on the loose. A man-eater at that. Not that you'd find a lack of those on the dance floor at the Christmas Hotel...

§

In the lavish foyer we run straight into the owner of the whole place. Attended by a horde of fit young men in tight-fitting elf costumes, Mrs Claus sits up in her wheeled bath chair looking like nothing else on earth. Her hair is fir tree green, teased to a point and studded with silver balls. Her frock is woven from strings of purple tinsel. Fairy lights bedeck every visible inch of her and her make-up is just like a clown's.

'Ladies! Welcome, dear ladies!' she shrieks at us. Her voice could curdle advocat. 'Take your places in the Grand Ballroom for the Barry Lurcher Experience!'

We are ushered past the yuletide hag by her festive minions and taken deep inside the Christmas Hotel. There is a surging crowd of pensioners, all eager to see the show. Effie seems just as excited as everyone else, but I can't see what's to get worked up about over a puppet show. I'm still new here. Perhaps Whitby is a town where novelty is rare?

Effie dashes among the cabaret tables to make sure we get a decent spot, fairly near the front. After a warm-up act from a poor impressionist on comes Barry Lurcher with his doleful-looking wife. She's wearing a magician's assistant type bikini and I reflect that all those sequins aren't doing anything for her hangdog expression.

Barry's act turns out to be music hall stuff – daft old jokes and ancient routines. Despite myself, I am kept in stitches throughout, just like the rest of the audience. Barry has a wicker hamper, from which processes a host of animal puppets, each with their own personality. Each of them banters with Barry, but the obvious highlight is when Tolstoy the Long-Eared Bat emerges from the darkest recesses of that hamper. Under spotlights the bat looks more fiendish than ever. He engages in nasty repartee with the audience – making individuals stand up so he can heap insults upon them, much to the hilarity of everyone else. Effie and I sit in a state of pleasurable near-panic, hoping that Tolstoy won't pick on us.

'What a marvellous audience you've all been tonight! Thank you so much for being terrific good sports! We're very grateful, aren't we, Tolstoy?'

'I've seen more life in a flaming morgue! Look at the state of you lot! What a bunch of frigging stiffs!'

It doesn't matter how rude Tolstoy is, the audience just laps it up. Barry Lurcher takes his bows to thunderous approval.

'Go and boil your heads, coffin dodgers!'

Then – miraculously! – comes the highlight of the act. We are all astonished and dumbstruck. It happens as Barry finishes taking his elaborate bows. He holds up the devilish bat, who flexes out his tattered wings – wider than a good-sized brolly. Then he flaps them and takes off into the glittering air. Tolstoy flies unaided up into the rafters...

He circles the ballroom three times and we all hold our breath!

'Look at me, you scabby old buggers! Just look at me go! Ha hahahahaha! How do you think we're doing this, eh? With strings? With smoke and mirrors?'

Then he's dive-bombing the audience. He swoops and makes lightning raids on particular tables. Screams ring out and glasses are smashed.

And I just know Tolstoy is going to come for me. I steal a glance at the stage, where Barry is beaming at his charge's naughtiness.

'Look out below...! Hahahaha!'

Effie is elbowing me like mad. Next thing I know those satanic eyes and the rest of the puppet are upon me. He's caught up in my beehive, slashing with his grinning mouthful of teeth. My hands grasp his furred and matted body. He feels surprisingly substantial and strong. Even muscular, beneath the dirty fun fur fabric.

The rest of the ballroom is silent for a moment, and then they all roar with laughter at my predicament. Effie tries feebly to help, but is rewarded by a slashing wing in the mush and falls backwards onto her chair.

Tolstoy is like a maddened beast, lashing out feverishly. A whole hank of my wig is between his jaws and I can see he won't let go. I won't give him the satisfaction of screaming. This is starting to seem like a struggle to the death. All played out against a soundtrack of mocking laughter.

Then – finally – there comes a cry from the stage.

'That is enough! Tolstoy – leave the poor old thing alone!'

The horrid claws relinquish their grip at once. I fall back on my chair, aware at once of the mephitic stench of the bat. Brimstone and fag ash. My eyes go a bit swimmy, but I'm aware of the beast flapping across the ballroom, to alight gracefully like a kestrel on Barry Lurcher's arm.

'A big hand, ladies and gentlemen! Let's have a huge round of applause for such an amazing sport! Wasn't she extraordinary?'

A blummin' spotlight comes on me just as I'm straightening my hairdo, which is in tatters. I'm still struggling for breath, but luckily the lights go down and the disco starts. This allows Effie to help me to the Ladies so I can repair myself.

I am at the sink, shaking. Effie makes me sip her vodka and orange.

'Eeh, that wasn't funny, was it? Are you okay, ducky? You look a bit – well – green.'

'It was the shock, that's all.'

'I'd have had conniptions if he'd come after me like that. You're a brave woman, Brenda.'

Then she's hoiking out her make-up bag and fussing at my face. I flinch when she touches my skin. I don't want her feeling the puckers and gathers of my scars. 'It's all right, Effie. I can manage.'

'Poor you,' she sighs. 'You know, something always happens at the Christmas Hotel. Oh, sometimes you can have a right nice night out. Other times it's like there's something in the air. Something... evil.'

She goes on, 'And it was *literally* in the air tonight. Tolstoy is much nastier now than he used to be on telly. It's like the mouthy, moth-bitten puppet of yesteryear has turned spiteful and bitter.' She empties her glass. 'I suppose that can happen to the best of us...'

But why would Tolstoy want to pick on me, I wonder? I remember Barry's attentions of the previous night. Now they seem more sinister than flirtatious.

I tell Effie, 'It's no ordinary puppet, you know. How on earth did he get it to fly like that? And do everything it was doing?'

'I don't know,' says Effie. I can see in the mirror that her eyes are lighting up. She can scent a mystery through all the vodka fumes.

'It was like a creature possessed,' I say. 'It was like fighting for my wig with a demon from hell.'

We exchange a half-worried, half-excited glance. Then a toilet flushes and some tipsy old dear comes out of a cubicle, making for the sinks. We put our conflab on hiatus. It won't do if word gets out that we investigate supernatural shenanigans. It's the kind of gossip that can easily spread.

But we both have an inkling that the famous puppeteer Barry Lurcher is consorting with dark forces.

'Let's get ourselves home,' Effie says decisively. 'I think we've had enough light entertainment for one night.'

§

I take Effie's advice and have a quiet day. I wave off my Todmorden ladies, having fed them a vegetarian smorgasbord and I have no more guests until Friday.

Effie and I take a walk four miles along the cliff tops to Robin Hood's Bay. She regales me en route with tales from her childhood. When she used to come here with her aunts it was a lot wilder. They'd pick up ammonite fossils and shards of jet. 'Did you know jet was meant to ward off demons, Brenda? It was said to emit vapours inimical to those of a satanic bent.'

'Perhaps we should stock up,' I suggest, only half-joking. In my dreams last night I was plagued by the flapping of velvet wings.

As we get to the hillier parts of our walk I am wishing I'd put on stouter shoes. The wind gets whippy as we toddle through the steep town, past cheery shops and bunting-strewn pubs, past displays of shark jaws, buckets and spades and sun-faded post cards.

I'm starting to shrug off my residual nightmares and enjoy that nicest of treats – the unplanned day off.

We sit on the beach with parcels of steaming fish and chips. Effie produces a hip flask of sweet sherry from her bottomless handbag.

I breathe in the whole horizon. All the fibres of my being are thrumming with something very like atavistic joy. I want to run about in the damp brown sand and into the freezing, foaming shallows of the sea. Effie counsels caution though, since it all looks a bit slippy. She's known a few come a cropper in Robin Hood's Bay.

We set about an afternoon's perusal of the quaint shops in the confusing alleyways. We duck under stone arches and creep along ginnels and I keep banging my head on hanging flower baskets. I'm wondering about somewhere for a cuppa when I realise I'm facing the bow-windowed front of an old-fashioned toyshop with a display that's been lovingly assembled. This is it! Grenoble's shop, just as the Marys described it – with toy soldiers and biplanes and teddies and locomotives. Effie totters up and has a look.

'I don't think I was very keen on toys when I was a girl,' she said. 'There wasn't much money for fripperies back then.'

'The sign says it's been open here since 1818!' I gasp. 'It's been here forever, just like the Marys said.'

Effie's not that interested. 'Where shall we go for tea?'

When I open the door there's a volley of tinkling bells and I have to hunker down to get inside, a bit like Alice squeezing into Wonderland.

All I see at first inside are wooden shelves stacked to capacity with coloured boxes. Then a mechanical humming bird whizzes past my head. When my eyes make sense of the place I realise I can see goggling glass eyes staring at me from every vantage point. The room is crammed with dolls, puppets, stuffed animals.

There is a ravishing smell of fresh paint and wood shavings, but also a hot tobaccoey scent – of ginger and rum and sunsets. Far away places, all caught up in the curling blue smoke.

The source of the aroma is a rumpled old man wearing a fez, crouching on a pouffe. His jeweller's eyepiece makes him look alert and suspicious. He's whittling a squirrel out of soft wood with a brutal-looking chisel.

'I've nothing here for old women.'

He gives us a glance that takes Effie's breath away, she says later. In fact, she adds, the whole place makes her feel very creepy indeed.

'Can't we just browse?' I ask. 'Everything's so marvellous and olde-worlde!'

He shrugs malevolently and Effie and I set about peering into cabinets and displays. We ooh and ahh over tiny robots beaten out of tin and toy mice decked out as Victorian gents and ladies. Crystal swans and geese and rubber clowns queue up for rides at a steam-powered fairground. There are no prices on anything.

'Too expensive for you. All this stuff isn't for you. What do old women like? Knitting and watching the wrestling and discussing death and disease and their horrible relations. You don't know anything about fun. You've forgotten what it is, haven't you?'

Effie is examining a Tomb of the Pharaoh playset and she gasps at his rudeness.

'What would you know? Nasty old man. I don't call that very nice customer service.'

Then he turns that clockmaker's eyepiece on me and it looks kaleidoscopic.

'And what about you? Why are you hanging about with a dry old stick like her? You look much more interesting than her. Who are you?'

Effie gasps.

'Brenda, I think he's making a pass at you. I suggest you get behind me and that we make for the door.'

But I am a bit mesmerised, to tell the truth.

'Tell me, my dear? Whoooo aaaare yoooouu?'

I'm teetering on the point of telling him exactly who I am. Then, just in time, I pull myself back from the brink. His attention is snapped off by the doorbells. Someone is coming in.

'Come on, Brenda,' Effie urges. 'There's something unwholesome about this place.'

But we are brought up short when we see who is entering the shop. It's Abigail Lurcher, Barry's catatonic wife. She's in a nasty tracksuit and her hair's in a scrunchy. She flinches visibly at the sight of us in this cavern of childish things.

Effie nudges me and surreptitiously points out what Mrs Lurcher is carrying. The shopping bag is crammed full with the ratty, furry form of a lifeless puppet. The end of a tattered wing flopping over the top tells us that Abigail has brought Tolstoy with her.

Effie and I bustle back out of the shop because it's time to take our cream tea. As we sip our heavily-sugared Assam we stew over our most peculiar visit. Effie loves a mystery even more than I do.

Late afternoon has us meandering the country roads back to Whitby. Cutting through the churchyard of St Mary's and down the 199 steps. I pick up some groceries and a bag full of minty chocolates from the chocolatier. We're both exhausted from all our walking and we say goodbye happily outside our neighbouring homes.

§

At last I can draw the curtains and slip on my housecoat, lock the doors and relax. Nina Simone on the turntable and sherry in a schooner with a heap of magazines and a couple of murder books Effie has pushed on me. I fall asleep in my chair and don't even wake when my reading matter falls onto the carpet. The gramophone needle hisses at the end the record and I don't turn a hair.

I carry on dozing. Or do I?

Do I instead stand up, all of a sudden, at eleven o'clock? Do I swap my slippers for shoes and pull on my good woollen coat? And then do I go stamping down my stairs, letting myself into the side passage, locking my Guest House behind me?

I might be dreaming but the sea breeze feels real. It doesn't wake me, and nor does the noise of the late night revellers I encounter on the sea front. The amusement arcades are as garish and grotesque as real life as I march past them. I find I am walking stiffly, mechanically. Does this look peculiar to passersby?

I can't stop myself stepping onto the pier, where it's much less busy and well lit. The noise of the sea blocks out every other sound. A shaft of fear goes through me as I realise I can't see the end of the pier. I have a horrible, confusing memory of somebody once trying to drown me. Strong, familiar hands attempting to hold my head under choppy, freezing waters. Waters just like these.

Right now I want to be back on my green bobbly armchair in my cosy attic. What on earth has possessed me to send me out here, this late at night?

Almost at the end of the pier, cloaked in darkness. Looking back at the town I see the tallest cliffs on either side and the lights of hotels, looking suddenly hellish rather than welcoming. Suddenly my head is spinning. It's as if my mind has come loose. There's a terrific flash of pain.

There is someone else in here with me.

Does that sound crazy?

But they are in here with me. Peering through a hole in my head. Into my very self.

I shout into the cold wind blustering off the North Sea:

'Come on out and show yourself! Who the devil are you? What do you want with me?'

The mocking laughter of gulls is my only reply, as they battle against the wind. The dark elements roar all about me. They soak me and push me down, stuffing up my ears with white, foaming noise.

My feet slip, taking me closer to the stony edge. Still that ghastly sensation of someone peeking into my skull.

'How can you do this? What makes you think you can do this to me?' After a few moments more of tottering about in the black air, at last a voice comes to me. It hammers into my head and its force pushes me to my knees.

'You've met me once already. Don't you know the sound of my voice?'

It's like the worst migraine I ever had. All at once I know who this is.

Barry Lurcher! It's you! Where are you? I thought you liked me!

There's an oily chuckle. I twist round as if I could find him. But I am pinioned at the very edge of the pier. There's no barrier between me and the tossing sea.

'I am inside you, Brenda. The sheer force of my will has penetrated every fibre of your shambolic mortal remains.'

'Shambolic? Who are you to talk to me like this?'

'I am the Puppet Master and you are my plaything. You find yourself in thrall to my ineffable will!'

So there you have it, I think. Just another silly man with a need to dominate women in order to satisfy his dodgy ego. He's playing mind games with me – literally, since I can feel his presence inside my mind and his physical self is nowhere to be seen.

'I could make you dance and pirouette your nasty old cadaver into the freezing briny and who would know? They'd think you'd topped yourself.'

I am horrified by his cruelty. I struggle to remain in command of myself.

'Mine isn't a miserable existence! I have a very nice life, as it happens! It might not look like much to the likes of you, with your showbiz lifestyle – and being some kind of wicked sorcerer to boot – but I'm actually quite content these days, thank you very much!'

He laughs and the pressure of his will relents enough to allow me to step back from the edge.

'I don't intend to kill you. Not yet. Not quite yet. Good night, Brenda. Good night, you horrible old monster.'

Then he was gone. He was out of my mind. And I was alone on the pier in a rising storm, but in full command of my faculties once more.

I knew that the so-called Puppet Master would strike again.

§

I wake up thinking: I can't let Barry win. He has proved he can blot out my thoughts and rule over me. I get up and do my exercises very quickly and I'm glad there are no guests to see to today. I need to concentrate on how to defeat my foe.

Effie is dozy in the morning and doesn't quite grasp the point when I tell her about the terrible events of last night. 'Are you saying you had a secret assignation with Barry Lurcher on the pier?'

I'm vexed by her leaping to conclusions. 'Do you think I go running about meeting funny men?'

She shrugs, cradling her coffee cup in her skinny fingers. 'I hardly know you at all, do I, ducky? You might be hiding all kinds of secrets. How do I know what you are capable of?'

Staring back at her, I realise Effie has been wondering about me. I try to give as little as possible away. I've grown good at it. Now she's squinching up her face into wrinkles and looks like nothing but a cross old coconut. If we want to be friends, she's saying, then she needs to know more about me.

'Effie, what I'm saying is that he did something supernatural to me, down on the front last night.'

She looks frankly sceptical. 'Maybe you're being swept off your feet by him. Maybe that's what it feels like when it happens.'

'There was nothing romantic about this,' I burst out. 'He seized control of me. He said I was an empty vessel and he could make me dance...'

'But why, ducky?' she asks. 'What would he gain from mixing his metaphors like that?'

All I know is I went to the very edge last night and was almost never seen again.

The two of us are jolted out of our conversation by a whole lot of banging at the door. We're both astonished when Abigail Lurcher comes stumbling in, more animated than we've ever seen her. 'Shut the door! He doesn't know I'm here!'

We both see at once how scared she is. 'What the devil's the matter?' says Effie, turning the shop sign to Closed and trotting off to brew more coffee.

'Only you two can help me,' says Abigail. 'I've snuck out of the hotel to bring you this.' She thrusts her shopping bag at us and we can see at once that it still contains the lumpen form of Tolstoy the bat. 'It's lethally dangerous. Mr Grenoble stuffed extra evil magic into the wicked thing. You two have to hide it and keep it away from Barry.'

'Hold it,' says Effie, trying to open the bourbons. 'What are you talking about?'

The distraught young woman points at the shopping bag, now resting on the breakfast bar. One wing has slid out. 'That monster needs to be kept away from my husband. Only then can Barry be free!'

Effie and I exchange a glance. Why should we trust her?

'It isn't just a harmless puppet,' says Abigail.

'I could have told you that,' I snap. Unconsciously I touch my hair, as if my wig is in danger again.

Effie says, 'What we want to know is how Barry makes it do such horrible things?'

'You've got it the wrong way about,' says Abigail. 'It's Tolstoy who controls Barry. He makes him comply with his will, drawing all his magic power from Grenoble's magic toyshop. It was there that Tolstoy came from, some forty years ago, you see. When Barry was just a teenager, on holiday with his mum. Tolstoy was a present, but poor Barry succumbed to a life of servitude to a dark, furry master.'

Effie and I stare at the single, gnarled claw hanging out of the bag. Could it be true? And yet it was Barry's voice I heard inside my head last night, not Tolstoy's. Right now I'm not sure who's possessing who.

'You're a witch,' Abigail says to Effie. 'You know what to do.'

'How do you know that I'm a witch?' snaps Effie, rather shrill.

'Mrs Claus told me,' says Abigail. 'She says you'll find a spell, somewhere in your old books of magic, to put this malignant beast out of action.'

Is it my imagination? Or does the claw that hangs half out of that bag start to tremble and flex? The sides of the shopping bag are swelling and rising and falling with the long-eared bat's sulphurous breath...

Effie grumbles. 'I suppose I might rustle something up. We'll need some black candles. And industrial quantities of salt to make a protective pentagram... And maybe there's something belonging to my old Aunt Maud which might be of some use...'

'How did you get the puppet away from Barry?' I ask.

'My husband was out for the count this morning,' Abigail says. 'Last night's performance wore him out. He had horrible nightmares and was shouting in his sleep...'

Around about midnight, I ruefully suppose. Right when he was shouting at me.

Abigail and Effie set about finding just the right protection spell to put Tolstoy out of action.

'The real source of this evil is in Robin Hood's Bay,' says Abigail worriedly. 'Mr Grenoble and his unholy Toyshop. That's where all the trouble began for my poor Barry.'

As she says this I am starting to feel most peculiar. Effie is fussing around with magical ingredients and getting Abigail to tie the bat puppet to a chair. But my thoughts are elsewhere. I am echoing inside. Chiming like a great hollow bell.

My feet start walking. I am heading to the door. I move without my own volition. I am responding to a summons I have felt, more than heard.

The other two don't even notice me leaving. They think I'm making a fresh brew.

But I'm not. I'm leaving the building. I'm sallying forth into the evening.

Utterly possessed.

§

It's a very brave man who tries to possess me, I'll tell you that for nothing. Over the years I've had svengalis and other brutes having a go at subsuming my consciousness and I've had to beat them all off.

Now I'm sitting on the bus and bridling. Underneath the worry I'm furious. How dare these men – this Barry Lurcher, Mr Grenoble and Tolstoy the Bat – how dare they assume they can meddle with my mind?

But I'm feeling peculiar. Like a thunder storm is raging inside my head. Many different voices are calling out to each other, overlapping and indistinct, each of them trying to be heard.

'This is the last stop, love,' says the bus driver. I'm the last aboard. My reflection in the dark window is horrible. I'm all pale and drawn.

We're at the very top of the sloping town. As I clamber off the driver looks concerned. He even asks if I'm all right. Why do I look strange to him? My feet are moving at a leaden pace. I'm walking like a robot. Maybe I look like a drunk old woman. That's what I feel like as I begin the steep descent into Robin Hood's Bay.

I don't have to consciously find my way back to the Toyshop. I know exactly which alleyway it's hiding in. My feet lead me there unbidden.

Soon I'm standing outside the illuminated windows and garish displays and the truth hits me. I am possessed by their wills at this very moment. I have been in their grip ever since I left my home.

My eyes well up with futile tears. I have been my own woman for so long now. It is many years since I escaped from the control of men. And yet here I am. Subjugated to a psyche not my own.

I kick open the door to the Toyshop.

Tinkle goes the bell.

Inside tea lights cast eerie shadows on the toys, making clowns and cats and china dolls seem infinitely sinister. By the counter sits Mr Grenoble, pixie-like in the shadow of Barry Lurcher and his gargantuan beard.

'How gratifying. You came here because I commanded it!'

Mr Grenoble chuckles at Barry's booming welcome. He's still whittling away at a piece of wood. I tell them both:

'I came here of my own volition, I'll have you know. I came here to get a few answers.'

'You shall have them, my dear. You shall know it all. Now that you have sacrificed your autonomy to my sublime potency...!'

'You're crackers! I've never heard such suggestive nonsense!'

'You know it's serious and real, Brenda. Last night you felt my voice inside your head, didn't you? You know that I can do what I will with you.'

I cast a glance at the still-whittling Mr Grenoble and see him sniggering there. I bark at him:

'What do you have to say about all of this?'

'I've known Barry since he was a little boy. He has grown into a great and powerful magician. He is the proud possessor of amazing powers.'

'Huh, you men always stick together.'

'I was only a child when I first came here. My mother dropped me at the door, thinking it was just an ordinary toyshop. She thought I'd waste my holiday pocket money on some trifling thing to keep me occupied. She never dreamed, I don't suppose, that she was sending me to face my ultimate destiny.'

'Oh, yes?'

'For here, in the gaudy recesses of Aladdin's cave I met this miraculous Toyman. When he looked at me he recognised my potential greatness at once.'

'Is this true?'

'True as true can be. I can see these things, you see. I can see into people. I can see into those who have larger, more powerful souls than anyone else. Like Barry here.'

'Well, bully for him.'

'Plus, I can see into the hollow interior of those unfortunates who have – for one reason or another – no soul at all. Such as you, Brenda.'

'W-what? I've got no soul?'

'Surely you know that already, my dear? After all the life you've experienced? You must know, deep down, in your heart of hearts, that there is no immortal soul in there. You're as hollow as an Easter egg. As hollow as a puppet.'

'No. Shut up!'

Suddenly I have to be out of that place. It's like dark tendrils are clawing at me. The tenebrous fingers of a heinous mind come writhing towards me and I whirl about, but I can't escape. This awful old man is saying nasty things but the nastiest thing of all is that, somehow, I know that he is speaking the truth.

You see, I've always been different to everyone else.

'You mustn't panic,' said Barry. 'Having no soul to speak of doesn't diminish you in any way. It makes you more special to me, in fact.'

'Let me out of this Toyshop, you maniacs!'

'How else do you think I can control you? How else can I slip so easily inside you, my dear? Why, because there is nothing else in there. It's only too easy for a Puppet Master like me.'

'No... I won't believe it! I can't! I'm a person! A real person!'

'But only just. And only because you really want to be. Barry, it's almost midnight already. We need to be prepared.'

'You're right. I think we've explained enough.'

'But you haven't explained anything! What are you up to? What are you going to do to me?'

'My stupid bint of a wife went to see you this evening, didn't she? She stole away with dear old Tolstoy. She thinks she can hide him away from me. Foolish woman.'

'How do you know?'

'I was looking out from behind your eyes...'

'Oh, come along, both of you. We have to go down to the shore. Down through the town and right to the very edge of the sea. And I must leave the door of my shop open to the night breezes, so that all of my puppets and toys can jump up and slip out and join in with the parade...'

'You two are bananas. What are you saying? That your toys come to life at Beltane..?'

'Not all of them, no. Just the most special ones. Just a certain type.'

'Ah – listen! Can't you hear it? That clattering... it sounds like bones and creaking old joints. That howling hullaballoo... Can't you hear them coming..?'

§

Mr Grenoble leads us out of the shop and into the alley and then into a steep street that curves about the outskirts of the narrow town and leads sharply down to the beach. And yes, all of a sudden, I can hear it. All the rattling and clacking of wooden limbs and metal joints, and the clacking of hinged jaws and glass eyes flicking in sockets. There comes the baying of wooden hounds and the roaring of monsters covered in dead fur.

Mr Grenoble laughs and claps with awful merriment and Barry becomes very solemn. I couldn't turn back if I tried as we step off the cobbles and onto damp sand. The moon is bright silver on the sea and the flat of the beaches looks endless. There is deep violet shadow beneath the savage crags.

From far over the hills and from goodness knew where comes the jaunty hurdy-gurdy of carnival music. It heralds the arrival of the Great Puppet Hunt.

'They're coming for you, Brenda,' said Barry. 'The puppets are crawling out of hell and they're enjoying their single night of freedom upon the face of the earth. Once a year they are allowed to dance through our skies and this year is special because they are coming for you, my dear. You – the most foolish puppet who ever lived. Or rather, who thought she was alive.'

'No... leave me alone.'

'You're a puppet made out of human parts, aren't you? Sourced from a dozen or more different graves and charnel houses. Stitched together with catgut and twine. That's all you are, isn't it, Brenda? A horrible hotch-potch. A female miscellany. A foul, reeking casserole of mortal remains. Oh, don't look like that. We know your secrets.

'Mr Grenoble and I know all about everything you have tried to hide. It's so pathetically obvious who and what you are. You're a puppet. A monster. Now. Stand on these sands, and watch them approach. They are coming for you now, dear Brenda.'

I'm standing there helpless. Struck dumb with fear and shock as Barry Lurcher steps away from me. Then I turn to look back down the long expanse of shoreline and I see that he is right.

All the masked goblins and dummies and marionettes, they have emerged from their own special hell. That portion of Hades given over to those who have no souls. Here they come dancing all out of time to discordant music, traipsing out of the churning sky...

At their head rides a man with a terrible bloated head and pointed chin. My captors laugh and tell me he is king of all the puppets in hell. Mr Punch rides upon the back of a glittering crocodile, whose scales are glossy black jet. Those flashing fangs are after me and I'm swept up into the charging crowd of effigies, homunculi and figurines. Princes and shepherdesses, dragons and mice, soldiers, nutcrackers and big bad wolves... In a trice I am a part of the horrible parade; I have ineluctably joined this dance of the dead. Or rather, a dance for those who had never really lived...

We ride along the headland and I resist, I twist and turn and struggle to break free. I see the faces of wildcats, foxes and owls all around me. A snarling menagerie with malevolent glass eyes. We swoop up the rocky crags and across the clifftops and we lift into the air like a dark skein of starlings. From the ground we must look like horrendous storm clouds massing above Whitby Abbey.

Down there in the town of Whitby – for that's how far we have flown already – the people are celebrating

Beltane, all unawares. They have a few garish fireworks and they indulge in some tame dressing up. There are bonfires and silly games and people out in the streets at midnight wearing Gothic finery. Yet here I am, a part of the most macabre show on earth – soaring through the skies with the Wild Puppet Hunt.

They want to take me away forever, I know. I understand that all this exhilarating stuff is just a prelude to what they intend to do. If they get their way they will take me down into hell with them. And there I will be in torment forever.

I can't have that, can I? I have a life to live on Earth, still. I might be two hundred years old, but I still have a lot to give. And so, as we sweep like a curse across the rooftops of Whitby I am struggling again, desperate to be free.

They hold me pinioned between them. A bear, a fox and an evil-looking hare with yellow buck teeth. They keep a tight grip on my chunky arms and my legs are pedalling madly high above the town. I am screaming and screaming for them to let go.

Then the Toymaker, Mr Grenoble, is with me, and so is that bearded brute, Barry Lurcher. They are both holding me tight and when I stare it seems that they are puppets, too, with painted faces and stringy hair. Now they're growing long furry ears and their eyes are like marbles stuck in their heads.

'Give in to it, Brenda! It's the most marvellous feeling. Giving up all volition and will. All these years of making your own way in the world. Decisions and choices and responsibilities. And all that time, all those years of dragging that gross carcass with you. All that mending and patching your unnatural body...!'

'Thanks a bunch, Barry! And there was I, thinking you fancied me!'

'Feel how light you are, Brenda. Feel how you can transcend all the rubbish and dross! Give up your will and your moribund flesh! You can dance forever with us on the very brink of being and non-being...!'

'You're talking a load of old rubbish! You're completely daft if you think I'd go anywhere with you, you creepy bugger!'

'But you're already here, Brenda! You're a part of the Wild Puppet Hunt this Beltane Night. You're here forever now. We will dance with you into the inferno...'

'What about your poor blummin' wife, eh? What about Abigail? You've led her a merry dance as well, haven't you?'

'She no longer matters. All that matters is you – and dragging you into hell with me! They are very keen, down in Hades, to get their hands on you – Brenda Frankenstein...!'

'Don't call me that name! I am not that name!'

'Oh, oh, but you are...! I know who you are. How have you managed it, you fleshy marionette? How have you kept yourself alive for all this time?'

'Shut up! Stop it!'

'How have you kept that spark of life force glowing within you? '

'Enough, you cheeky devil! As if I'd ever deliver up my secrets to the likes of you!'

'We will hear it all... when we get into Puppet Hell..!'

'Nooooo!'

I fight like a mad thing this night and screech like a banshee. Not for a long time have I been quite so scared. I don't doubt for one minute that this hairy occultist will do exactly what he threatens to. I know where this horrible flying circus is bound for...!

So I clobber him. I wrestle myself free, out of his grip, and that of the wretched old Toyshop owner. Up in the howling air I struggle out of their grip, and I clobber the bugger. Yes, he might be strong, and possessed of unholy determination. But I am stronger because I'm even more determined. I want to live and carry on living, exactly as I choose. I want this with every fibre of my being.

I think my inner goddess has been woken by the almighty shock of these unfolding events. Barry knowing my true name – my father's name – was the biggest shock of all. He flung that filthy epithet at me from out of the blue. The true horror of my heritage fell full force upon me all over again.

Cursed to be a member of the Frankensteins!

But if I am a monster then I am possessed of a monster's vim and vigour. And so I batter Barry Lurcher. I punch his blummin' lights out. As we fly through the skies across Whitby I give his fat arse a bloody good kicking. And all the puppets laugh maniacally at the way we're carrying on.

Then, just as I am starting to wonder how I'll ever get out of this predicament, we are joined by a horrible, fanged and flapping creature who brings with him a whiff of brimstone and death.

He comes sneaking up from the rooftops. I can hear the bruised and bleeding Barry call out to him.

'To me, Tolstoy! To me! Save me from this dreadful woman!'

And, true enough, it is Tolstoy the Long-Eared Bat, swishing those satiny wings and hurrying to keep up with us all. With all of his ghastly teeth on show he screeches some choice names at me, but I am in no mood to argue with a glove puppet. I seize him by the throat. Weirdly, he's jangling. He's wearing some kind of necklace that he didn't have on before. But there's no time to be thinking about what this might signify.

'Aaagghh! Get off me, foul harridan! Barry! She's got me, Barry! She's got me by the throat!'

'I'll rip his bloody head off! I swear it!'

'I think she means it, Barry.'

All the puppets are squealing with laughter.

'This is your revenge, isn't it? For the rough ride we've given you?'

'She's squeezing harder, Barry! I can hardly breathe!'

'My life for his, Barry. You can have your rotten bat back, but only if you set me free.'

'Aaaagghh! She's choking me...! I've gone all limp!'

'Do it, Barry! Set me free!'

'All right! Just don't hurt him! Tolstoy is all I've got!'

Barry is as good as his word. I stop throttling Tolstoy. I hand him over like the hostage he is. Then Barry hugs the bat to his chest and, in that moment, relinquishes the magical power he holds over me. For a second he looks stricken with defeat as I fall away. I am free of the Wild Puppet Hunt!

I feel exultantly free as his will flows out of me. I see that parade of puppets streak off across the sky without me. Through a bright breach in the midnight clouds they go.

I hear their manic, chattering, hullaballoo, and the voice of their leader crying out his eternal mantra:

'That's the way to do it! That's the way to do it! That's the way to do it!'

Somehow – in the very nick of time – I have avoided being sucked into hell.

All these thoughts flash through my mind in an instant. Then – as if gravity is the least of my worries – I start falling. Falling fast, arse over tip. Down through dark fathoms of air. I start off higher than the Christmas Hotel and higher, even, than the very top of the abbey.

I have such a long way to fall, and it's over extremely quickly.

I land very loudly in the black water of the harbour with one hell of a splash.

At first I think I'm a goner, but of course that isn't so. As Barry Lurcher kindly reminded me, I've survived all kinds of awful to-dos. I've hauled this old carcass through two hundred tumultuous years.

A drop in the briny isn't going to stop me now. I hold my breath and belly-flop and because it's Beltane there are still folk up and about. A gaggle of startled Goths ends up with the job of fishing me out. Working in gloomy unison they have a struggle to get me ashore onto dry land. But they make it! And I am saved!

I thank them and make up an excuse about being out on a bender. I've been a little drunk and disorientated and I've fallen off the pier. A touch too much of spirits this Beltane. I'm awfully ashamed. The Goths seem to believe me, though they look perturbed at having to dredge old ladies out of the harbour.

I hurry on home, avoiding further questions. Hoping that no one happened to notice me streaking through the sky tonight, in the grip of those horrid creatures. What an evening I've had!

§

I'm sopping wet. I'm like an old dishrag. I'm holding my wig on with both hands, but I'm jubilant. I've fought my nemesis to the bitter end and I've won!

When I traipse up Harbour Street I see lights on in Effie's junk shop windows so I bang heavily at her door.

She quails at the terrible sight of me.

'Whatever's happened to you, ducky?'

'If you let me in I'll tell you all about it.'

In her sitting room I survey the wreckage. The protective pentagram she drew in salt with Abigail has been scuffed over. The black candles have been snuffed out and there's a big scorch mark on the net curtains. One of the windows has been smashed.

'We tried to contain him as long as we could,' Effie says. 'He had all this daemonic power inside of him. He was thrashing about, shouting that he couldn't let the Wild Hunt go without him.'

I nod grimly. 'I had to fight him off... That creature was terrifically strong.'

Effie's eyes are bright. 'Remember when I told you about jet? About the vapours it's reputed to give off? And how they combat the forces of evil?'

'Why, yes,' I say.

'I dug out my favourite antique necklace that used to belong to my Aunt Maud. This was very quick thinking of me. While Tolstoy was imprisoned here, Abigail and I held him down and wrapped the beads all round his wings. He was tangled up and furious. He couldn't get rid of it before he raced of into the night.'

I stare at Effie. 'You clever old thing! You weakened him! That's why I was able to defeat him – even as I was being dragged through the skies in that terrible throng...!'

'Oh, Brenda, you must have been through a right ordeal,' Effie says. 'Are you saying they flew you up into the skies over the town..?'

I nod. 'And I fell into the harbour, too.'

'Let me get you some towels and a dressing gown.'

Abigail fishes around for a hanky.

'I'm free of Barry at last! He got to ride with the Wild Puppet Hunt after all. That's all he ever wanted. It was all he'd wanted to do ever since he was a little boy and he first fell in love with Tolstoy. And now he's gone and buggered off to hell. I'm footloose and fancy free, aren't I? Free of this marriage, which has been the bane of my life.'

Effie comes back dragging towels, blankets and an old hot water bottle, catching the end of this. She stares at Abigail.

'Couldn't you have just gone in for a trial separation?'

'He was an obsessive control freak.' cries Abigail. 'He had to be in complete possession and command of everything!'

Now I'm thinking about that malign presence in my head, that night on the pier. I knew he would stop at nothing. My heart goes out to this limp, dowdy woman on the settee. Goodness knows what she's had to put up with.

Effie dumps the towels on me.

'Eeh, can't men be weird? It's all power games and domination with them.'

I start towelling my wig and suddenly I'm shivering. I'm sitting in Effie's front room, stinking of the sea. 'I'd better get these sopping things off.' Before I head off to Effie's spartan bathroom I ask Abigail, 'So what will you do now?'

The Puppet Master's wife shrugs happily. 'Oh, well. There are still seven nights booked and paid for at the Christmas Hotel. Seven nights of cabaret to put on. Barry would never listen to me, but I've got the most amazing voice. So what I thought I'd do is hook myself up to the karaoke machine and put on a wonderful show for everyone!'

Effie punches the air. 'We'll be there, won't we, Brenda? We'll be in the audience, cheering you on!'

It's only later, as I'm pulling on Effie's too-small spare fluffy dressing gown that I wonder. Do I really want to applaud the warblings of the woman whose husband sought to deliver me to Hades?

Then I think, oh never mind. We can't be held responsible for the doings of dodgy partners, can we?

§

That night I have the most lurid nightmares. I'm in a kaleidoscopic whirl of bodies. Feathers and claws and horrible appendages. I'm back with the empty-eyed puppets and we're soaring over the clouds.

I wake with a shout.

I make myself spicy tea and sit up in my attic, reassuring myself with familiar surroundings. You got away in time. You haven't been sent to hell just yet. You've snatched yourself a bit longer on earth...

I'm glad because I've decided I like it here, after all. Twenty decades in, and I'm enjoying my life at last.

I've got new guests arriving today, so I'd better pull my socks up.

At eight pm Effie comes calling. We're both glammed up, ready for Abigail's debut at the Christmas Hotel. The spring evening is all golden light. It's May Day and there's a lovely, rinsing breeze, washing all of the cobwebs away.

I haven't told Effie half of what went on last night. I'm relieved she wasn't there to hear my darkest secrets divulged by Barry Lurcher. And she never heard him accuse me of having no soul.

What a terrible thing. I've wondered for two hundred years whether this was true. What do I really have inside me? Why am I even alive? What's to do, if there isn't a divine spark inside this old body?

But all that is just philosophical folderol, isn't it? It doesn't really impinge on my day-to-day life, or my nights on the town. Who really knows anything about our souls?

Effie and I link arms all the way up the winding road to the West Cliff and the Christmas Hotel. Where the pensioners are excited, wearing their party hats again and Mrs Claus is booming at her willing elves and she's bedecked in fairy lights. And all the fluorescent posters of Barry and Tolstoy have been replaced by pictures of the brand new singing sensation – Abigail Lurcher. She's going to sing us all our very favourite hits in the grand ballroom.

Effie and I grab ourselves a vodka and orange and hurry to a nice table. We settle down to be entertained.

The lights go down. Her spotlight awaits. And out comes Abigail, singing 'The Wind Beneath My Wings.'

About half way through the first song Effie nudges me with her bony old elbow. 'Eeh, that's a bloody awful voice she's got. I've never heard nowt like it, have you, ducky?'

I know by now that you can't shush Effie.

## 3

# Spicy Tea and Sympathy

Hello, there. Well, obviously I'm not where I want to be. I'm afraid I am narrating this from a slab. Or some sort of operating theatre. A flat surface, at any rate, cold and ominously smooth, and I'm blummin' well strapped to it. Not very comfortable. I'm used to narrating from the comfort of my attic sitting room and after the event, so to speak.

But here I am, entering into what I hope is the climax of our latest adventure. This time I don't even have the luxury of blaming Effie for dragging me into the fray. This time I've no one to blame but myself. I'm in the murky underground base of my enemies and I'm alone ... oh, apart from that desiccated old corpse over there. She who's hooked up to all those tubes. They're filling her veins with an unholy mixture of my blood and a very special herbal infusion, hoping she'll return to life. Oh, it's a filthy tale. And while they've left me on my tod I might as well occupy my mind. While I'm lying here, all tied up and with the life force draining out of my vitals, I suppose I could regale you with the details...

It begins... with a new tearoom that's just opened in Pannet Park, quite close to the creepy old museum. It is a delightfully sunny afternoon and perfect for sitting inside what was once a botanical hothouse. It's called *Tipple* now, and it's still florid with exotic blooms and rubber plants. As we wait by the 'Please Queue to be Seated' sign, Effie idly remarks on the Ancient Egyptian theme, fairly evident due to the fact that the waitresses are got up in bandages like mummies. The air is rife with the myriad buttery, crumpety, fruity and spicy, toasty and smoky scents of teatime.

Effie reminds me about a lavish article in our local paper about the man who has started this venture. He was pictured in the colour supplement, sipping a cuppa very elegantly, under the dewy fronds of a tropical bush. Professor Marius Keyes is – Effie and I are in agreement about this – something of a dish. One-time antiquities handler (a phrase which prompts a giggle from Effie) Professor Keyes has now retired to Whitby. He is wealthy, handsome, and lavishly coiffured. Everything about him speaks of quality and polish: from his golden cufflinks to the leathery woodsmoke of his aftershave. According to the write-up in *The Whitby Gazette*, anyhow.

We are shown to a table in a secluded corner, with a view of the hilly, wooded park and the Japanese pond.

I start examining the menu. It's quite complicated, with names for the teas that look like anagrams and dollops of over-rich text describing their flavours, origins and properties.

'His overheads must be atrocious,' Effie says, glaring about.

'It says here the tea will revive our ailing spirits,' I tell her.

'They'll want to, at four pounds ninety-five a pot. At that price it had better knock our socks off.'

We choose. Blue Flower Moonrise for Effie and Mango Whimsy for me. When it comes it's in glass pots of fearsomely trendy design. Effie looks cross, but is mollified by the quality of the china.

The tea tastes unspeakably awful. I very nearly gag.

'What's the matter with your Mango Whimsy?' Effie looks severe.

Next thing, she's actually spitting her tea into her saucer. She is mortified. 'Just goes to show. All this fuss about nowt. I've never had such a despicable brew.'

Her tea looks pretty in its glass pot, though, with the blue petals opening out and swirling. The waitress brings our bill, which Effie snatches out of her hand. At the tables around us I notice other tipplers seem to be grimacing and complaining to each other, about the vile tasting speciality beverages. Typically English, no one says a word to the staff. We all assume this is the way it's supposed to taste. Plus, it's meant to be doing us some good, and therefore must taste horrible.

We catch a glimpse of Professor Marius Keyes as he weaves about the tables, looking very pleased with himself and more corpulent than he did in the Gazette. Everyone smiles and congratulates him. 'They're succumbing to his obvious charm and charisma,' I observe, peering keenly through the rubber leaves.

'Hmm,' growls Effie, and I can sense her bridling. She wants to call him over and give him a few home truths. 'My Blue Flower Moonrise tasted like piddle.' I really hope she doesn't make a scene.

I long to be home and enjoying a pot of my own Spicy Tea. I adore that blend of ginger, pepper, garam masala, cardamom and cloves. It's like Christmas Eve and the Arabian Nights all in one. Homely and exotic as anything. And far nicer than the fancy nonsense they're dishing up here.

§

Effie and I part company down on Harbour Street. I have a suspicion that she's dabbling with the spells in those Books of Magic she has hidden away in her upper rooms. There's a glint in her eye that tells me she's been exploring her witchy roots of late.

While I'm enjoying a decent cuppa on my own, I'm having another read of the newspaper profile of Professor Keyes. This time he comes over as a bit smug, as if he's bringing civilisation and sophistication to the unwashed hordes who dwell upon the North Yorkshire Coast. I must have skimmed the article earlier, because now I'm finding out about his fixation on Ancient Egypt.

'It all dates back to my earliest boyhood and my up-bringing at the hands of my Great Aunt and Uncle. They allowed me to accompany them on their expeditions to some of the most fabulous and hidden regions on the planet. As a child my playgrounds were in ruins and among treasures lost to time. We girdled the world many times over, staying in the most luxurious hotels and the humblest encampments. We drank a lot of tea, wherever we went. We tried every kind of tea that the world has to offer. A fascination with tippling was born in me, and it has endured all my life. I am as obsessed with the reviving properties of the humble leaf as I am the dusty relics of bygone eras.'

What a show-off! Like anyone cares about his blummin' back-story! Still, he is quite a dish, with his streaky auburn hair, his pink cheeks and that lavish moustache.

§

That night I sit up in my sumptuous bed with a murder
mystery and a tot of sherry. When I drop off I dream
about being back in *Tipple*. Professor Marius Keyes
himself comes over to our table. The stars are bright
through the spotless glass of the conservatory. His head is
bent over Effie's upturned teacup and we are in suspense.
Then he whisks the cup away, revealing a mound of wet
leaves, to which he gives careful consideration.

'What have we here? What spicy secrets do these leaves
divulge?'

Effie rolls her eyes and gives a highly sceptical tut. Even
in my dreams she is borderline rude to people.

'Ever since antiquity folk have believed much truth has
been revealed by the leaves left at the bottom of a tippler's
teacup.'

'My Aunt Maud was a dab hand,' Effie tells him. 'What
do you see in my dregs, then?'

'Tea leaves aren't just something to discard. They were
in your cup. You blew on the tea and sipped and sipped
until it was all gone. And so these fragments of leaf are
inextricably bound up with you. They are connected to
your very soul.'

'And what do you see there?' Effie snaps.

'I see... Why, a glowing cat! Prowling the dark and
misty streets. And I see... an evil bat with long velvety
ears...!'

'That's the past,' I tell him.

'I also see... terrible things in your future. I see blood... and suffering. And meat pies. And garden furniture that has been manufactured from evil bamboo. And I see... the undead! They are rising out of their tombs and seeking out a reckoning with you two...!'

Professor Keyes looks at the pair of us, appalled. I'm just glad he hasn't had a peek at *my* dregs. At this point I'm glad to remember that this is all just a dream.

Except, the next morning, I'm up and about serving Full English Breakfasts to my half dozen guests and Effie gives me a tinkle. It turns out that she's had a dream, too, and we were having our leaves read by Professor Keyes.

'Is it possible to share the same dream?' she squawks. 'Without something nefarious going on?'

I muse, still holding a plateful of congealing Eggs Benedict. 'What did he foretell in your dream?'

'That I'm going to be a Vampire Queen! And that a great big brute of a man whisks you off your feet! And we're going to be on a TV show about haunted houses!'

As I finish the call I'm glad that we never had the precise same dream. I just know that I don't want to be sharing all my thoughts with my neighbour.

In my break I reread the article about the Professor. Something snags at my memory. Oh, this memory of mine. Did I ever travel to the exotic places he mentions? I don't think so. I can't recall ever being taken up the Valley of the Kings.

Effie phones later in the day, having decided we're using some vouchers she's had popped through her front door. Two-Eat-for-One at the Hotel Miramar. She tells me she could just murder Scampi-in-a-Basket.

'I thought you always said the Miramar was insalubrious,' I say.

'There's always been a lot of scandal about that place,' she agrees. 'Swingers' Weekends and things. I remember one, when the fire brigade got called in. It was the talk of the town.'

'Perhaps it's more respectable these days?'

She harrumphs. 'It's still owned by the same blousy, common, bloated old bag. They call her Sheila Manchu.'

'So why are we going?'

'Like I say, ducky. I've got a voucher. Plus, I've heard tell it's where a certain Professor Marius Keyes is staying.'

Effie has her investigating head on. It seems she's avid for dirt on our mystery hunk.

We meet at six pm, both reasonably dolled up. Tramping through steep and convoluted streets, I can see Effie's ran to more effort than yours truly. She's sprayed herself with something musky, but that could just be the whiff from the harbour.

When we reach the Miramar we're both a bit lathered, but there's some picnic benches out in what might make a nice beer garden, if it was done up properly. It's pleasant to sit in the breeze, but for some rowdy-looking youths at the other benches.

When Effie opens the door to the bar to place our orders all this music comes out. Thrash metal, they call it. I feel conspicuous in my lilac woollen two-piece amongst all this black leather. Never mind. And I won't have a word said against Goths after a gaggle of them fished me out of the harbour last week during Beltane.

It's while Effie's at the bar that I spot our quarry. Professor Keyes is in a linen safari suit, being flirted at mercilessly by a largish woman in a tangerine polyester nightie. They're standing by a half-hearted rockery, looking very much in cahoots. The early evening light makes her nightwear well-nigh see-through, but the Professor seems not to be embarrassed in the least.

Effie brings our drinks and I point them out. 'She's far too common for a man of his ilk. Unless he's capable of being overcome by sheer animal lust.'

I nod. 'Do you know, I've a feeling he is?'

'Florid complexion and big hands,' Effie shivers and picks up her glass. We both take great big swallows of our freezing vodka. And just then – the object of our curiosity advances on us across the lawn.

'Ladies! Didn't I see you sampling my wares at *Tipple* the other day?'

'You did indeed, Professor Keyes.'

'Marius, please...'

'I'm Brenda and she's Effie. Yes, we were both very favourably impressed by your café. We feel thoroughly refreshed by the whole experience.'

Effie gives me a look as if I'm laying it on a bit thick.

Such delicious tea. Very unusual.

Like many a vain man he responds atavistically to any form of flattery. He just can't help himself expanding like a dinghy as he warms to his favourite subject.

'There's a little drop of magic in every cup. Though I'm forbidden to reveal its source. An arcane mystery out of antiquity.'

He taps his mighty aquiline nose and Effie goes: 'Oh, really? Secret ingredient, is it?' I can tell a barbed comment is about to make itself felt. 'That's the kind of thing Health Inspectors can be very funny about, you know.'

'My dear, I didn't mean it literally! It's all a bit of flummery and nonsense. Why, the very thought of slipping something untoward into my infusions...'

He laughs long and hard, then kisses my hand and then Effie's. His lips leave a cool mark I find I don't want to rub off. We watch him link arms with Sheila Manchu and re-enter the Miramar via the public lounge.

'I know two things,' Effie murmurs. 'Those two are having it off and – he's lying through his false teeth. I've got an extremely refined palate and there was something about that wissy cup of tea I had the other day that wasn't quite right.  He's up to no good and I sense the presence of dark forces at work.  Don't you agree, ducky?'

I nod, but a part of me is still thinking about his warm, wet lips on the back of my hand.  And the fact that my skin there is tingling...

§

I've often made a fool of myself over men.  Tingling inappropriately and having my head turned.  I'll have you know though, that my nascent attraction to that patrician purveyor of gourmet beverages is not, actually, the reason for my present incarceration. My predicament has nought to do with any libidinous urges. Those I have placed under firm control, though I have, in fact, wound up under the wicked man's power.

Wait a second. What's that?  I heard something.  Is it the recumbent female form in the mummy case in the corner?  Oh heavens, is she returning to life while I'm lying here, utterly helpless?

There.  Definitely something in here.  A rat maybe.  A very soft footfall.

Oh! I recognise that scent. Shalimar.  It's Effie.  She's a godsend. Effie, Effie – you managed to find me! Oh, well done, dear.  Can you help me with all these straps and tubes things? Quickly, quickly... before he comes back...

While we struggle to escape I shall narrate the rest of the events that brought us here... to the scene of our near-demise...

§

Our scampi turns out to be delicious, hitting just the right spot. While Sheila and Marius Keyes are in the bar with a whole bunch of Sheila's cronies, Effie and I get up to a bit of investigating.

We take advantage of an abandoned reception area to check the reservation book. Then Effie's pushing me into the lift and we're shooting up to the third floor.

'He's got her most lavish suite,' mutters Effie. 'It's booked out for a month.'

I admit that I have a flash of envy of Sheila Manchu.

We hunt about the corridors at the very top of the Miramar. The monogrammed carpet's so plush we are soundless as we hunt for his door.

'We can't just break in,' I gasp.

Effie produces a skeleton key and starts fiddling like mad with the lock. I hold my breath and – we're in.

It's wall-to-wall chinoiserie inside. Lacquered cabinets and fancy wall-hangings and stuff made out of bamboo. Quality items of apparel are chucked and rumpled anyhow over the unmade bed, along with books and papers and trays of half-eaten snacks.

'What if they come back and find us?'   I whisper hoarsely. 'What are we even looking for?'

Effie is hunting and pecking through all of his intimate stuff. 'Clues,' she says. 'Anything.'

She hoiks out a luxury suitcase and flings it open.

'He's got such wonderful things,' I say, gazing into his wardrobe. 'Look at all these beautiful shirts.'

'Never mind all that,' Effie snaps.   Then she finds something interesting at the bottom of his case.  It looks like a tin tea caddy.  She opens it, sniffs the contents and wears an expression I've only ever seen before on a police tracker dog.

I dither round his gentleman's requisites – they're like relics from a more gracious age.  Then I turn to the bed and realise that the covers aren't just heaped any old how. They are bulging in a distinctly human shape.

'Erm, Effie,' I begin, but my throat has gone dry and I can feel my scampi starting to make its way back up.

Effie is still sniffing tea samples. She's found some other caddies and one has made her gag.  Even from over here I can smell something sweetish.  A hint of ancient must and mould.

I find myself reaching out to touch the bed clothes...

And – 'Aha!'  – at that very moment comes Effie's shout of triumph. 'What do you think of this, Brenda?' She plucks out a nasty rootlike object to show me – a horrid, gnarled thing.

But my attention is elsewhere. It's as if my fingers have developed a life of their own as they suddenly snatch the bedclothes away.

Revealing the slumbering form of a mummy.

Swathed in none-too-clean-looking bandages, flat on its back on the queen-sized mattress. I give a hearty shriek at the sight of the thing and Effie cries out too.

The mummy twitches in response and starts to sit up.

Effie pockets the dried-out root and grabs me by the arm. It's down to her that we exit that suite before the mummy can do anything other than sit up in bed.

Down the corridor and stairs we thunder, sure that the thing's going to be coming after us. We get downstairs and clatter through reception and push through a crowd on the doorstep outside. We hurtle down the street together, without looking back.

'Why was it in his bed?' I ask, wildly.

'Didn't I say I thought he had issues?' says Effie.

'Mummy issues?' I ask, and laugh, though I don't mean to. Something about Marius Keyes' mummy has put the willies up me, even though I'm usually more sanguine about dead things coming to life.

Once back on Harbour Street, Effie announces that she's going to do some tests on that funny root she's found. 'Scientific and magical tests,' she says, a bit pompously. 'I think it's what he's putting in the tea, ducky, and I want to know what it does. Coming?'

I demur. It's getting late and I've got a spot of reflux from the scampi and vodka. Besides, there's something I want to check.

'Please yourself,' says Effie and we say goodbye. She shoots off and I know she's going to be up all night poring over that purloined scrap of whatever-it-is.

Meanwhile, I've got some thinking to do.

You see, the sight of that mummy plus the ghastly aroma of desiccation and bandages have combined to stir my old memories around. I fancy that my mind is just like an old teapot, filled with murky infusions. It needs a proper swirl.

Egypt, mummies, gnarled old roots and pots of tea...

Once home in my attic rooms I open up the safe in my living room wall, hidden behind the Turner painting. Here I store the keepsakes from a hundred adventures. It's all here. Fragments I have hoarded. I hunt through cryptic stuff and I don't even know what it's supposed to mean – a severed monkey's paw, a half-burned Bible, a Rubik's Cube, a weird piece of electronic circuitry, scrolls of yellow paper, a black carnation, clippings from exceedingly old magazines. And a stack of old diaries spread out over years, all written by different hands.

As if by providence a volume from the 1940s falls open. A utilitarian thing with flimsy pages, covering five years from the middle of the war onwards. Where was I living then?

Yes... yes... it's starting to come back... a little...

Oooh, I need a sit down. I stagger to my armchair, clutching the little book. It's charred along one edge. Acrid-smelling. When did it get burned? Many pages are missing. What I could do with now, I think, is a nice, reviving pot of char...

§

And suddenly – here I am. I'm warming the pot. Spooning in the tea leaves. But this isn't my cosy kitchen at the top of my B&B in Whitby. Oh no, indeed. I'm in a different kitchen altogether, in the past. A stone-floored scullery in a house in another town altogether.

I look the same and I feel the same, but I'm wearing a dowdy maid's outfit and I'm a... a servant. I'm working for a cross old man. A Professor. Suddenly I'm back to who I was. I am housemaid to Professor Reginald Tyler, who's a dab hand at the Olde English. I'm making afternoon tea and loading up the hostess trolley. Salmon paste sandwiches and walnut cake. Riches, during this time of rationing.

Today it's Thursday and the Professor is hosting a meeting in his study. The fire is lit and the curtains are pulled against the autumn afternoon. I push the trolley into the room and its wheels squeak as I make my circuit, serving refreshments to the various members of the Professor's writing club. They ignore me, and carry on listening intently, fuming the place out with their pipes and baccy. Here comes Brenda, not listening to Professor Tyler's droning voice as he regales them with another chapter of his book about the elves and wizards and whatnot. I concentrate on the seated men – a dozen of them, donnish and tweedy, their faces blurry and soft with fading concentration.

They are the Smudgelings.

They're having one of their special story-telling afternoons again. Professor Tyler clutches his papers and looks piqued by my intrusion.

My favourite of the bunch is Professor Cleavis. He's the only one who treats me like a human being, thanking me as I load him up with tea and cake and sarnies. He has wispy hair and the proportions of a giant teddy bear. When it's been his turn to read, I've lingered by the door to listen. Of all their queer, phantasmagorical tales, his are the best, I believe. He writes about an impossible land called Hyspero, where magic and adventure walk hand in hand. Professor Tyler usually berates him for churning out silly stuff for children and for not writing the true stuff of legend and myth.

Henry Cleavis beams at me while the others keep their attention fixed on Tyler's incantatory narrative. Same old gobbledegook, it sounds like to me. Dwarfs it is, today. A dragon this time, too. Maybe that'll liven the story up. While I'm going round with the fish paste sandwiches the old prof gives a meaningful cough. So I plod away, back into the kitchen. I know my place. I decide that I might as well do some washing. I could give the venerable Professor's smalls a good rubbing through, since I imagine they'll be tied up for ages hearing about his dragon.

That's just what I'm doing when I hear the dreadful ruckus coming from outside. I hear a sharp cracking noise in the walled garden outside. At first I think it must be local children, scrumping for late apples or dragging a guy about perhaps. Then I see it. Thorough the pebbled glass of the outside door. A tall shape. Man-sized. Bulky. It's five o'clock and the garden is filled with dark shadows. Is it really someone out there?

Then there's a noise of a body stumbling into the bins. My next thought is of German spies. I pick up my bucket of hot soapy water and carry it to the back door. I take a deep breath, grasp the handle, and fling it open.

And then...!

I am face to face with one of the most awful creatures I have ever seen. Its blank face is covered with mucky bandages, with hollow depressions for eyes. Its shambling form is coming towards me and I realise its twitchy hands are raised because it's about to seize me by the throat.

At this younger age my reflexes are pretty good. I leap backwards, slinging into the face of my assailant the first thing that comes to hand. This happens to be an armload of Prof Tyler's soggy underthings.

The mummy crashes through the back door to the sound of splintering hinges, undeterred by the weight of old underpants.

I cast desperately around for a weapon. The mangle? The mop? I'm backing away now, dread almost overcoming me. There isn't time to consider where such a musty brute has come from.

Then it turns out he isn't after me at all.

It's my hostess trolley he wants.

The revenant lumbers forth and tries to take hold of the still-warm teapot. I'm standing there astonished, watching on, as the kitchen door flies open. Help is at hand!

'I heard something untoward in the vicinity of the scullery!'

Henry Cleavis comes bounding to my rescue. He is astounded at the sight of the monster, now trying to drag my entire hostess trolley out the back door and into the misty garden beyond.

'Cease and desist at once!'

'That trolley is an heirloom!' I find myself yelling, and feel such a fool once the words are out.

The mummy gives a dreadful, guttural snarl and then he's gone, quick as you like. We can hear china cups and saucers tinkling like mad as he makes his escape.

We try to follow but to no avail. The back garden is suffused by an evil brown fog. The gate hangs open and the lane beyond betrays no sign of the bandaged miscreant.

'Are you all right, my dear? What was that thing?'

'Buggered if I know,' I burst out, and feel like collapsing into tears. I should have put up more of a fight.

'It looked very much to me like an Egyptian mummy come back to life.'

Professor Tyler's dry, acerbic voice comes from behind us and we whirl around to see my employer. He's standing in his shirtsleeves and puffing thoughtfully on his pipe.

'You saw it as well?'

'I was right on your heels, old chap. How very alarming. Our tea things have been carried away by a cadaver some half dozen millennia old. He must have a most ghastly thirst on. Brenda, you look as if you're about to keel over.'

I admit that I feel a good deal better when we are back indoors and out of that perishing fog. The gentlemen bring me to sit by the study fire. Prof Tyler disbands the Smudgelings' meeting and dismisses his fellow scribblers. They seem concerned and disappointed to have missed the fracas in the kitchen.

Henry Cleavis makes some rather nasty tea in some old mugs.

'I wonder why our mummified chum would want our dregs.' Tyler leans against the mantelpiece musingly. I can recognise the excitement in his thin-featured face. He doesn't give a hoot about the smashed back door or the expensive trolley. There is a mystery and he is cockahoop.

'I wonder if it's all to do with our meeting?' Henry Cleavis is examining the packet of tea I've been using. It is purple cardboard and decorated in foreign symbols. Rather exotic.

'Do you believe whoever controls the mummy was thinking of poisoning us?'

'You had some senior dons here tonight, Reg. Not that I want to flatter us unduly...'

'We'd already finished the tea. Little point in poisoning the pot after it's been emptied, is there?'

'Fair point. What a whopper though, eh? I've not seen a reanimated corpse like that since... well, a very long time indeed.'

Discussion of our frightening visitor comes to an abrupt end. Tyler stumps off to spend the remainder of the evening writing, and Professor Cleavis says his goodbyes, pulls on his hat and coat and goes off into the murky night. I clear up the disturbed kitchen and, just before bedtime rolls around, I take Prof Tyler his usual nightcap.

I find him scratching away in one of his old ledgers. He's working on the book that will eventually take him thirty-four years to finish. At this stage he is teetering at the halfway mark and quite grumpy about it. I tiptoe up behind him, put down his whisky, and turn to scoot back out.

'Poppy Keyes' Herbal Infusions.'

'Pardon, sir?'

'The people you bought that tea from. They are based in this very city. I read the back of the packet. Do you know what, Brenda?'

This old man always manages to make me feel nervous...

'I think there might be something in this tea leaf business.'

'I've only been using this new kind quite recently, sir...'

'Yes, the quality of the tea round here recently has been bloody awful. I've been meaning to have a word with you about it. There's something rather nasty in the leaves, I think, and I intend to find out what it is.'

I nod, reflecting that Professor Tyler only turns his massive intellect upon spooky mysteries when they disturb his comfort or when his magnum opus hits a sticky patch. Judging by the crossings out in his ledger, I'm guessing he has double the cause for thinking about this mystery tonight.

§

In the following few days there are reports of several incidents involving the tea leaf thief. A bandage-wrapped spectre is spotted in numerous locations all over the city as high teas and breakfasts are rudely interrupted. Each time there are ructions in the houses of brilliantly learned scholars as tea pots and cups and saucers are dragged ruthlessly away.

One luckless Reader in Applied Ethics puts up a fight for the sake of his wife's best china. Both of his arms are torn out of their sockets and the astonished academic bleeds to death on his dining room carpet.

When I hear this I'm glad that I never put up more of a struggle on the night my hostess trolley was manhandled away.

I'm relieved... everso relieved... oooh...

This is the moment that I come back to myself.

Right then. I mean, all these years later, standing in my attic. Brewing my tea. It's a bit stewed and awful now. But it was worth it. The fumes took me back through all those years.

To the first time I was menaced by mummies in a tea-drinking-related escapade.

I must tell Effie about this at once, I decide.

§

'Ooh, Effie. Thank goodness you're here. How did you manage to free yourself?'

She's gasping, 'I don't have time to go into that, Brenda. They're right behind me!'

'Who?' I ask, as she struggles with my bonds, sawing away with a pair of handy pinking shears she's taken to carrying about in her handbag. I already know the answer.

It's Professor Marius Keyes and Sheila Manchu. They're descending into the dimly-lit crypt where I've been incarcerated.

They've realised that we are on the point of escaping!

'Wait! Brenda, stop!'

'You wait till I get free, buster. You won't know what's hit you.'

'Please... you must listen to me... I never meant to hurt you. Either you or Effie, or anyone else. I just wanted to help my aunt... my poor old aunt Poppy.'

'This?' I ask, pointing to the hideous and withered up old thing in the casket. 'This old mummy is your aunty?'

'She is indeed, Brenda. And, really, it's partly your fault that she's in this state... '

'My fault! Well, I like that!'

'Yes, indeed. But to understand why that is so, I believe we must return to the tale of how you first met Poppy Keyes, many years ago, in Darkholmes...'

'Hold on, sonny. This is my flashback. I'll tell it the way I think best.'

'Very well, then…'

§

Three nights after the mummy's first visit I wake in a muck sweat. I have suddenly remembered how I came by Poppy Keyes' special blend in that purple packet. It was given to me as a free sample, by a rather severe and glamorous woman in a head scarf. She had a bike with a basket on the front, and it was full of these packets of tea.

She claimed to be pedalling free samples for the most august professors in the vicinity. Would I care to try this new blend her firm had perfected?

Well, nothing ventured, nothing gained, I thought, and thanked her kindly. At the time I didn't suppose it odd, the way she came to the door like that.

And something else has come back to me, too. It's to do with the tea leaves themselves. I believe that the fact that the mummy was nicking dregs was significant. It isn't really about poisoning people at all.

Prof Tyler is already out that morning, but I run into Henry Cleavis in the town. I happen past his favourite hostelry just as he comes tripping merrily into the autumn sunlight.

'Brenda, dear!'

He does look a treat in his green velvet jacket. A bit of a dandy on the sly, is Professor Cleavis.

I tell him about the sample, and how I have met the glamorous Mrs Keyes. And how she was particularly keen that the learned Professor Tyler properly sample her wares. Henry is thinking deeply, chewing on both ends of his moustache.

'But why collect leaves afterwards? That's what I don't understand. What's in tea leaves after you use them?'

'This is what I've been stewing over for days. And... well, you know how some folk can read fortunes from your tea cup?'

'Go on, my dear.'

'Well, what if there really was something magical about what's left at the bottom of your cup?'

'How fascinating! My dear, in your lumpen, proletarian simplicity, I think you may have strayed onto something! Why, I've read of something similar to this in old Icelandic mythology...'

'The leaves have been infused, you see, with the future fortunes of the tea drinker...'

'Yes! Yes! Inspiration! The leaves are filled with the very inspiration of very brilliant men! Good god, my dear, but I think you have it!'

Henry Cleavis invites himself over to Professor Tyler's house this very evening. He primes me so that I will be ready with a pot of special tea. Tyler is surprised but pleased to see his fellow Smudgeling. When I bring in the tea Henry and I exchange a wink of complicity.

'Oh, you've made this horrible concoction again, Brenda.'

'It's that special blend, Reg. I want to try out an experiment. Indulge me.'

'An experiment, eh? Ugh. Filthy stuff. Now, what is it you want to see me about?'

I return to my tasks in the scullery, pottering about, though I soon fall asleep in the old armchair. Don't blame me – I've been up since five this morning, riddling the grate and boiling porridge. I am dozing by the heat of the stove when there comes all this brouhaha from the living room. It sounds exactly like someone kicking the French windows in and then getting caught up in the velvet curtains and that's precisely what it is.

I wake with a cry and stagger into the hall, hearing Professors Tyler and Cleavis shouting at the tops of their voices. A tea cup shatters and then several more follow suit as I fling open the door onto a scene of utter chaos.

Henry has taken up arms. He has a poker and a pan shovel from the companion set I polished yesterday afternoon. He brandishes them fiercely at the figure still struggling amongst the folds of the curtains.

'We have captured the blighter, Brenda! Let's pin him down!'

'Is that wise, sir? If he's strong enough to kick in doors and yank off the arms of Readers in Applied Ethics?'

'Is this another of these mummified fellows?'

'Yes! He's covered in curtains, though.'

'We lured him here!'

'Are you saying you purposefully lured this creature here?'

'With the aroma of the tea...'

'That filthy brew!'

'We need to know what they want with used-up tea leaves...'

'Do we? Why do we?'

'Just help me, Reg! Help me with this confounded devil!'

All this while Henry Cleavis is battering away at the shrouded monstrosity with both dust pan and poker. The mummy is letting out some savage and disturbing – though muffled – cries of vengeance.

Then all three of us are upon him, and wrestling the creature like mad.

'Hold him steady! Good girl!'

'I've never been involved in anything so ridiculous!'

'Watch yourself, Reg! This chap's a killer!'

Then, all at once, the mummy goes very limp. It's as if all the life force suddenly drains out of it. We stop hitting and it slumps the ground. Henry drags the curtains away and hastens to prop up the damaged curtain rail.

Then the three of us are staring at the hideous revenant as it lies completely lifeless on the oriental rug. There are bits everywhere and I can picture me having the devil of a time with the ewbank later.

'It's given up the ghost.'

'Just moments ago it was possessed of the most diabolical vigour. Someone is dabbling in supremely dark arts, Reg. You know it as well as I. And we pledged, didn't we? To combat those forces wherever we encountered them.'

Professor Tyler mutters to himself and suggests that we unwrap the creature and have a look at what's underneath the bandages. Not being overly fond of this idea I head off to make tea and, when I return with the second-best pot I am confronted by a heap of dirty bandages and a lumpy form lying on the dining room table. They've covered him up with a spotless tablecloth muggins here spent her time ironing.

'Well, we've established that it's a cadaver of the correct sort of vintage.'

'I'm just glad my Nancy's away at her sister's. She would be livid seeing a nasty thing like that hanging about the place. I shall phone the museum at once.'

'I don't think they pick up donations this late in the evening, Reg.'

'Shall I phone the police?'

Both gents turn to stare at me like I'm mad.

'The thing is, what if it comes back to life in the night?'

'We shall keep a vigil by its side!'

I volunteer to take my turn, naturally.

'Certainly not. You have more important duties to attend to than mummy-sitting. I insist you get a proper night's sleep.'

When I glumly go off to bed I can't help feeling I've been cast out of the boys' gang. Actually, though, in my tiny housemaid's room, I sleep wonderfully well.

In the morning I find the house empty and abandoned. The mummy and its dreadful wrappings are vanished, as is the second-best teapot and both Professors. I could weep with frustration. How dare they go off without me? Haring off into adventure like that. Or perhaps, they had no choice in the matter? Maybe something truly dreadful has befallen them? I start to panic, shivering in the breeze that wafts through the broken French windows.

Then I see the note propped up by the clock on the mantelpiece.

'Brenda dear – the mummy awoke! We even managed to get some sense of out the brute...!'

'I am the servant of... Princess Ayotep... long-lost queen of my tribe... I followed her into the land of the dead in order that I may protect her forever against...'

'Yes, yes, we understand all of that. But what is it she wants with all the tea leaves?'

'I must follow the aroma of the tanna leaves... I must take out the pots... bring the mystical infusions...'

'Oh, dear. He's a bit slow.' said Henry. 'But, look here, old man – do you think you could show us to where you must take all these used tea leaves and so on?'

'Take you... take you to Princess Ayotep...'

'Well, that would be most awfully kind.'

'You have a real knack for talking to monsters, Henry.'

'You will... come with me...'

'Marvellous! Well, there you have it, Brenda dear. This mummy chap is taking us to the secret hideout, apparently. So – if we're not back at Prof Tyler's house before you get this, then I suppose, er, we might need your help. With my very best regards, Professor Henry Cleavis.'

His handwriting is as diabolical as the whiff of grave mould that still haunts the dining room. But never mind all that upset just now! The Professors need me! They surely need my help!

I surge at once into action... but the room around me is fading...! All colour and light are draining away...

§

And then all at once I'm back in the present day. Strapped to the sacrificial slab deep underground in the villains' lair and everyone looking at me.

Slightly awkward moment.

'I've had another flashback!' I cry out, before I can stop myself. 'I've seen all this happen before! It's all been flashing past my mind's eye! I know the secret at the heart of this mystery!'

'Oh!' gasps Effie. 'Do you, Brenda?'

'Do you indeed, Brenda? Do you really know the secret of our activities in Whitby today, as well as when you were investigating in the Forties with Professors Cleavis and Tyler?'

'Yes, I believe I do. I believe my frangible and delicate memories have lifted the veil of forgetfulness just enough to allow me to peek into your nefarious doings...!'

'Oh, not that nefarious at all, my dear. If there is anything mysterious going on, then it's all in the cause of love.'

'Love, he says! And do you think it's right to commit murders in the name of love, eh?'

'There has been no murder here. Ah, maybe in the past. When the mummies were too unwieldy and over-zealous, perhaps. But not now. Now I hope that there will be no harm to anyone.'

'You've already caused plenty of harm. Look at this! Look at how you've had me! All trussed up in your secret base underneath your rotten tearooms! Leaching the blood and life force out of me!'

'But you are a special case, Brenda. A very special case indeed.'

'You wanted more than just my used tea leaves.'

'Yes, that's very true. You see, you have so much to offer, my dear...'

'My own special blend.'

'I'm afraid I can't let you leave, you know.'

'What? Oh, help!'

Suddenly the mummies are advancing out of the shadows. They're seizing hold of Effie and me again. Sheila Manchu has the decency to look perturbed as her fancy man rocks with silent mirth.

It seems that we aren't about to escape at all! And they're hooking me back up with the tubes that will drain away my precious life essence!

All for the sake of that withered up monster in the casket!

But let me tell you how we came to be here, tonight, and in this horribly disadvantageous situation...

§

'Whoever heard of a combined tea room and massage parlour?' Effie is frowning.

We are back at *Tipple* in the park and Effie is staring at a sign advertising this curious combination. It seems that Professor Keyes is keen to offer services no other Whitby tearoom can, and rumour has it that strapping blokes swathed in bandages do the massaging in a secret room under the café.

We spy Sheila Manchu bustling through the park, on her way to a rendezvous, no doubt. Effie and I confront her on the footpath.

'You know what he's up to, don't you?' Effie asks her sharply.

Sheila looks distraught. 'Oh now, look, girls. I know you're both intent on ridding this town of everything occult and untoward...'

'What?' I cry. 'Who told you that?'

The buxom hotelier looks shifty. 'Word gets round. I've heard tales about your recent adventures.'

I glare at Effie. I'm not very happy about us getting a name for ourselves.

Sheila goes on, 'I don't care what you ladies have got against him, but Marius Keyes is the first decent fella to look my way in donkey's years. And he's not even after my business or my loot. He just wants me for who I am. And I won't have you telling me that he's up to no good.'

Effie coughs. 'We found a living mummy in his bedroom at the Miramar. It was in his bed, Sheila! Plus, we found some very peculiar herbal samples and things.'

She looks scandalised. 'What were you doing poking about among his private things? He said he thought someone had been in.'

'That would have been the blummin' mummy!'

Sheila looks disturbed. 'The mummy isn't real, you know. It's just a bloke dressed up. It's a gimmick. He's got them giving massages in the basement.'

All three of us are wondering, if that's the case, how come Marius had a masseur hiding under his bed sheets? But neither Effie nor I press the point. We've given Sheila enough to chew on for one day.

We both suppose, though, that it's through her – the blousy harridan, as Effie calls her – that Professor Marius Keyes gets wind of the fact that it was us rummaging through his belongings.

The reprisals come fairly quickly and brutally after that.

But we don't know that at the start of the evening, when I cook dinner for Effie at my place. We've having a lovely shepherd's pie and I'm telling her everything that came back into my head when I had my flashback into my own past life.

Effie is at once on the alert. I'm just dishing up seconds when I realise that I've perhaps given too much of myself away.

'The 1940s, Brenda?' Effie asks sharply. 'You were a housemaid to Reg Tyler in Darkholmes during the 1940s? Just how old *are* you, ducky?'

She laughs then, as if I have simply made a silly mistake with the dates.

I blush, because of course I haven't. It's just that I have hardly aged a day in over two hundred years. And that's a secret I've been hoping to keep locked up a little longer than this.

Effie is staring at me as I hand her plate over, heaped with more of that delicious pie. She narrows her eyes suspiciously.

I brush her chronological quibbles aside. 'Never mind all that now. The point is, I've seen all of this before, back then. When Professors Tyler and Cleavis and I smuggled ourselves into a tea warehouse in the north of Darkholmes, late one Autumn night... and there we did battle with mummies and a certain Mrs Poppy Keyes.'

Effie purses her lips at me. 'Are you sure you didn't just have a funny dream, Brenda? You've had a stressful couple of weeks. Setting up a new business, and embarking upon some strange investigations...' She reaches for the brown sauce and lavishes it on my pie.

Actually, Effie's unctuous concern is starting to make me feel cross. I hurry off to the kitchen to make us a pot of tea. My favourite spicy tea, naturally. I'll make it spicy enough to blow the top of her patronising blummin' head off.

She can forget all about dessert. I was going to do a trifle, but my heart's gone out of it, frankly. There I was, offering up a glimpse of my shrouded past, and Effie was looking like she didn't believe a word of it...

And, as I sniff the gorgeous aroma of my tea as it brews, I think it might be possible that I'm going off into a reverie again... and slipping back into the past...

§

I'm in a leafy back lane, checking out the walled perimeter of Poppy Keyes' tea warehouse. I won't go into the intricacies of how I have to shin up a horse chestnut tree to get my legs over the top of the wall. Suffice to say, I get myself inside the tea compound. I think I must be rather nimbler back in these times.

I dodge between wooden crates and the place seems oddly peaceful. All that can be heard is the sleepy whickering of horses in the stables.

Then, as I approach the rear of the warehouse itself, I can see lights and burly figures working into the night, moving huge loads in their bare arms. It seems that the tea company employs a mummified work force.

Now. Where do I think the Professors will be held?

I manage not to be noticed by my lumbering foes and inveigle myself into an office crammed with paper folders and receipts. I have a quick look through and can't find much evidence of a thriving business. It seems that this tea company doesn't much care for profits. All they do is give the stuff away.

In the bottom drawer of the filing cabinet I find a selection of withered-up gourd-type things. Nasty-looking objects. They have a strange scent about them. It's familiar because it's the scent of Poppy Keyes' special blend in concentrated form.

Oh my, what have I been brewing for my old Professors?

Speaking of which – it's they who I should be looking for. I turn to go – and that's when I'm captured by the mummies. I thrash about a bit so they don't take me too easily, but it's no use. These revenants are possessed of an inhuman strength. As they carry me off into the murkiest recesses of the fragrant tea warehouse I believe I recognise the specimen who was, of late, supine on Prof Tyler's dining table. His bandages are still half-hanging-off.

'You will be silent... until you come before the mistress...'

'Yes, but you're him, aren't you? The mummy who came bursting into our house. The special servant of Princess Ayotep...'

'You must be silent and stop wriggling...'

'Where are you taking me? Who is this mistress, anyway?'

'All will be revealed...'

Well, perhaps. But for the moment, as they lug me into their secret hideout, this mummified minion is keeping things firmly under wraps.

And then... all of a sudden... I am in an underground lair. A huge blazing lake of what looks like lava takes up most of the space. There are great golden statues of gods and creatures that I suppose came out of ancient Egypt. Lots of conspicuous wealth on display. I find it all a bit showy, to be honest. I've spent a lot of time in secret hideouts by this point in my life and I'm not easily impressed.

'Brenda! You're here!'

'Oh, so they captured you too, then.'

'Did you get my note?'

'That's what brought me here, Professor Cleavis. I came here to rescue you both.'

'The mummies are too strong. We're at their mercy.'

'I rather think our pessimistic friend is right, Brenda. They're going to do something terrible to us, I imagine.'

'Well, at least we're all together.'

'Harrumph. I don't see any benefit in that. What a terrible way to die. What an awful waste! And my magnum opus only half-finished.'

'He's been going on about his magnum opus quite a lot.'

Just then there is the noise of a gong and a kind of brassy fanfare. We realise that someone rather grand must have entered the place...

'Oh, yes. Over there, look. By the sacrificial altar sort of thing...'

'It's Poppy Keyes!' I burst out.

'It's who?' asks Tyler.

'The woman who came to your door, Professor. Offering free samples. She's all dolled up tonight though, isn't she?'

'She certainly is,' gasps Henry.

'Like a kind of Egyptian Queen... or the reincarnation of one..!'

And that is the long and the short of it, really. Poor, silly Poppy Keyes. She is only a purveyor of fancy beverages, but something has gone a bit wrong in her noggin. I suspect it's down to all the time she spent in hot climes and poking about in tombs for a hobby. But somehow she has convinced herself that she is the ancient princess got up in a new incarnation... Oh dear.

'Avast and avaunt!'

'What's the Professor doing?'

'Trying to cast out her demons,' Henry tells me. 'He always has a go at this. He's rather good at it. It's worked once or twice in the past...'

'Even when he's tied up? Doesn't he need his arms free?'

'He's got a very carrying voice.'

'Out, foul demons! Leave this innocent woman in peace!'

Well, even I can see that it isn't working this time. Through her kohl-lined eyes and golden headdress,

Poppy Keyes is smirking at him. She's grinning at him madly. She's raising a cup and saucer to her lips and toasting him with her special blend.

That's when I look into the molten lake of lava, ringed by fire. And I see that it isn't lava at all. It's a swamp of used tea leaves. A quagmire of old dregs.

The mummies step forward and help their mistress disrobe...

'Goodness me!' Henry shouts.

'The woman's a decadent piece of work, and no mistake! Gracious!'

She delighted in appearing before us naked. She Who Must Be Obeyed. She For Whom Everything Stops. We watched her step into the lake of tepid tea leaves and swim there luxuriously...

'Aaagghhh!'

'Aaahh—owww!'

'Professors, what is it?'

'It's... agony..!'

'What's the matter with you?'

'She's... she's inside my mind, Brenda... we're psychically linked...'

'What? Through tea leaves...?'

'A-absurd though it seems... yes!'

'Do something, Brenda! She's absorbing our brain-waves! And the minds of every tea drinking intellectual in Darkholmes..!'

'Quickly, Brenda! She's destroying our minds!'

Once again, everyone is looking to me to sort it all out. The two old Professors are screeching fit to burst. The invidious Poppy Keyes is currently doing the backstroke in the lake of tea leaves, kicking up her legs and showing off madly. She gives a carefree laugh and her whole body glows as she leeches off their mental energies...

And I stand up. I've got to step into the breach, and rescue my professors.

The mummies see that I'm on my way. They come lumbering towards me. I roll up my sleeves...

'You must fight them, Brenda! You must...'

'You must put a stop to Poppy Keyes, Brenda!'

'Help us, my dear...!'

§

Well, it's just at the most exciting bit when I come back to myself. I'm standing in my kitchen feeling very peculiar.

Was I really involved in a terrible punch-up and fracas in that weird sepulchral place? Did I batter mummified revenants that night in order to prevent my professor chums from having their life force drained out?

And did I really wade into that rock pool of tea dregs in order to grab hold of Poppy Keyes and box her ears bloody? Reincarnated Egyptian Princess or not – I foiled her plans good and proper. Silly old tart.

And here we are again. All these years later. And she's raised her spooky self out of the dregs once more...!

Along with her spooky – though handsome – nephew.

This tea's stewed, I've been in such a state of abstraction. I must...

Hang on. What's that noise?

There's a scream, and I recognise Effie's voice. Then there's all this running about on the staircase. Very heavy, muffled footfalls. Who've I got staying? Just a few elderly ladies, who'd surely be hard-pressed to cause such a racket on my stair carpet?

I gird my loins and hurtle into the hallway. And I'm just in time to see Effie fending off three huge mummies with my ewbank. That carpet sweeper's got a lovely action, is all I can think, absurdly, as my neighbour takes her life into her hands. I hope she doesn't break it. At that very moment it gets smashed to smithereens and Effie herself is grabbed by the rampaging monsters. At once she is hoisted howling into the air above the banisters.

The third mummy whips around as I shriek and shoves his horrible, clothy face right into mine.

'Keep your nose out of our business!'

'I will not! I've put a stop to you lot before, and I will again!'

The mummy snarls and I see that his hoodlum chums are carrying my best friend off down the stairs. She's very quiet. Have they snapped her spindly neck? I think she's simply fainted. Quick as a flash, the three of them lumber out of my Guest House and down the side passage into the darkness outside.

Of course I thunder after them, thinking surely someone out there will see them and blow the whistle? Even in a town like Whitby three bandaged corpses making off with an unconscious antiques dealer can't go unchallenged? All of a sudden I feel alone and helpless.

Just then a dark silhouette detaches itself from the shadows of the alley. He rears up before me. The dashing and handsome Marius Keyes himself.

'So this is where you live.'

'I'm not so hard to find. It *is* called Brenda's B&B, after all.'

'Perhaps we had better go inside to discuss this.'

'I'm not letting you in.'

'As you like.'

'Where are you taking my friend?'

'I'm afraid I'm having to be so vulgar as to take her hostage. She will be escorted to my secret hideout and kept safe by mummies until you give me what I require.'

'And what can I give you? I'm just a harmless old woman. Same as Effie. What can you possibly require that I have?'

'You're rather more than a harmless old woman, my dear. Let's not beat about the proverbial bush. I know that you know that I know you were present in

Darkholmes in 1943. I know you were at the warehouse when my aunt was concocting her plan to live eternally.'

'Oh yes?'

'I know you thwarted her by wading into her pool of eternal youth and punching her lights out.'

'I did, did I? Well, she was a dreadful woman. She wanted to drain all the genius and life force out of my old professors...!'

'She was – she is – a wonderful woman! After my parents and my uncle died she was all I had. And so what if she was insane and believed that she was the reincarnation of an ancient Egyptian princess? She kept me fed and in fancy clothes and took me around the world with her. The soul-sapping activities she got up to, involving raising bodies from the dead and stealing vital energies from the living, that was all by the by, really. She was marvellous and beautiful and the most thrilling woman I ever knew.'

'I think you might have an aunty complex as well as a mummy one.'

'But now she's bitter and twisted and hideously deformed. And it's all because of you, Brenda! Because you denied her access to that pool of eternal life essence!'

'By punching her in the mush?'

'Don't you remember? You knocked her out cold and you pulled the plug. Literally.'

'Did I?'

'You saved the lives of all those boring geniuses. You doomed my poor aunt to a shrivelled and embittered afterlife.'

'Good!'

'And now you are going to come with me.'

'Never!'

'You will if you want to see your nasty best friend again!'

Oh dear. And that, you see, is how I ended up following Effie into captivity. Into the mysterious crypt-like place beneath *Tipple* Tearooms in Pannet Park.

And here we are now. With me all tied down and my life essences draining out... into the desiccated body of the Aunt of Marius Keyes.

§

'Oh, Princess Ayotep! We beseech thee! We have done all that we have done in order that thy nefarious will be done! We have caused to be brought forward before you this shambling wretch! This woman known as Brenda! May her strange and mysterious life force bring you back to full strength!'

'Don't count on it, buggerlugs!'

'Silence, woman!'

'Well, this was a right to-do. I had thought we had a chance of escaping, back when I started this narrating lark, and then Effie came and found me in this evil massage parlour of doom. However, things don't seem to be going our way, do they?'

'For all these years we have tried to find you, Brenda. We have followed the traces for decades now...'

Effie hisses out of the corner of her mouth, 'What's he on about, ducky? Why is he saying they've followed you about?'

'My aunt and I have known for many years who and what you truly are! We know what tremendous, occult forces are surging round in your immortal body...'

'Oh, now, I wouldn't go that far, Marius...'

'That night in Darkholmes – my aunt knew. She knew that her hopes lay with you and your blood and inspiration, Brenda. She knew she had to find you again.'

'Now you've got me.'

'We have indeed! Behold – she arises..!!'

'Now that's torn it,' says Effie.

We are reduced to cowering on the slab as a brilliant violet light suffuses the casket wherein lies in the dried-out husk of Aunty Poppy. Sheila Manchu is on the floor somewhere, moaning and gasping at these queer developments.

I'm feeling ever so depleted, what with my vital life-energies flowing into this... this monstrosity!

'Welcome! Welcome back to the land of the living, Aunt!'

Her voice is very raspy, when she speaks.

'You took your time, didn't you?'

'Forgive me, aunt. It took so long to find her, and to set up the optimum conditions for your revivification...'

The Egyptian Queen waves aside his protestations. 'Never mind all that. I arise once more..! That's the important thing! I feel the life force surging within me!'

'You are eternal now! You will live by my side forever..!'

'Yes, Marius, dear. Your aunt is with you again. You have done very well. What is this place?'

'It's the secret base beneath my new tea rooms in Whitby.'

'Ah yes,' says the ghastly revenant. 'I came here once for a weekend with your uncle. Many years ago...'

'I have done everything that I promised. I brought you Brenda... This half-alive monstrosity on the slab here before you...'

Hang on a moment, I think...! But I am too weak to budge an inch or say anything in protest.

'Ahh,' says the snooty cadaver, and all at once she sits up. 'Brenda! You thwarted my plans all that time ago. All those decades ago when I tried for the first time to make myself into an Egyptian goddess and take over the world.'

'Not this time, aunt Poppy! She won't get in our way this time!'

Suddenly Effie is on her feet.

'Well, now, look here,' she shouts, in her bravest voice. 'I don't know everything that went on in the past, but what I do know is that this time is different! This time I'm here!'

'Get out of the way, you silly old fool. Guards! Mummies! Take hold of her!'

But Effie is adept at giving the lumbering masseurs the slip.

'Who is this woman?' cries Aunt Polly at the top of her voice.

Effie is at work on the many tubes through which my life force is being drained. She's yanking on them and I'm not so sure that's a good idea... as they come loose and start spraying horrid ichor about the place... and my poor tortured form starts thrashing about on the slab...

'Stop her!'

'Kill her at once!' shrieks the would-be Egyptian goddess.

'Come here, you..!'

Marius himself grasps hold of Effie, who wriggles, pinioned in his powerful arms. He commands his mummies to fix the damage she has done.

'You stupid old woman. You have endangered the life of your friend as well as my aunt...'

In my weird delirium, this scene is distorted and macabre... Everyone seems to be covered in my blood... my consciousness is fading... and then the horrible laughter of the woman once known as Poppy rings out in the underground massage parlour...

'I am reaching my apotheosis!' she cries. 'And here, in Whitby, the historical location of the infernal Bitch's Maw... I will have access to unlimited power! I stand at the manifold gateways to countless dimensions...!'

'Yes! Yes! Just as you foretold! Drink! Drink, Aunt Poppy! Drain this monstrous female of all her diabolical juices!'

Naturally, since things aren't going too well at this point, I'm starting to wonder if my end isn't in fact nigh.

'Hahahahaha!' howls the Egyptian princess, swaying atop her casket. 'Behold my apotheosis!'

'You will rule forever via the Gateway to Hell!'

But there is one person we have all forgotten about.

Marius's forgotten lady-friend who has been cowering on the floor of the subterranean den for some time, is astonished out of her wits.

But now Sheila Manchu is coming to her senses. She is shivering in horror, clutching her peach-coloured negligee and her flimsy dressing gown about herself. She's coming to the rapid conclusion that her fancy man Marius isn't quite the reliable fellow he has presented himself as.

Sheila Manchu sees what he has done, and realizes that her true loyalties must lie with her two fellow Whitby residents. Myself and Effie, who are so close to pegging out at that precise moment.

Sheila gathers herself up and casts about wildly for inspiration. She has to do something. She has to stop these awful people.

'Don't worry, Brenda and Effie...' she gasps. 'I'll save you...'

'Come to me, Aunt. Step out of your casket! Leave your tomb behind once and for all!'

Sheila is a quick-thinker. She knows that desiccated and revived corpses fear one thing above all else. And, to that end, she rips into a boxload of tea room supplies that she finds in the corner of the room.

Doillies! Hundreds and thousands of paper lace doilies! Quickly, with trembling hands, she opens the supplies and whips out her cigarette lighter...

Marius Keyes is the first to sniff the smoke...

'No! What are you doing? You foolish woman...!'

The doilies catch light astonishingly quickly...

'Stick that in your pipe and smoke it, Marius!' shouts Sheila Manchu. 'You were just using me, weren't you?'

'Of course I was, you blousy old cow! But that doesn't mean you have to set my massage parlour and tea rooms ablaze!'

'Noooooooooo!' howls the would-be Princess Ayotep. 'The flames! The flames! Keep them away from me!'

The brainless mummies stop what they're doing at once – ie, guarding Effie and I – and hurry to swat out the fire. The flames leap at them – catching at the musty cloth and their flammable preservatives.

'My god...! No...!'

But it's much too late. The place is filled with choking fumes and burning mummies...

'Keep away from me...!' wails the woman who was once Marius's aunt as she thrashes atop her casket. But now the flames reach out to her and a tremendous sizzling fills the choking air...

Effie shrieks in my ear, 'Brenda...! We have to go! We have to get out of here. Right now!'

Then I am being hoisted from the slab and the lurid, deadly scene tilts and swirls all about me. I am aware of Effie taking one of my arms and Sheila the other and we lurch towards the stairs in the corner of the cellar.

The cellar is filled with the screams of the long dead...

'Don't leave me! Don't leave me! You cannot die!'

'Marius – you have to come with us. You'll die if you stay here!'

'Get away from me. You devil woman! All three of you! You're monsters!'

'Leave him,' snarls Sheila. 'We've got to save ourselves.'

The last I see of Marius Keyes before the smoke blots everything out is him standing before the blazing wreckage of his aunt's casket. He flings himself into it, soundlessly, determined to share her fate.

And then Effie, Sheila and I are struggling for our lives and hurrying as fast as we can go to the exit.

Until we're outside.

The night air is cool and fresh and impossible as we burst out of the cellar's concealed entrance outside the conservatory of *Tipple*.

We topple across the gravel and get as far away as we can...

WHUMMMPP goes the explosion behind us.

The aftershock knocks all three of us off our feet.

We lie there, deafened, in each other's arms.

Then we turn back to see the fire raging throughout the fancy new tea rooms.

The place is one big cleansing inferno.

'Sheila,' gasps Effie. 'What have you done?'

But Sheila's face is set in a grim expression. 'They needed to be stopped. She was reaching her apotheosis, she said. That didn't sound good. And I didn't like all that talk of a gateway into hell...'

'Me neither,' I agree, and realise that I'm bleeding still, from where those wires and things were sticking into me.

Effie says something about getting me to A&E but I bark out in protest. No way. I'm not letting anyone else poke about, looking at my workings. I just need to get home. To my attic. I can tend to my wounds myself.

'All right,' agrees Effie.

The first sirens can be heard. No wonder. The conflagration must be visible from miles away.

'Who'd have thought doilies could be quite so deadly and effective?' Sheila gasps. Then she says, 'Let's scoot before anyone official arrives. Then we won't have to answer any awkward questions...'

She's already going, galumphing away across the dancing shadows of the lawn. She's got a great instinct for self-preservation.

So have Effie and I.

'Marius Keyes' secrets will die with him,' Effie says. 'And his infernal Aunty will trouble the world no more.'

'I'll drink to that,' I say, as we lumber heavily through the park, away from the flames and towards Harbour Street. 'Come on, Effie. Shall we revive ourselves with a pot of Spicy chai?'

She pulls a face. 'I think I'm off tea for a little while, ducky.'

## 4

# Brenda has Risen from the Grave

I've tried telling her.

Honestly, Effie. Listen, will you? No, the Elephant Man didn't have a trunk and huge big ears. He just didn't.

But will she listen?

NO. She'll never listen when you try to talk sense. I've known Effie Jacobs for nearly two months now and sometimes there's no reasoning with the woman.

And this is one of those times.

You see, Effie has had her head turned. She even tells me – when we're having coffee and cake this afternoon – that she suspects she might even be in love.

'You've only known him a week!' I gasp, catching my breath on a fragment of hot, buttered tea cake.

'That's how it goes sometimes, ducky. I've been caught up in a whirlwind of amour.'

Usually you'd be hard-pressed finding a more cynical old woman. She can't stand anything sentimental. She reads Romantic novels only so that she can laugh at them and pour scorn on the hopes and dreams of the rest of humanity. Or so she says.

And now look! After only one week of knowing Keith she's gone head over heels.

I've only met him once. It was yesterday evening. Effie's been keen to get my opinion. She's been raving about him ever since Monday. That night she was at a special fitness class at the Christmas Hotel – Gumba or something. It's for ladies and gentlemen of a certain age. Well, I'd told her no, thanks, I'm not about to don a leotard in public and go throwing myself about in a chockablock ballroom, which is where, apparently, it all goes on. I know my limits.

Anyhow, that's where she met Keith the latterday Elephant Man. He took her for fancy cocktails afterwards at a swanky new place on the sea front. They had a number of Mojitos as they sat there in their tracksuits, sweaty as anything. They quenched their thirsts and ate each other up with their eyes, she says. When I heard about this I was astonished.

'Erm, why do they call him the Elephant Man?' I ask her, dreading some saucy kind of answer. I brace myself for smut. I'm asking this as the two of us ascend the 199 steps below St Mary's church. We're on our way to meet him.

'You'll see why. But you mustn't flinch or react at all, Brenda. You see, he has a slight – what d'you call it? – facial disfigurement. He's quite self-conscious, so you mustn't make it worse for him.'

How could I make it worse? How can she think I'd be so tactless? Here's me with all my scars and my own bodily oddity that I feel so self-conscious about and try to conceal from the world. How could I ever react in an untoward fashion to some else's peculiar looks?

Mind, it *is* a bit of a shock, when he opens the door of his caravan and reveals himself in all his glory.

The fact that he has an actual elephant's trunk and huge flapping ears *does* give me pause for thought. On the bright side, at least I have an answer to my question about where his nickname comes from.

He wears a scarlet dressing gown and over its silken folds hangs his pendulous trunk – which is prehensile, too! As he mixes the three of us vodka and tonics his trunk is gently prising ice cubes out of the plastic tray and dunking them into our tumblers. I can't help staring and Effie nudges me.

'It's such an honour to meet you, Brenda. I've heard about all the adventures you and my new girlfriend have been having.'

'Really? I hope she hasn't told you too much...!'

'Oh, we don't have any secrets from each other,' Effie sighs. 'I already feel like I've known Keith all my life.'

Now, this is serious, I realise. Both Effie and I have secrets neither of us want broadcasting. It won't do if Effie gets slapdash while she's in the throes of love.

The caravan is very modern, just as Effie bragged it was. But it's not very spacious. Squeezed into the corner of Keith's breakfast banquette I can feel the beginnings of claustrophobia coming on.

Effie's practically sitting on his knee, which I find embarrassing. As his great big ears flap the two of them look happy as anything. Perhaps I should stop being so mean-spirited. Why do I have to doubt the truth of their love?

Then Keith is telling us all about his fascinating life and times. How he's spent most of his life on the road, travelling round the world in a series of mobile homes.

'Yeah, I've seen some really amazing places. The world has such variety, you know. So many wonderful things to see. You get so blinkered and small, living in just one place.'

'It must be wonderful,' says a doleful Effie, cradling her glass. 'I've been nowhere. In all my life I've only lived here in this tiny town that hardly ever changes. In the house where my aunties brought me up. I've never known any excitement whatsoever.'

I raise both eyebrows at this. No excitement at all? Isn't she forgetting the hair-raising excitements of recent weeks? I suppose nothing is any cop compared with the excitements that the globe-trotting Keith and his prehensile trunk can offer.

Now Keith is talking about his illustrious lineage and the terrible things his forebears suffered as a result of their genetic legacy. 'They all had the same, erm, features,' Effie explains.

'One time I'll show you my family album. The earliest recorded member of my family was the famous John Merrick, who had such a terrible life as part of a travelling freak show. His travelling wasn't a matter of fancy and whim like mine is. He was a prisoner of his own deformities and he was treated abysmally in that ignorant age.'

Effie cries out, 'Just think, Brenda! A relative of John Merrick, the Elephant Man, himself! I'm going out with one of his actual descendants!'

'He was my great, great uncle.'

Keith gives a mournfully jubilant toot on his trunk. And the evening continues in this vein, with us crammed into that caravan, listening to Effie's new beau blowing his own trumpet. Honestly, he doesn't really seem to have any real interest in either Effie or me. I needn't be bothered about Effie airing our secrets. Keith is only interested in his own self.

At midnight I decide that it's time I went. We've had a few vodkas by then and a whole box of French Fancies. Effie holds them out one at a time for Keith to tenderly take in his trunk. I'm woozy and looking forward to a brisk walk home across the harbour. 'Coming with me, Effie?'

She jumps up and starts fastening up her mac. She has already told me that she and Keith have stopped short of becoming 'physically intimate', as she puts it. She has revealed to me however that she is powerfully attracted to him despite his deformities. And you can tell.

We bid him farewell and he waves from the doorway of his caravan. It's parked in the long grass, rather close to the ruined abbey. Our way home takes us through the rather frightening graveyard, where we are soon knee-deep in sea mist. I dearly hope there's no dog muck about because we can't see the ground at all.

Effie is keen to know what I think of him. I manage to answer in general terms and don't mention his awful boastfulness. As we descend the 199 steps I foolishly mention something that's been bothering me. As soon as it's out I'm regretting it. 'You do know, don't you, Effie, that the Elephant Man was a poor fella with a horrible condition? He didn't just look like an elephant, like your Keith does.'

We are passing under a Victorian gas lamp just as I say this, and Effie's furious expression is illuminated for me.

'How dare you, Brenda? How could you be so awful? How could you deny Keith his birthright? How could you doubt his word for one second?'

'Well,' I say. 'The thing is, the original Joseph Merrick looked nothing like your Keith. You see, I happened to know him personally.'

My words are out before I know it and Effie looks at me like I'm completely crazy. In that instant, I feel it, too. Did I know Joseph Merrick? Where did that memory come from? It has risen from the darkest, murkiest depths of my memory.

'Brenda, what are you on about? How can that be true?'

'I-I don't know,' I stammer, and then the two of us concentrate on trotting down the rest of the steps, careful not to trip after all the vodka and excitement.

At the bottom on Church Street, under the smoky light of another lamp, Effie surprises me with a bold question:

'Just how old are you, Brenda? And how many different lives have you lived?'

§

Later that night I'm having one of my strange flashbacks. I'm heating some milk and while I project myself on the astral plane the pan boils over and the attic is suffused by an acrid stench. But the whole house could be in flames and I'd be none the wiser. For I am standing there like a lemon and my mind is elsewhere.

I am in old London town, where it's foggy and stinky and slimy underfoot. This is where I used to eke out my days living in a dreadful warren of back allies. I was a seamstress, wasn't I? The hands I had then were so nimble and skilled. I lived in Limehouse, where I had a miserable existence for a few years. No wonder I've blocked it all out of my memory.

But what's this I see before me? A boy on the corner with a pile of newspapers shouting out the headlines:

'London Monster Throttles Victim Number Nine!'

A horrid chill runs through me. I remember now how we all lived in fear of that killer. I forget when he first became known as The London Monster. Maybe after the third body was found. She turned up on the filthy embankment, tossed there like an old rag. She was a respectable girl. An employee of the pie shop, only four doors down from the rooming house where I slept and spent my days running stitches through fraying garments. I had bought a hot pie or two from her myself and I did feel queasy at the thought of her demise.

They said that she had horrible contusions. All over the exposed parts of her body. Her neck, face and arms bore awful red weals. She had been strangled, by all accounts, but not by human hands.

Tentacles, some said, had claimed her life and we all started imagining a vile, suckered, leggy thing come crawling out of the squalid river-murk. Perhaps a squid or octopus had come seething inland? Or maybe it was a mad person's pet? Or a vengeful eel? We talked about nothing else for weeks, it seemed, because ours was a life of misery and only murders – the grislier the better – could ever penetrate our gloom and get us excited.

Friday nights we were all down the pub. The 'Masks of Satan' was my local then and I remember once when we were having our usual singalong, there came this godawful ululation from the street. The most dreadful gurgling scream we'd ever heard. The pianist stopped playing at once. The singing died down. Even the pint the barmaid was pulling dried up at once.

We piled outside en masse and a thick bank of woolly mist met us head on. Hurried footsteps were clipping away in the opposite direction. Then we all saw him. A man with – believe it or not – a trunk growing out of the middle of his face. About as long as a baby's arm, flapping away as he fled the scene. We forgot all about pursuing him down that dark alley because next thing was we found his victim.

She was the old flower seller who'd spent most of her working life outside the 'Masks of Satan', plying her withered-up blooms. Now she lay face-down in the gutter, heaped in elderly daffodils. When the doctor in our midst turned her over she was found to have those same ghastly contusions all over her throat.

The facts of the case were bruited all over London. The monster had a lethal and prehensile trunk, with which he choked the life out of unwary ladies.

The last image I glimpse before I snap out of my flashback is that newspaper board again, with the headline about the latest death. Yes, I knew that I had seen a trunk just like Keith's before. Such a very long time ago, but somehow the memory has surfaced. In order to *warn* me, I suddenly think.

I stand blinking in my kitchen, becoming aware of the aroma of scorched milk and burning pan. I'm troubled because there's something else about the Elephant Man. Something I'm not remembering yet. I can't quite put my finger on it...

I turn off the gas, throw the pan into the sink, and mop up the mess as best I can. Then I go to bed, hoping to dredge up the rest of my memories concerning my life in the late eighteen-hundreds.

However, my sleep is deep and, for once, quite peaceful.

§

The next morning Effie talks me into taking a morning off and we idly check out the charity shops on Silver Street. I'm always on the look-out for unusual knick-knacks to display in my new home. I'm examining a collection of capodimonte kittens and Effie keeps up a barrage of commentary about Keith.

In the end I burst out: 'Yes, Effie, I'm sure he's a lovely man, once you get to know him.'

'He's so masculine and self-reliant,' Effie gabbles on. 'You know he customized his mobile home himself? It used to be a horse box. And he's ever so cosmopolitan. He's been all around the world and back again. Places I've never even heard of, let alone spent time in.'

'Yes,' I say, examining the largest of the china kittens for cracks. 'Yes, I heard quite a lot about him last night.'

Effie goes frosty. 'What's that supposed to mean?'

I sigh. 'He's a bit fond of the sound of his own voice, isn't he?'

She looks flabbergasted that I could even think about criticising him. 'How could you, Brenda? Don't you realise how shy Keith is? Can't you tell how hard he's had to work to overcome the prejudices that his unique physical deformities have forced him to face?'

She's gone all pious. It isn't my favourite of Effie's various moods, I must say.

'People are so cruel. And I think it's marvellous that he has managed not to retreat into himself and become a broken, reclusive man. I am grateful that he's as outgoing and as sociable as he is, and that he can talk so confidently about his life. Why, I think we could all learn a lot from the way Keith has lived his life and overcome...'

'All right, Effie! Enough!!' I shout at her in the middle of the Sue Ryder shop. Instantly I feel ashamed. She has a look on her face like I've smacked her one. Other browsers are staring at us and I decide on the spot I'd better buy each and every one of the capodimonte kittens, because the ancient shop assistant is looking at us daggers.

'What are we doing squabbling?' I smile at my best friend in all of Whitby.

She still looks sore. 'I don't know. I think maybe you're jealous of my happiness with Keith. Why else would you be so nasty about him?'

I hasten to the counter and wind up spending ten pounds on more china cats than I'll ever have use for. The volunteer sales assistant takes a terribly long time to wrap each one in used tissue paper.

Effie and I don't exchange any more words until we're out on Silver Street again. The morning sun feels lovely and I wish we weren't at loggerheads. And especially over some silly man. Then a new thought strikes me about something she said and I make things even worse by bursting out: 'Effie! I meant to tell you! Keith's condition isn't unique at all! I've seen the very same thing before!'

She glares at me sideways. 'What are you saying to me?'

'It was a long time ago, and far away from here.'

Effie tuts. 'Is this more of your dreary lies?' she asks fiercely. 'Like last night, when you were three sheets to the wind on poor Keith's vodka? You were babbling on about being back in Victorian times!'

This brings me up short. 'Yes! You're right! I was, wasn't I? I really was. Thank you for reminding me!' Suddenly I feel like hugging her. She guesses this and backs off. 'But what I wanted to tell you, Effie, isn't about that. It isn't about Joseph Merrick. Like I say, he never had a great big flapping trunk hanging off his face. Of course he didn't! But someone else did, back then in Victorian times. Someone who looked just like your Keith! The London Monster, Effie! And I saw him with my own two eyes!'

Effie is looking at me like she thinks I'm the one who's the monster.

§

Late that very night – after a wearying afternoon I've spent doing heaps of laundry – there's a loud banging at the door in my side passage. I assume it's Effie come round to apologise for being so shrewish, but it isn't.

'Keith!' I burst out. His appearance startles me somewhat. Under the porch light his trunk casts most of his face in deepest shadow. He's wearing a tatty pork pie hat and his eyes are narrowed at me. I didn't realise he even knows where I live. 'This is a surprise!'

'Can I have a word, Brenda?'

All of a sudden I've got a bad feeling about letting him in. I look him up and down, taking in the fact that he's wearing a ghastly shell suit that's seen much better days. As I let him in and lead the way upstairs it strikes me that everything about him is quite shabby, including his caravan, whatever Effie says about it. I wonder if he's latching onto her because he fancies she must have a few bob stashed away?

Up in my attic sitting room he refuses to sit down, or to accept a mug of tea.

'I shan't beat about the bush, Brenda.'

'Go on, then.' I try to sound as cool and businesslike as he does.

'I thought we could be friends. But it seems we are destined not to get on.'

He tosses that trunk of his arrogantly. Its pink tip quivers at me and I feel revolted, I really do. What can Effie see in this man?

I tell him, 'I'm very easy to get along with, actually.'

He chuckles and fingers his absurd hat, thoughtfully stroking its brim, though he doesn't remove it from his head.

'Oh, I saw your expression last night as we sat in my mobile home. I could see all too plainly what you thought of me. I'm not good enough for your precious bosom buddy. I'm a freak! A mutant! A loathsome monster!'

'That's not what I was thinking at all!'

'Pah!'

He trumpets, looking furious.

'I would never let anyone's looks prejudice me against them,' I shout. 'Even yours!'

He snarls at me and his ears flap.

'I might have a low opinion of you,' I tell him. 'I might think you're a chancer and a seducer of defenceless old ladies, but it isn't because you look like an elephant that I don't like you.'

My dander's properly up now. I hate to be accused of being something I'm not.

'I don't think you're right for Effie, no,' I tell him. 'And I don't trust you a single inch.'

'Well! Thanks for being honest with me! The feeling is mutual, I might tell you. There's something I don't like about you, Brenda. When I look at you all my deepest instincts run riot. I detect something rotten and from beyond the grave. What it is I don't know yet. But I will find out, and expose you for the freak show that you are!'

He advances on me throughout this horrible speech until he's waggling that horrid trunk right in my face. Flecks of spittle are flying off it.

I keep my voice calm. Unflappable.

'Please will you leave my home at once.'

'Got you frightened, have I?'

'I – er, no,' I say. Though my heart is pounding and I expect he can hear it with those ears of his.

'You know what I should do? I should do away with you. Just put you out of the way – right now!'

Before I'm even aware of the danger I'm in, he lashes out with his trunk and it winds its way around my neck. He starts to squeeze and squeeze tighter. It's like being got at by a boa constrictor. With every deadly little squeeze Keith's murderous face draws closer to my own.

He says dreadful things. Though they sound rather congested.

'You wid die id hoddible abony, Benda. Jud like all my udder vittims.'

The edges of my vision are spiralling, turning into a black kaleidoscope of impending mortality. But what can I do? I was foolish to let him get this close. And when he gets as close as this – just the length of his lethal appendage – then there's no stopping him. Just like the London Monster!

After all this time, I have invited this homicidal pachyderm into my sitting room. But surely I can't die like this. I simply can't let this be the end of me.

Throughout my prolonged strangulation my free left hand has been scrabbling away on the wall unit behind me. I draw upon my final reserves of strength and take tight hold of the heftiest object that comes to hand.

Then I bring my arm round as hard as I can. I'm like a demon bowler as I smash the ornament down on Keith's head.

He shrieks in pain and his trunk loosens its death-hold.

I see at once that I have brained him with the biggest of my capodimonte kittens. And it hasn't even broken! What a fortuitous purchase and a bargain to boot!

My assailant is staggering about on the rug, making a bigger deal out of my retaliation than he needs to. There isn't any blood, after all. The pottery kitten hasn't even broken his leathery skin. He's shouting and swearing and lashing his trunk about. This time I make sure that I keep well back.

'You were going to throttle me to death!' I cry, rubbing my throat, and knowing before I even get to a mirror that I'll have the same tender pink marks those poor girls in London bore. 'You must be descended from the Limehouse killer, aren't you? What was he? Your great grandfather?'

Keith seems in no mood for a spot of 'Who Do You Think You Are?' with me.

'That was just a taster. If you go anywhere near Effie and tell her about this, or try to warn her about me – I'll do you in. And I'll finish you off next time, as well!'

I can't believe that he's still issuing threats! I must prove to him I won't put up with any more of his nonsense.

I make a quick dive for the mantelpiece and snatch up the first thing that comes to hand. Unfortunately it's the furniture polish and he sneers as I brandish it in his face. I soon wipe that sneer of his face with a quick spray of lavender-scented wax.

'Oooowwwwwwwwwww!'

He starts backing off towards the door and I know I have won. His hat's fallen off and I notice that I have, it seems, left a curiously-shaped mark on his skull with that ceramic kitten.

'Go on! Get off with you! Get out of my Guest House!'

Then he turns tail and thunders into the hall and down the stairs. The outer door crashes behind him. I'm still yelling: 'Go on, you great big Nelly!'

And that's how my B&B guests find me, at the top of the stairs, waving my furniture polish and bellowing at the top of my voice. As they come to console me I burst into noisy tears. It's delayed shock, I suppose, at the awful violation of my home's sanctity.

§

I don't – as my worried guests suggest – report my attacker to the police. Best if I deal with this in my own way. Though I don't at the moment have any idea what my own way might be.

Then I think – I have to make Effie aware of what she has on her hands here.

This man is a potential killer, just as his forefather was.

I ring her and she doesn't pick up. I leave a breathless message begging her to ring back, but she doesn't. All at once I know that terrible man is in there with her, in her dusty and junky house.

I can't stand this. I'm dithering late at night. Should I go next door? Should I chance my neck? Would she even listen if I tried to warn her? I just don't know. What if he's wringing the very life out of her skinny old body right at this very moment?

I sit at my writing desk, where each night I update my journal. This window looks out over the back of Effie's house.

I can see her bedroom lit up all warm and peachy. The curtains at the side aren't drawn yet and I realise that her net curtains are giving a kind of puppet show. Oh, my goodness! Yes! There are two silhouettes standing in her bedroom. I'm frozen here like an awful Peeping Tom.

Yet I can't drag my eyes away from this horrible scene. As she crosses to him!

Effie in a slinky negligee...! Keith in his pork pie hat and a vest!

And his prehensile trunk – reaching out to Effie...!

§

Days pass by and I can't seem to shake those awful images. My imagination keeps embroidering them. Effie in all sorts of ghastly congress with her gentleman friend. She never replies to my phone messages. She never comes round and, when I bang on her door, she never answers. Her emporium remains closed. I decide that Keith must have fed her disinformation about me, and is busy turning friend against friend.

What can I do? I know that he's dangerous. She might even be dead already. I realise this with a shock. Maybe that's why I've seen neither hide nor hair! But then – each night – I peep out and see – their silhouettes standing at that bedroom window. The scene exerts a hideous fascination over me. Effie never struck me as one who'd have her head turned so easily by a bloke.

Meanwhile... I am continuing with my strange tussle with my own memories. Perhaps because I now feel so settled here in my new life, the old recollections come trickling back...

I am flabbergasted by the lifetimes I have led – and the extent of them. They come back in dribs and drabs and dreams...

What I am seeing most in these memories is a face. A kindly face, full of understanding. A strong and complicated face, staring back at me down the years. It's a beloved face, and one I knew well, once upon a time. His misshapen nose, his bulbous brow and sunken eyes. The lopsidedness of that face as a whole looks as if it has been thrown together by an inept sculptor out of clods of clay.

It's a face that is very dear to me, and not at all frightening.

It is the face of the actual Joseph Merrick. Not John, as they often got it wrong. Joseph. The real Elephant Man. He's sitting up in his bed behind the thick red drapes. Hidden away in his carriage. He's chatting away with me. Easily, freely, or at least as easily as his impediments and catarrh will allow.

I used to nip into his caravan to see him, didn't I? I'd sit on a wickerwork chair beside his bunk and we'd talk up a storm. We'd talk for hours. It was that tour we did, all round the country. A whole summer in caravans, in what was essentially a freak show.

Oh, goodness. It's all coming back. That's how we two knew each other, all that time ago. They put us on display for the gawking, peanut-crunching crowds. I'd listen to them gasp and cry out in horror at Joe when he shuffled out to stand before them. He met their appalled stares bravely, but I could see that it was killing him inside, these days and nights in this horrid circus.

Joe was the star of our show, along with the much less spectacular bearded lady, Siamese twins, dancing midgets and alligator men. At the start I was just an usherette, flogging my tubs of melting ices and tarry cigarettes under the flaring gas lamps. Then, sometimes I would be shoved out before the crowd, when our owner, Mr Diodati was feeling particularly cruel.

I would be The Half-Dead Woman.

'It's Amazing That She's Still Alive...!'

All my scars and monstrous deformities were put on show. All for the price of a tuppenny entrance ticket.

I was a fool to fall into the hands of Mr Diodati.

At that time in my life I was at such a low ebb. I thought all I could do with my life was parade my ugliness. I had no other gifts or skills, I thought. Only my hideousness. Which human beings would shriek at. Laughter, fear – it was all the same to me. Their reactions meant that Mr Diodati graciously allowed me to stay in his circus of freaks.

It was Joseph who befriended me. He saw the *me* in me.

He gave me back my self-esteem.

I watched him and saw his indelible grace and his massive dignity. His great good nature and humour. Nothing could dent it. Even when they stripped him and jeered and called out to him. Nothing could truly touch him inside.

And he would talk to me. Long hours in his caravan, when we weren't required by our task master or the crowds. Joe would tell me about his life and his past, and then he'd coax my stories out of me.

I was much younger then. Why, even less than a century old. My memory was much less full and patchy. Gradually I told him my various tales – all of them hair-raising – and he accepted everything without question.

He never expressed shock or disbelief. Even when I told him I had been a grave-robber, a vagabond, a woman of ill-repute, a warrior, a witch, a handmaiden to a queen, a Sorcerer's assistant, and a lady pirate. All these things I'd been before barely came as a surprise to Joe.

I told him how, at last in 1879 I had fallen into the wicked hands of Mr Diodati, at a time in my life when I'd run out of resources, energy and ideas. I'd run out of ways to save myself by reinventing my life. I had no gumption to keep me going. At that very moment Mr Diodati presented himself and I found myself joining the freak show. As usherette and occasional exhibit.

Here's what I did, to persuade the crowds to take notice of me.

I showed them how I could remove my feet, my legs, my hands and my arms.

I made myself into... *The Discombobulated Woman*.

Crowds flocked. Word spread.

Folk couldn't quite believe what they were seeing.

This woman, coming apart at the seams. Turning into smaller and smaller fragments. This woman... *was still alive..!*

Joseph thought that the act I developed was astonishing. He was amazed at my growing confidence and my nascent showbiz patter. But he counselled against showing off too much. He thought I was giving too much of myself away.

Then I found I was getting addicted to all the attention. I did a show in which I came completely to pieces – I was... The Atomised Lady! And at the end I was nothing but a talking head on a plinth!

Not only women passed out at this unusual and unique sight. I grinned ghoulishly and down came the curtain.

Great physicians of the day and other scientists gathered to see me. Mr Diodati wouldn't let them get too close and discover my secrets. 'It's all trickery done with mirrors and smoke and black magic,' they claimed, but the folk from the freak show knew better. They knew that every bit of me was for real.

At night Joseph and my new young assistant, a country boy called Basil, would spend many hours stitching my limbs and constituent parts back together again with the strongest catgut they could procure. They knew they'd have to do the same thing again the next time I performed my increasingly famous act.

'You'll do yourself a mischief, Brenda. I think you're growing mad for all the applause.'

Oh, he was right. But I couldn't stop myself. I, who used to skulk among the shadows. Now I was happy in the limelight, doing the most extreme strip-tease of all!

How well I remember the night I elected to go one better and give them all a new novelty to thrill to. And how their reactions gratified me!

That night, when my limbs lay scattered around the stage, at the climax of my performance when my head was on the plinth... I did something no one had ever seen before. I wriggled my nose and made my disembodied parts set to twitching. I made them jerk about. Then I made them jump up in synchronised motion. They danced and capered all around the stage, chasing each other around the plinth on which rested my grinning head.

Perhaps it would have been less disturbing if there wasn't so much blood splattered about?

The audience were on their feet and screaming. They ran pell-mell out of the shabby venue. I laughed like a drain to see them go.

Joseph was appalled.

'You're going too far. You're doing things only Beelzebub can do. They'll accuse you of being in league with Satan. Their admiration will turn to fear and hatred. They will say that you're an abomination...!'

As he said this he was busy stitching my lower left leg onto my knee, hunching forward, breathing painfully. And I was all vanity and foolishness, I am afraid to say. All I could hear in his concern was unwanted criticism. I jumped up at once – and almost fell over. And then I accused him of jealousy.

Oh, what a callow and ungrateful wretch was I! I let him sew my lower leg back on. I seethed impatiently until it was secure, and then I lumbered out of his gypsy caravan without another word.

'Brenda, come back! I'm only trying to help...!'

The very next day the owner of us all, Mr Diodati, announced that I was to replace Joseph at the top of the freak show bill. My fame had eclipsed even the Elephant Man's. My cankered heart thrilled at this news.

Joseph took his demotion with good grace. He was also rather ill. Something bronchial. His breath was sounding chokier and more congested. But I pushed those concerns aside and thought only of myself, and how my billing would look on the new garish posters that were being printed up. I imagined them posted everywhere when we pitched up for shows in Leeds. York, Lincoln, Derby, Norwich... working our way back down the country and finishing up once again in London. I pictured myself in lights – in Drury Lane! Brenda, the Discombobulated Lady..!

And that is who I became.

Joseph was gurgling and fighting for his breath. As his lungs filled with fermenting mucous he was slowly drowning. We were hardly talking, but still he and my assistant Basil wielded their expert extra-strong needles after every show. I might have been in a huff with Joseph, but I still needed him to put me back together again.

I found at about this time that Basil was stealing from me. Not just coins and notes, but souvenirs. By that I mean bits of me. Bits of my body. He was one of the few souls on earth I had entrusted with the knowledge that I had an old wooden trunk lined with silk and stuffed with bolts of soft wool. And this trunk contained spare parts. Ears, eyes, fingers... and the occasional organ.

Basil had been quietly appalled, the first time he had come upon them, one night when he was searching for a fragment of my exiguous stage outfit. He laid his hands on the flimsy veil I used for my 'Arabian Nights' themed dance and then he opened my trunk and fainted dead away at the sight of what lay within.

Joseph Merrick wasn't perturbed at all by this. He had heard so much about my past that nothing at all could frighten him. Or put him off me. Even my rotten behaviour.

I learned a lot about loyalty from my Elephant Man.

How could I ever have forgotten him?

§

Effie is going to marry Keith. That's the next thing I hear.

When this titbit comes my way my heart sinks with a solid thunking noise like it's come loose in my chest. I imagine dashing round her house and flinging myself on the floor. 'But you mustn't, Effie! Over my dead body will I let you..!'

But that wouldn't do any good.

All this month there have been murders in Whitby. The nightly radio bulletins tell the tales and keep up the grisly tally. Now, I know some of them are down to the Crispy Cat. That radioactive feline is still patrolling the town's back allies. For weeks on end this phantom with claws has been claiming victim after victim. I realise that Effie and I have let this glowing demon slip out of our minds a little.

But in recent days there have been other deaths as well. Victims have been found in the dingiest of streets, and these women's necks have borne the livid red marks of strangulation. I listen in shock as a DCI Aickman takes to the air on Whitby F.M. to describe these contusions. I sit there holding my breath, knowing that the great-great grandson of the London Monster has embarked on a killing spree in my newly-adopted town. Mercifully he failed in his attempt upon my life, and it seemed that these murders are a fervid outpouring of his true nature. Badness will out, I fear and Keith has embarked on a reign of terror. And poor old Effie doesn't know what she's got herself into.

Now that news of their impending nuptials is in the public domain, I can hold back no longer. I go to the police. I tell them I think I know who is behind the rash of recent killings. They don't seem altogether convinced by my accusations. I suppose I look and sound rather wild, pointing the finger so determinedly at my ex-best friend's new fiancé. Without a shred of hard evidence of his guilt, other than pointing out that he is the possessor of a prehensile trunk.

'A trunk? Are you quite sure, madam?'

Then I make myself sound even less plausible by gabbling about Keith's inherited facial deformities and his relation to the London Monster of old, and if the police cared to look up that unsolved case from the 1870s, then they would certainly see some correspondences…

'An Elephant Man, then, would you call him? Ha haha hahaha.'

'No!' I cry. 'The true Elephant Man was a lovely fellow and one I let down rather badly with my vain, silly, showbiz ways. He died before I could tell him how wonderful he had been to me and before I could say – you were right, Joseph! The crowd and the circus folk *did* turn against me in the end! Driving me out of town. Driving me out of Norwich on the last night of our engagement there! Just as you warned me, Joe! They said I was a freak of nature!'

The two policemen are staring at me now across the interview table and I can see I'm giving them far too much information. They think I'm barmier than a fruitcake. (Or brack, as they call it in these parts.) But when the memories come welling up I can't hold back. My every waking thought and all my dreams are teeming with Elephant Men these days. The evil ones and the marvellous ones.

'Shall we go and question this Keith, then?'

They treat me with kid gloves, thinking I'm on the verge of a breakdown. I accompany them to the abbey, where Keith's mobile home is still parked. It's Sunday morning and Keith and Effie seem very surprised to have a police car pulling up on their doorstep.

She's in a pinny, in the middle of frying sausage sandwiches on the Baby Belling. Keith wears a very surly look as he faces the police and myself.

'We'd like to ask you a few questions concerning your movements on some recent nights.'

It's rather impressive, I think, that DCI Aickman and his friend both manage to be cool when confronted with the sight of Keith's unmistakable trunk.

'Have you got a warrant for my arrest?'

'Well, no, we don't...'

'Then this is a case of sheer harassment. This is prejudice against a minority. That's what I am, and I've got rights. Can you hear all this, Effie?'

Effie comes to the caravan door and glares daggers at me.

'You've set the coppers onto him..! How could you do this, Brenda? Is it just because I've found myself happiness? Couldn't you just be pleased for me? Why do you have to stir up trouble?'

I hit back quickly. 'He's a murderer, Effie! I've seen his sort before – with that trunk of his! Plus he tried to do me in when he was in my sitting room. He's a wicked, violent man, just as I've been trying to warn you for weeks!'

'Are you making an official complaint against this person?'

'I suppose I am, yes!' I say, and the next thing is, they're taking him off to the station for questioning. Keith looks like he wants to kill me all over again, as Effie wails about their trip to Scarborough for wedding outfits being ruined.

I've got to follow the police so I can give a proper statement, but I linger to tell Effie, 'It's not about your happiness. It's about the women who've been strangled to death by that trunk of his.'

'Rubbish! He wouldn't hurt a fly!'

I'm feeling my own neck self-consciously. 'I think he could.'

She turns on me rather nastily. 'Anyway, lady. You think you're so superior. Keith's been telling me all about you. He says that when he went round yours the other night it was you who were out of order. He says that you made a number of obscene suggestions to him. And tried it on.'

I can't believe my ears. 'What? Why would I ever fancy a little scrap of a thing like that? Plus, he's deformed.'

Effie reacts like a cat dunked in a deep fat fryer. For a moment I think she's going to hit me. 'He's the best thing to happen to me for years. And you know what? I thought you were too, Brenda. I thought it was wonderful because I'd made a new friend. But I can see now it was all a lie.'

'What do you mean?' I gasp.

'Keith says that you put me at unnecessary risk, Brenda. Time and time again you've got me involved in macabre adventures during which I could have been maimed, possessed, disturbed for life, or even killed.'

'So could I!' I shout back. 'We both know the risks. You aren't some helpless little puppet. We set about our investigations together, don't we? We can't help getting involved, can we?'

Effie goes quiet, but I can see from her face that she knows I am right.

'But Keith says...'

'Keith is a homicidal maniac,' I tell her. 'I just can't let you go marrying him.'

She staggers back inside the caravan, which is thick with fumes from blackened sausages.

She whirls around, eyes blazing. 'Get out! Get out of my life! You've interfered enough, you abominable woman! You're a monster! That's what my lovely Keith calls you!'

I can see I'm not going to get any sense out of her. Not tonight. Maybe not ever. I back away and hurry across the scrubland, stumbling in the long grass with Effie's awful words ringing in my ears.

I dash home not caring who sees me on the streets looking so distraught.

She's right. I can't help thinking that Effie's right. Who do I think I am?

I'm the one who's a monster...!

Then, later that evening I'm killing time watching a silly costume drama I can't even concentrate on. DCI Aickman rings me and tells me that Keith has been set free. They won't be taking my complaint seriously and won't be requiring any more statements from me. I can tell from Aickman's tone that he is convinced by whatever line Keith has spun them, and that they suspect I am mad or even jealous. I get ticked of for wasting police time.

Oh, Effie. This is terrible.

Is he innocent? Did I get it all wrong?

I'm so confused. My head's been all over the place.

Did he try to kill me? Did I hit him with the kitten first? Was he just defending himself? Passions were running high...

All these flashbacks I've been having... they've got me all in a tizz.

I don't know what to do about it. If only I had someone else to talk to. Henry Cleavis, say. Or Joseph Merrick. But all my old friends and allies are long dead. That's the thing about being as old as the hills. You end up sitting alone in an attic with no one to mull things over with.

§

I'm surprised to learn that Effie takes up Mrs Claus' offer to hold the wedding and reception at the Christmas Hotel. What is Effie to her after all?

From my window at the top of my house I can see Effie and her fancy man darting hither and thither. They're dealing with florists and bakers and dressmakers. I feel rather left out of it all.

There's nothing I can do. I keep picturing horrible scenes. Effie lying in her four poster bed and that terrible trunk inching its way towards her, tensing to throttle her where she lies.

And what happens when Keith finds out she's not as rich as he evidently thinks? Surely that's why he's marrying her, after all?

I can't help thinking the worst of him.

But maybe it's just that I'm jealous. Maybe it's my nasty unconscious that's demonizing the bloke.

The big day comes round at last and I receive a last minute invitation shoved through my door. It's a fancy, lacy card hastily scribbled on by Effie. She says she'll forgive me for what she calls over-protectiveness. She'd rather I was there to witness her happiness first hand.

I've got mixed feelings, of course. I've got to be there, but I must get my skates on if I'm to make the ceremony in the Grand Ballroom at eleven. I swear that I don't mean anything by it, but my black velvet is the smartest, most suitable frock I've got. I quickly don it, titivate myself and fluff up my wig, surveying the results before my cheval mirror.

I think, once more I am the outsider again! Just as I always am. Here I am, like the spectre at the feast, encroaching upon the happiness of a friend.

Luckily, I find I don't have to attend alone. As I lock up my side door I bump into Leena and Rafiq, the nice couple who run the grocery on the ground floor. They're both dolled up – Leena in a rather festive sari. She's eyeing me in my best party dress.

'We weren't sure,' she says. 'Whether you'd be attending or not. I said you would, no matter how badly you had both fallen out. Friendship means something, even if you did call the police out on them.'

I gawp at Leena. I'm finding that this is a town stuffed with keen gossips.

'Now then,' Rafiq tells her sternly. 'I'm sure that Brenda doesn't want the more shameful aspects of recent events digging up on Effie's big day. Look! It's a lovely morning and we're all going to a wedding!' He's holding what looks like a kilogram bag of basmati rice. 'I'm sure we've brought too much to throw.'

They invite me to walk along the sea front with them, past the novelty and gift shops, the swanky cafes and amusement arcades. I wish I could join in with things as whole-heartedly as other people.

'Well, Brenda,' chirps Leena. 'You've certainly had a busy time of it since moving in upstairs!'

I agree guardedly. 'Running a B&B can be awfully involved. More work than I even thought. But I don't mind rolling up my sleeves.'

'Not just that,' says Leena craftily. Her dark eyes are twinkling. 'I mean all the spooky stuff, too. You've had some strange encounters, innit?'

I'm startled, but I won't be drawn. 'Is there a lot of spookiness here in this town..?'

Leena chuckles. 'Yes, there is, but just lately it has been quite astonishing. You seem to have been at the heart of a spooky maelstrom.'

'Oh, well,' I say, trying to be modest.

'But we think you've done rather well, Raf and I. Innit, Raf?'

He nods, smiling brightly. I'm not very happy to be the subject of their discussions.

We yomp up the steep hill.

At the top we find that there is a theme of Arctic white at the Christmas Hotel. White roses and ribbons and twinkly white lights bedeck the front of the Edwardian palace. Within, the festive elves are in white and gold velveteen. It's in danger of seeming tasteful.

We are each given a Kir Royale as we step through the revolving doors and I recognise a few faces gathering in the foyer. I feel like they're looking at me and they all know the gossip about mine and Effie's ructions.

Like a gigantic seal dripping in theatrical jewellery, Mrs Claus is bundled up in white fur atop her motorised bath chair. She's carrying on like she's the star of the show, which I can't see Effie being very pleased about.

Then I clap eyes on the happy couple. They're on a love seat beneath the biggest Christmas tree I've seen in my life. They're surrounded by gifts and both look immaculate in matching ivory satin outfits. Jump suits, I'd call them.

'Brenda,' says Effie, at my approach. 'I hope there's going to be no bad blood between us.'

'Humph,' I say, which is really the best I can do. It's the most gracious I can sound. I look at Keith and he's sat there flapping those huge ears of his. He's still wearing his daft little hat. I bend closer and whisper, 'I'm giving you my blessing. And the benefit of the doubt. Perhaps it isn't you doing all these murders...'

Keith smirks at me. 'That means a lot to me, Brenda. Thank you.'

'Yes, well, just you look after my friend. She deserves the best, you know... and... and...'

Keith is holding my hand and I have a very strange sensation creeping over me. Even here... even in the teeming foyer of the Christmas Hotel, with all these wedding guests milling about me... I feel like I'm slipping into one of my reveries about my own hidden past...

'Brenda?' Keith's voice is distorted, echoing.

And I am in a different place.

In a blizzard, on a mountain pass. I'm at the rooftop of the world and sitting on a yak, or some such smelly creature.

Many, many years ago. The gentleman in furs on the path ahead of me... it's Henry Cleavis, I'd know him anywhere. And Professor Tyler sits astride a donkey further down the path, haranguing sherpas in his most querulous tones.

We are in the Himalayas... on the trail of a deadly cult... we have pursued them across continents, by train and boat... finding horribly strangled, sacrificial victims left in their wake...

And their leader was... their leader was a man such as Keith. With the ears and the trunk. He was the London Monster. Chief worshipper of a loathsome Death Cult. We came face to face with him in the Himalayas... in a terrible temple in the most remote place upon the Earth...

where they practised certain vile rites beneath the statue of their many-trunked Goddess – Effulvia!

'Noooo-ooooo!' I cry, recalling just how narrowly those adventurous professors and I escaped with our lives.

Seeing again as the deadly cultists worshipped like crazy, and the London Monster led them in their wicked prayers. When he removed his hood we could see him in all his revolting glory.

How his followers howled with joy to see his ears and trunk and little tusks.

'See?' Professor Cleavis whispered to me, as we peered out of our hiding place. 'On top of the monster's grotesque skull – there's a very dark tattoo. His mark of belonging. A stylized representation of his own features. All of the monks have one, you see? The icon is on the walls of the temple and all the corridors leading us here. Everywhere! Something I never dreamed of seeing outside of the ancient texts. It is the ghastly face of the demon elephant goddess of destruction - Effulvia!'

Professor Cleavis was lecturing me a little too excitedly in our hidden nook and it was at this point that we were spotted...

'Quickly, my dear Brenda!' cried the Professor. 'We must flee! What's that my dear? You've got what? A... a bazooka...?! And a hidden supply of... rock buns..?!'

Then suddenly – SNAP! – and I'm back at the Christmas Hotel on Effie's wedding day. The Himalayan adventure and its bizarre conclusion are relegated all at once to the distant past. I am left very troubled indeed. And what's more, I'm holding up the queue to meet and greet the happy couple.

I wander away, to snag a second cocktail, and then the rest of the event passes in a blur. We get ushered into the ballroom and there's an extravagant fanfare and scads of flowers and rapturous applause. I stand somewhere near the back, finding myself beside Jessie, the gloomy waitress who serves high teas here. On her other side is her nephew Robert, a handsome boy who doesn't look at all impressed by the proceedings. The two of them make catty remarks throughout the service – a little too loudly – and they even manage to make me smile.

'Such a shame,' Jessie hisses out of the corner of her miserable mouth. 'When a sensible woman lets herself down and falls for the blandishments of a ruthless maniac.'

I gasp. 'You know the truth about Keith too, then?'

'Oh yes,' she says. 'He had a go at me, you know. Late one night he jumped out at me when I was coming along Frances' Passage. I only saw him in silhouette before I scarpered. But those ears and that trunk are unmistakable.'

Her nephew Robert puts in, 'She only just managed to get away.'

'I beat him with my brolly,' Jessie says. 'I can defend myself. I'm strong as anything from pushing hostess trollies through carpet with deep pile.'

Then she starts telling some complicated story about – believe it or not – a hostess trolley she once thought was possessed by its former owner, but I'm not really listening. I'm thinking about the corroborative proof of Keith's perverted activities.

'Have you told the police?'

'What's the point?' moans Jessie. 'I'd had all sorts jumping out at me in this town. You can't go putting in complaints about them all.'

'Folk have been killed...' I whisper, but there comes another fanfare and it seems the ceremony is over. I've missed the bit when I could have shouted out my just cause and impediment and caused pandemonium. Next thing, Effie is gliding back down the aisle looking extremely pleased with herself.

The silly mare has gone and done it.

§

One of the worst things that the Monster he created ever said to my father was: 'I will be with you on your wedding night.'

Well, at first, naturally, Herr Doktor Frankenstein had no idea what the heinous creature might mean. Obviously it was a threat and all became clear only when the Doctor found his bride dead on the bed, murdered by the monster, who was revenged at last.

Now I find that I am making the same promise. Not out of vengeance or anything nasty, but out of friendship and a desire to save Effie from herself.

In the Christmas Hotel the celebrations go on all evening. It's a raucous place at the best of times, but tonight the old age pensioners are kicking up their heels even more wildly and the whole place is jumping. Effie is proof to them all that love and excitement and romance can come to anyone, no matter how old, embittered and shrivelled up they may be.

All I can think is that the clock is ticking for Effie in more ways than one. Now that Keith has stuck that ring on her finger, everything she has is now his. Surely he won't tolerate her for long. I feel sure that he's going to do her in on her wedding night.

I've already learned from Mrs Claus that she has donated the use of her finest suite for their honeymoon. While she was bragging about that, I made my decision. I knew just what I was going to do.

About fifteen minutes before midnight, here I am creeping out of the shindig. I am out on the freezing prom with the music pounding at my back. I nip round the back of the Christmas Hotel. There's no one about. There's no one to hear me clanging and banging my way up the network of metal fire escapes. I'm not too fond of heights, but it's too late to think about that. I have to think about getting my mission accomplished. I duck past windows and haul myself up frozen railings.

I know that the best suite is highest on the tall, gabled roof of the hotel. Six storeys up. From here I can see the sprawling lights of Whitby. The fierce breeze makes my head spin as I stagger about looking for the skylight above the fanciest room in town.

There. About ten feet beyond the end of the ladder I'm on. To reach it I must balance upon the slates of the roof itself.

Across the harbour the tinny chimes of St Mary's come drifting. It's midnight. Mrs Claus said she was going to make everyone applaud the newly-weds and send them up the wooden hill precisely on the cusp of the witchy hour. It's a tradition at the Christmas Hotel, she was saying, for brides to go off in this manner. To be dragged off amid the tumultuous applause of the guests. I'd rather die, I think, than face such mortification. Effie has surprised me today, with her relish of being centre of attention.

So – I shin carefully along the guttering, praying it will take my weight. I'm hanging on by my fingernails, it seems. I could expire on the spot and lie here forever without anyone knowing. Don't look back, Brenda. Don't look down. Don't look blummin' anywhere. Use your strength. Use your amazing powers of endurance.

Call upon the freakish abilities with which you are mysteriously endowed! I bully and cajole myself and manage against the odds to drag my sorry carcass to the window that looks down into the bridal suite.

The elves have done a magnificent job. Candles are flickering in the purple room, and rose petals are scattered on the silky sheets. Champagne stands on ice. All of it would be lovely, if I wasn't thinking about Keith having his wicked way and throttling the life out of Effie. The poor old cow will be expecting the time of her life, not its abrupt cessation!

This is when I hear the *growl*.

Quite close by. A deep-throated growl. Out on the rooftop with me.

I look around and can't see anything. I decide it must be the weird acoustics up here; distorting the sound of the sea.

Then I get distracted by sudden activity down below in the room. The newly-weds have arrived, it seems. The door flies open and, heaven help her, Effie is being carried into the suite by Keith. Keith appears to be trumpeting their arrival with his trunk. He dumps Effie on the bed and she lies there, resplendent in her ivory satin jumpsuit with her hair done up in that chic little turban. She seems to luxuriate in the rose petals as Keith dashes off to the bathroom.

I'm about to draw her attention to me, when I hear that growl again.

Much closer this time. It's right beside me. And unmistakable. It's not an aural hallucination, after all.

It's the Crispy Cat.

And it's caught up with me at last.

The phantom moggy has bided its time. It has followed me all about the town, and at last to the top of the Christmas Hotel. There is no mistaking this green and orange, crackling feline form, baring its yellow fangs at me. I stare into its swirling, radioactive eyes and I know I am about to become its next victim.

It crouches, with its whole body tensing up. I open my mouth to say something pathetic, like promising it special cat food. But I know it's about to pounce.

Down below Keith has emerged from the bathroom in a kimono. I am only dimly aware of what's going on down there, while my attention is focused on the Crispy Cat. Nevertheless, I am aware of Keith flomping onto that heavenly bed beside my friend and whispering sweet nothings while she giggles.

And then I see something absolutely awful.

For once Keith isn't wearing his hat.

His massive skull is bare as I stare down from above.

And there, right on the top of his head, is a very old, dark tattoo. A stylized icon of an elephant's face. The face of Effulvia – the many-trunked destroyer and demon goddess from the Himalayas!

I was right! I was right after all!

Keith is guilty as sin, and up to his neck in that ancient cult!

And poor Effie is squashed underneath him..!

And here on the roof tiles, the Crispy Cat is making the most horrible noise. He's going to pounce any second.

In the suite Keith is rolling about on top of Effie. She's all abandonment and bliss. She wouldn't be if she knew what I know about him.

Then his deadly trunk flexes itself and, as he leans down to kiss her, it wraps itself – at first tenderly – all about her neck...

And this is when the Crispy Cat springs.

I jump in alarm and the full weight of my body drops onto the skylight. I am spread-eagled on the glass as the cat sinks his claws into me.

Effie is staring up at the ceiling. Her eyes are popping out of her head as she realizes Keith isn't caressing her, he's strangling the life out of her.

And now she can see me up here, face down on the double-glazing with a glowing cat on my head.

Effie screams. Keith tries to shush her and choke her quiet.

And then the glass breaks beneath me. It smashes and I'm falling through it, with a glowing, sabre-toothed kitty ripping my black velvet finery to ribbons.

There's a mad scramble below as Keith lets go of Effie and they both roll off the bed in time.

Surely this can't be anything like what she imagined her conjugals would be like?

Keith himself is screaming now, as I land with an unholy racket and safety glass flying everywhere.

The Crispy Cat is dazed only for a second. Then he's rearing up and preparing to tear my face off. Luckily, I still have enough fight left in me to fend him off with a hefty wallop in the chops. I've got deeper reserves of strength than anyone might think.

This is when Keith makes his fatal mistake. He picks up an antique chair and brandishes it at the ghostly puss. The cat howls and swings round on the startled groom. Effie shrieks as she realizes exactly what the assailant is. I roll across the furniture like something out of the SAS and try to shelter Effie with my battered and bruised body.

'What's happening, Brenda?' she shrieks down my ear. 'What on Earth have you done..?'

I don't even try to answer this. Besides, it's much too noisy in here. Keith and the Crispy Cat are slugging it out. The cat's claws flash and Keith bellows in pain. His trunk grabs the cat by the throat and begins its deadly squeezing... but is it even possible to throttle a phantom?

Effie calls her husband's name, even though he has just tried to murder her. She still feels concern for him. I tell her that she oughtn't to look. The battle is too horrible. Too fierce and bloody.

There is frantic knocking at the door. People outside have realised that something ghastly must be going on. This is way noisier than any honeymoon this place has ever borne witness to.

Suddenly Keith drops. He's bleeding badly and is cut to pieces. To me he looks mortally wounded. The Crispy Cat howls its primitive triumph and bats Keith's trunk about a bit, until it's quite sure he's defeated. The cat's badly injured too. His glowing seems dimmer somehow in the candlelight.

The candlelight! This licking flame isn't just from nightlights. Everything was knocked over when I fell through the roof. Sheets of flame are springing up all over the honeymoon suite. The silk sheets turn out to be polyester and there's a horrible smell as they melt and burn. Black fumes are starting to engulf the blummin' lot of us!

'Brenda!' Effie shrieks. 'Where are you?'

I stand up and take stock. The Christmas Hotel is on fire and the latterday London Monster Keith is dead. I check his pulse. Poor Effie. The door flies open and shocked-looking elves come storming in to rescue us. Effie's passed out, which is probably for the best.

At the very last I lock eyes again with the Crispy Cat and all I can see there is feral hunger. A horrible sight. Then it fades away, suddenly, as if it had never been.

A new urgency overtakes me. Just what we need – another inferno! We have to get out of here at once.

By rights I should be half dead. But I heft up Effie – bony, unconscious, disappointed Effie – and I get us both out of there.

The Christmas elves bring hoses and extinguishers and are trying to resuscitate Keith, but it's too late.

I drag my best friend out of that hellish bridal suite at last.

Mrs Claus and all the guests are waiting outside the Christmas Hotel. They've been hurriedly evacuated at the first signs of fire. Now they're in the freezing cold, looking shocked and terrified.

An ambulance comes screaming to a halt and Effie is loaded aboard. She's all right. They just want to check her over for smoke inhalation. My heart goes out to her. Strapped down to a gurney in her flashy wedding outfit, her turban partially charred and her face white and wild-looking.

'Keith didn't make it,' I tell her, as they push her stretcher into the van.

'W-who?' she asks, in a vague sort of tone.

So she's lost her memory. The shock has robbed her of her wits. Well, perhaps that's just as well.

The paramedics want me to come to hospital too. But I roughly refuse. No one's getting a look at me. This one looks after herself.

I watch the ambulance race off and then, before anyone can ask me anything else at all, I stumble off through the back alleys to my B&B. My blessed sanctuary.

§

And so... It turns out that the Christmas Hotel isn't razed to the ground after all. It just gets a nasty hole in the roof and has to have a new bridal suite put in. Mrs Christmas is, of course, insured up to the eyeballs.

The only thing I care about is Effie's safety. They let her return home on the following day. She looks pale when I see her. I can tell that the memory of recent events has returned to her. And she's in mourning for the mad cultist who briefly married her and tried to finish her off with his trunk.

'You were right, ducky, and I was wrong.'

'Never mind that now.' I pass her a small schooner of sherry. I change the old jazz record on my turntable. Nina Simone will buck us up, I reckon.

'I should have listened to you, Brenda. You're my best friend. I've never had a best friend before.'

I have, of course. I smile as I sit back in my armchair and bask in the cosy warmth of my attic sitting room. I don't tell Effie about the wonderful best friends that I had before her. Joe Merrick. Henry Cleavis. I don't want to hurt her feelings. I've had a good many friends in the course of my long, long life. And the thing about those friends is that you have to be able to trust them absolutely and depend on what they say. Sometimes that can become a matter of life and death.

And the other thing about being best of friends during the course of a very long life is that things change. People change, times change. Things go wrong. Sometimes things go right. Sometimes you can drift apart forever. Sometimes you're left all on your lonesome again.

But today's not a day for thinking like that. Today we're listening to good music and finishing our sweet sherry and thinking that maybe it's time to head down to the harbour for a quiet fish supper in *Cod Almighty*.

We chink our glasses together in a toast.

'To old friends and narrow escapes!'

And also: 'To best friends and further adventures!'

I pull a rueful face. 'And maybe a bit of peace and quiet, too? At least, until the next spooky mystery comes along?'

# 5

# Mrs Hudson at the Christmas Hotel

*From the Journal of Dr John Watson.*
   *November, 1925.*
   This morning I received a rather large envelope postmarked Sussex.  Of course I knew at once that it came from my old friend and, sure enough, amongst various yellowing papers and envelopes there was a jar of his finest home-engineered honey, wrapped in a protective bundle of muslin.  Holmes' bees' honey is a rare treat and a welcome addition to our breakfast table, though my beloved does object to the occasional dead Hymenopteran found suspended in the sticky stuff. Digging deeper in the brown paper parcel proved there to be a further bundle and this was a padded box, such as might contain an item of jewellery. Indeed, inside the box there were two splendid multi-hued crystals.  They looked rather like a pair of eyes.  I passed them to my

beloved wife across the table and she gasped. 'Whatever is he doing, entrusting such things to the Royal Mail?'

I couldn't answer her satisfactorily without first absorbing the import of his note, which was folded neatly underneath these packages. I do enjoy my former colleague-in-adventure's sporadic missives, touching as they often do, upon events in our shared past of which even I am not fully cognisant. It seems that adventures and investigations were going on continuously all around us, and I wasn't aware of even half of them. His letter of this morning – in rather shakier handwriting than ever, I am afraid – consisted of the following:

'Watson – please find enclosed the latest production of my recalcitrant livestock. Cajole them as I might, they are very slow and perfectionist and what is contained in this jar represents almost a full year of squeezing and cudgeling of their small selves. I trust you will find it delicious. I also enclose the Eyes of Miimon, which belong to the people of Finland. They were smuggled here in the early 1890s by extraordinary means and the manner of their theft is still, I am afraid, a closed book. However, they have recently come to light again and were sent to me by the nieces of one Maude Sturgeon, a deceased spinster from the North Yorkshire coastal town of Whitby. They are a superstitious folk in that part of the islands, and will believe any silly piece of nonsense when it comes to matters of black magic and necromancy and so on. The nieces of this elderly, formidable lady – known as the local wise woman, apparently – believe that their ninety four year old aunt was whisked away before her time at the behest of dark forces. (Before her time, I ask you! At the age of ninety four...!) As you know, I will have no truck with such things as magic and dreadful sentimental drivel about daemons and so on, especially at my time of life.

Nevertheless we must respect the beliefs of others – at least, in terms of how those beliefs might lead their owners to behave. Maude Sturgeon, I am informed, fully believed that these jewels are capable of exerting an influence of great evil. They had been in her possession ever since they were smuggled into this country, in 1895 – some thirty years ago. Her nieces found them amongst her precious belongings after her demise and they have decided to be rid of them. And so – in their great good wisdom - they have sent them to me. I was appalled to find that Maude Sturgeon never presented the jewels to the authorities three decades ago as she was plainly instructed to, but as you know, I have no faith in the doings of womankind. Especially not the kind of women who instruct their surviving relatives to sprinkle their ashes illegally and unhygenically around a national monument such as the ruined Abbey at Whitby.

Anyhow, I am too old and decrepit to run about the place with supposedly-magical crystals. Would you,

Watson, please see that they are disposed of correctly? My initial thought was that you should present them to my brother Mycroft, for official restoration to the Finns, who would no doubt be delighted. But then I thought... why not give the things to Professor Challenger, that old charlatan? If they are indeed magical stones – and I know you will guffaw at my entertaining the very idea, old friend – well, at the very least Professor Challenger might squeeze a little entertainment and amusement out of them. As might his new housekeeper, Mrs Hudson. She might even recognise the Eyes of Miimon, and be reminded of an escapade of her own from 1895.

An escapade which the also-enclosed packet of letters and postcards rather chaotically details. They are all addressed to you, my dear Watson, though somehow they have ended up amongst my many jumbled papers and effects.

Do you remember these rather strange communications which we received from Mrs Hudson during her holiday in the early summer of 1895? We both thought – as we read each one during our breakfasts at 221B – that our absent housekeeper was losing her mind.

Well, perhaps not. There is certainly something very odd about these twin jewels from Finland. Do you not find they give off a rather odd vibration? Don't they make you feel that there might actually be something in the superstitions of the wild North-Easterners?

With great affection,
Holmes.

§

*June 17th, 1895*
  *Whitby; The Royal Crescent, The West Cliff*
Dear Doctor Watson,
   Now I hope you two sillies are seeing to yourselves
properly. I put some nice jam on the kitchen counter,
did you see? For breakfast. Damson. Home-made. I
won't be away for more than a week. My sister Nellie
could never put up with me for longer than that. Today
we have had a trip out to Scarborough, where folk go
to take the waters. I much prefer the quieter seafront
here in Whitby, though. Far more civilised than all that
hullaballoo further down the coast. Here, life is much
more sedate and genteel. As you yourself told me, Doctor,
my nerves need soothing, rather than exciting further.
Frazzled and malcontent, I think were the words you used
to describe my recent moods. How your epithets rang
in my ears when you left me on the station platform on
Monday morning.
   Anyhow, relax I must, the good Doctor tells me. To
that end Nellie and I have been enjoying rather lazy days
strolling about the intricate streets of this town, on both
sides of the harbour. During yesterday's rather gusty
afternoon we even took a bracing walk up the 199 steps to

the old, broken down Abbey. I am sure you approve of a little light exertion, though I must admit my legs were trembling this morning. Not that either of you wish to hear of my sundry complaints, of course. As far as the pair of you are concerned, all I *ever* do is run and up and down staircases.

This evening we attend a special musical evening at one of the grander hotels on the West Cliff. Nellie has promised an evening of wonderment and enchantment. Nellie often exaggerates, though I must say, Whitby thus far is everything she has been promising me. Do you know this neck of the woods, Doctor?

I do hope all is peaceful at home. The two of you are, I imagine, embroiled in one of your dreadful investigations, I am sure. Ruffians of all kinds will be tracking muck up and down my stair carpets. I would not dream of asking a man of your elevation to run around with the ewbank, Doctor Watson, but you would lighten my load considerably if you could manage it.

Now, please give Himself my warmest good wishes, and do save some for yourself.

Oh – the picture on the reverse shows the ruined Abbey and St Mary's Church, at the summit of the winding upward slope of 199 steps which Nellie and I doughtily tackled yesterday. You will be amused to note that, from this elevation, the stairs describe a reversed question mark upon the face of the steep, grassy cliff. Mysteries everywhere, you see.

Yours,

Mrs Hudson

§

Dear Doctor Watson,

As you know I practice moderation in all things and I hardly ever touch a drop of alcohol, and so I don't know quite what came over me last night at the Christmas Hotel. There was, I think, a feverish and hysterical atmosphere about the place, and a sense that things were running ever so slightly amok.

Nellie and I arrived for dinner at the grand, imposing edifice of the one hundred year old hotel and I admit to marvelling at its palatial splendour. It was painted pink and its windows were lit up charmingly with golden light. Inside, however, it was clear that all the guests were awash with the party spirit. There was dancing and hectic activity in every direction one cared to look. We found a foyer trimmed with every kind of gaudy Christmas decoration and barely room between flushed and over-dressed guests to manoeuvre ourselves. As you know, my sister is lame and rather short, and so we had something of a trial, scuffling past the vast Scots fir and making for the ballroom at the far end of the first floor.

Nellie had already explained that the owner of the Christmas Hotel went in for these festive excesses all the year round. This was how she and her customers liked it. I found it all a bit much for a warm night in June. I did think it possibly irreligious, too.

Things are different in the North, as we both well know, Doctor, and though, had I been alone I should have turned on my heel and quitted the Christmas Hotel at once, I felt I ought to linger a little for poor Nellie's sake. I don't believe she gets out much on her own, being as disfigured and generally malformed as she is.

Having said that, I was astonished that Nellie didn't seem perturbed by the abandonment and revelry all about us. It was a kind of cross between a rough Parisian dance hall and scenes from Bedlam. In fact, as she led the way into the ballroom, I realised that she seemed quite eager to take part in the dancing and the various hi-jinks in evidence.

Here there was a band, all the members of which were attired in green and scarlet outfits befitting of some species of pixie or elf. The music they were playing seemed unearthly and vulgar to my affronted ears.

Nellie must have noticed the expression on my face, for she turned to me, laughing. How strange, I thought, to see her so unselfconscious. Laughing, like this, in public. She must indeed feel at home here in this insalubrious place. Under the glittering lights of the ballroom her makeup seemed horribly garish and there were points of light dancing nastily in her single eye.

'The mistress wants to meet you,' she told me.

I was duly introduced to the proprietress of this extraordinary establishment. It was a vast, blousy female form that came shunting towards us, her bloated body surmounting a kind of mechanised bath chair. Her revolting gown revealed a surplus of powdered bosom and broken veins crisscrossed her face like contour lines on the Ordnance Survey Map for this part of North Yorkshire.

She cackled at me, 'I am Mrs Claus,' and the force of her breath was vile. She reeked like a pudding hot with flaming sauce and I took against her at once. 'I feel honoured to meet poor Nellie's infamous sister.'

'Infamous?' snapped I. As you know, Doctor, I do try not to be short with folk. But the fatuous remarks of others sometimes make it impossible for me not to snap at them.

'Oh, certainly. We all know who you work for, dear, and we're all very impressed. We keep up to date with his exploits through the scribblings of the good Doctor Watson. We aren't so remote from the metropolis that we aren't bang up to the minute on unspeakable crimes in the south.'

What a coarse way of referring to your various literary productions, Doctor Watson! Suddenly, I felt exposed before this heinous female in this parochial pleasure parlour. I felt as if our entire lives had been laid bare. In that moment I knew that no matter that her hotel was geared to continuous celebration of the birth of our Saviour, there was an unholy stink of corruption about it and also about the occupant of that steam-driven bath chair.

Such was the extent of our discourse last evening, for Nellie swiftly dragged me away to sample the Christmas punch, which was being dispensed from a crystal bowl by another pair of waiters decked out as elves. We drank, and then we danced. Gentlemen gallantly offered themselves. We whirled about under lights to music I had never heard before. We made several return visits to the bottomless tureen of that delicious brew. We slaked our thirsts after our exertions and I marvelled again at Nellie's fleet-footedness on the floor. Never had I seen her less ungainly, with her clubfoot banging the sprung floor in perfect time. I think we both imbibed a little more of the heavenly beverage than we ought to have done.

Luckily, Nellie's compact cottage isn't far from the Christmas Hotel. We tottered easily down a few back allies when it was time to drag ourselves away.

It had been a far more enjoyable evening that I had expected and really, Doctor, I am only telling you about it now in order to prove that I am taking seriously your exhortations that I should relax during my northern sojourn and do my level best to let down my hair.

This morning we are in disarray. My head and that of my sister are both pounding with the echoes of queer music. Nellie has made several large pots of tea to help us stir ourselves. Uppermost in my mind is the needling impression left upon me by that grotesque hostess, Mrs Claus. During our unexpectedly energetic dancing, I caught her watching us once or twice, through the crowd. She even had the nerve to waggle her fat fingers at me.

Also – and I haven't breathed a word of this to Nellie, of course – I happened to glimpse a poster advertising the very thing that you and Himself have asked me to watch out for.

In the ladies' lavatory there was a garish notice for An Extravaganza of Exorcism to be held at the Christmas Hotel. It's on every Tuesday night, apparently.

§

Dear Doctor Watson,

It was evening before Nellie and I ventured out again and, in nostalgic vein, Nellie wanted to reminisce about our distant shared childhood in the Borders. I have no interest in looking back at a time when I was small, helpless and at the mercy of neglectful parents, and I can't see why she would care to dwell on such times when folk would call out names and throw rocks at her in the street. But my sister seems depressed and sunk into herself. Her flesh appears to hang off her distorted skeleton and her spirit is out of sorts, and so I indulged her for a portion of the evening, roving stiffly over old times. I also made half a dozen discreet enquiries about her health and state of mind, but about both my sister has not been forthcoming, poor mite.

Gabbling about a childhood expunged of all distressing details she led me through the harbour and there we found a crowd gathered around a certain whaling vessel at the jetty. There was a flurry of excitement and kerfuffle going on as the ship docked and naturally we paused to see what was occurring. Nellie pointed to the cause of all the over-stimulation and it turned out to be a dark, dripping, unidentifiable carcass that was being roped into a harness on the deck of the ship. The sailors had brought something horrid out of the freezing sea. Some multi-limbed monstrosity that sent shivers through each of the observers, none of whom had seen anything like it.

We wandered to the swing bridge over the harbour and, even from there, we could see the nasty thing as it was hauled aloft and we were standing downwind of its evil, brackish stench. I stared straight into its monstrous and sightless eyes.

And how do I explain this without sounding like a raging loon? Ach, Doctor Watson. You will think that no more than two days away from Baker Street has turned me into a silly woman. For I looked into the eyes of that beast. Eyes as large as side plates they were, and I felt I could see whole galaxies expand in their swirling depths. I saw stars blooming and worlds colliding and time telescoping into nothingness. I felt the whole of the future and past were laid out before me as I stood there on the bridge in the middle of that town, with the turbid North Sea all chilly around me. I experienced a small thrill of excitement, I have to say.

All of that I saw in the queer cephalopod's eyes.

Anyhow, then we had a very pleasant fish supper. Much, much better than the rubbish we get in London. I hope you and Himself are having a pleasant week, Doctor, and that there have been no untoward investigations thrust upon the two of you. You know how I fret. Tomorrow is Tuesday, as you know, and I shall be attending the Extravaganza of Exorcisms, just to see what it is like. I will report forthwith.

§

Dear Doctor Watson,

Oh by jingo.

Why on Earth did you ask me to go there? Why not leave a poor woman alone to potter about at the seaside and enjoy old ladyish things? Why make me undertake a mission of this nature?

I wish I had never gone.

Nellie is upstairs in her bed. It's past one in the morning. She's whimpering in her sleep, I can hear it through the floorboards. I'm just praying that she won't be permanently damaged by what she has been through tonight.

I'll tell you what it was. It was cruel, is what it was. It was shameful cruelty on the part of that woman and I blame myself. More than you and Himself, I blame myself, for letting my poor sister come along to the Christmas Hotel with me this evening.

But how was I to know?

I mean, with things of this sort, you expect them to be a den of charlatans, don't you? There's nothing in it, is there? All that table-rapping. Spirit world mumbo-jumbo. Why, I recall several occasions when you yourself and Himself have been called out on cases complicated by the carryings-on of fakers of psychic phenomena. I had assumed that much the same would be going on at the jamboree held at the Christmas Hotel and, indeed, when we first went in, it did seem like a fairly innocuous affair: a kind of bazaar for the feeble-minded. There were gypsies everywhere, reading palms in tents and at tables; there were Arabs and Jews and Chinese flogging their exotic wares; there were foreign folk consulting crystals and scrying mirrors and all types of occult artefacts. The very air was singing with the mystical mumblings of the fey folk crowded into the hotel's public rooms.

It was for the demonstrations of Exorcisms that we were there, however, as you well know, Doctor Watson. I guided my lumpen and somewhat sullen sister in the direction of the ballroom and there we were witness to a most peculiar performance. He was rather like a magician on that stage, with his assistant in a glamorous, beruffled frock. Denise and Wheatley, they were billed as and, when they got going with a volunteer from the audience, I saw that it was the female Denise who took the lead. She was the one shouting and exhorting the devil to hie himself out of the volunteer elf. Mr Wheatley simply stood to one side, mumbling verses from a black-bound Old Testament and casting worried sideways glances at the supposedly-possessed young man when he started vomiting on the stage.

It was a revolting spectacle, but my sister was enthralled. When I turned to tell her that I thought we had seen enough, I was startled to see that Nellie had an avid expression on her face. Her whole, twisted body was rigid and on the very point of surging forward through that crowd. 'N-nellie..?' I asked.

She looked at me and I saw a light in her eyes that I had never seen before. A wicked light, I thought.

We were interrupted then by the next act. Denise and Wheatley had, apparently been successful in de-

demonising the vomiting elf, and they were replaced by a formidably ancient Romany woman in hooped satin skirts and jet black hair. She was hard-faced and sinister and she appeared to be slipping into a trance.

'There are devils among us,' she intoned, in a curious accent. 'Beelzebub walks among us.'

I turned to my sister to make a dry and jocular remark and was startled to find that Nellie had gone. She had slipped neatly through the press of bodies and was hauling herself onto the stage area. There was a roar of approval from the crowd.

'He is in me!' Nellie declared. She held out her arms and faced us, with a beatific smile upon her usually rather miserable-looking and crumpled face. 'The devil is inside me! He has always been inside me! I have always been his plaything!'

The applause grew wilder, as if my unfortunate sister had won the approval of her fellow townsfolk; as if she were confirming the truth of something they had always suspected about her.

There was a string of words stuck in my throat. I tried repeatedly to shout them out at the stage, but they wouldn't come. I was suspended in horror, jostled in the crowd and helpless.

Now the Romany woman was laying her coarse, dirty hands on my sister and chanting some very strange verses indeed. I watched as Nellie went stiff as a board and started to froth at the mouth. That made me sick to the pit of my stomach. I could feel the Seafood Surprise from our early dinner start to rise in my gorge.

The gypsy woman's chanting was reaching a crescendo. I could have sworn I saw Nellie's eyes roll back and turn red.

Then there was a round of applause and it was over. Nellie was helped down from the stage and she was smiling shyly and nodding, acknowledging the applause. She wandered back through the crowd towards me.

On the stage the Romany exorcist flung up her arms and said, 'The demon is powerfully strong! He will not leave this woman so easily. Nor will he leave any of you. All of you must buy...' And here she produced a pink jar of some kind of snake oil that she insisted we must all queue up and buy for four guineas a pop. Well, I was having none of it, and practically dragged my still-shaking and frothy-mouthed sister home.

So – thank you, indeed, Doctor Watson. As if you even needed Nellie and I to investigate those charlatans at the Christmas Hotel. Naturally they are fakers. We knew that even before attending this macabre charade. But Nellie needn't have been frightened out of her wits in aid of your pursuit of knowledge. I wish you had never read those accounts in the first place, of the miraculous and mysterious events reported here in Whitby at the Christmas Hotel. I don't know why a sensible man such as yourself would have been at all bothered in the first place.

§

Dear Doctor Watson,

This morning my poor sister was no better. She has gone a very odd colour indeed. Her usual hue isn't all that healthy-looking, but this is downright alarming. I asked her if there was anything I could do for her.

'Maude will know,' she said, tremulously. 'Fetch Maude.'

Well, it turns out her friend Maude Sturgeon lives down by the docks and she is what used to be called a local wise woman. Actually, there is a whole family of wise women, as it turns out, and these sisters occupy a tall house not far from the harbour. Downstairs it is a kind of herbalist shop – reeking of spices and curious unguents. I cast my eye around with some interest at the things they had on display. But I was there on a mission. 'Maude will be able to help me,' Nellie had insisted.

Now I was confronting the formidable Maude Sturgeon herself, in her witchy emporium. She listened disapprovingly as I described the previous evening's events. She seemed to take a very dim view of anything that went on at the Christmas Hotel.

'There's always someone dabbling with dark forces and things they should know better about,' said Maude gruffly. She was more like a schoolmarm than a witch, I thought, in her plain grey suit and her steel grey hair pinned up like so. It was reassuring to be in the presence of her stolid good sense. She asked me to come and sit in their parlour, where I found three of her rather more fey sisters engaged in a very odd task indeed.

Maude was fetching her shawl off the hat stand. 'Oh, don't mind them,' she told me. 'They're stuffing it for the Whitby museum.'

I looked harder and realised that the slippery dark thing they were all sewing wasn't some svelte garment after all. It was the gutted remains of the monstrous sea beast that had been landed yesterday. Those witchy sisters appraised me as they went on stitching, and I was very careful not to look into the behemoth's eyes again.

Then Maude was ready and I was glad to get out of the fishy smell of that back parlour. The wise woman led the way through the narrow streets towards Nellie's house, pausing on the way to buy her a fancy cake from a favoured bakery.

'How long have you been friends with my sister?' I asked conversationally.

'Ever since she's been here,' said Maude, beaming brightly, and brandishing her walking stick as we passed familiar faces. 'Your sister has proved quite a reliable helper on a number of my more terrifying investigations and adventures here in Whitby.'

Well, of course, you could have knocked me down with a feather. Our Nellie? Having adventures? Involved in investigations? Helping out a personage such as this Maude? For a second I experienced a slight dizziness. Did everyone I know get themselves involved in curious adventures behind my very back?

'Do you mean... crimes?' I asked, lowering my voice as we came within sight of Nellie's cottage.

'Crimes, indeed,' nodded Maude. 'Also supernatural and unexplained phenomena of all kinds. Whitby seems to be a kind of magnet for occult and devilish practices, schemes and unholy beings, y'know.'

'Really?'

'Oh, yes,' sniffed Maude, giving me a very dark look indeed as I fumbled for my keys to Nellie's house. 'It's to do with the presence of an interstitial dimensional gateway known as the Bitch's Maw in the grounds of the old Abbey, you see. A kind of gateway into hell. Very nasty indeed.'

I'm afraid my mouth dropped open at her words and I busied myself with letting us into the cottage, which smelled reassuringly of newly-brewed coffee and fresh wood smoke. Convinced I was bringing a raging lunatic to the rescue, I was delighted to see that my sister had risen from her bed. She was shuffling about in the kitchen in her nightie and pouring coffee for us all.

'I'm so sorry to call you out, Maude,' she said, as her visitor produced the Victoria sponge from her shopping bag. 'Ooh, lovely. I'll fetch plates. No, I thought I'd better call you over, because of this funny do that we had last night at the Exorcism Extravaganza.'

'You were fools to go to such a thing,' Maude growled, slicing the cake and dolloping wodges of it messily onto dainty china.

'I know, I couldn't help myself,' said Nellie. 'And we all know these things are about charlatans fleecing the public. But the thing is... I went there because Raphael was worried. He had felt a vibration. There was a genuinely powerful psychic up there at the hotel last night. He could feel them at work. They were malevolent. Harmful. Hiding their wicked selves away amongst the usual fakers. That's why we were there last night. So I could flush this person out.'

I sat there with my wedge of cake halfway up to my mouth, staring at my sister. My malformed and shy younger sister, Nellie. Nellie with one eye, a crooked back and a clubfoot. Nellie who would never say boo to a goose. My poor Nellie was sitting there in her nightgown, eating cake for breakfast, and coming out with all of this gobbledegook, easy as you like. And that bullish Maude woman was simply nodding at her. Nodding as if they had little chats like this all the time. Nodding as if they were discussing something entirely reasonable.

Before they could carry on saying other things to uproot my sense of the stability of all things, I broke in, 'Erm, who is Raphael?'

My dear sister Nellie looked at me and I was astonished to see a hint of pity in her single eye. She was pitying me! 'Oh dear,' she said. 'Well. I suppose needs must. After all these years, I must come clean. I must tell you the truth. After a lifetime of concealment.'

'I think you're right,' said Maude. 'It's about time your sister knew the truth.'

Nellie took a deep breath and looked at me dead in the eye. Both my eyes. With her single one. Which was wincing with pity. She said – in a very calm voice indeed – 'You see, Raphael is my inner demon. And my spirit guide. He's been inside me all my life and he's been my little secret. It was he that that dreadful woman tried to exorcise last night. It gave Raphael quite a turn, I can tell you.'

I stared at her. I really didn't know what to say. What does one say, Doctor Watson, in circumstances like these?

§

Dear Doctor Watson,

I hope both your good self and our mutual friend, Himself, are faring rather better than I am this week. I have been in a whirl of perturbation for several days. Never have I been so steeped in strangeness and such eerie goings-on. Well, it turns out that my malformed sister and her bluff and hearty best friend are very well accustomed to all manner of supernatural things. Things I assumed simply should not be. I, being, like our good friend Himself, a creature of rationality and good, plain commonsense am having problems. Here in the North I am finding more things in my philosophy – as the Danish prince would say – than I could shake a stick at.

Today is Thursday – honestly, I don't know where the time is going; I'm being led around all passively by my sister, who seems to have a renewed vigour about her, now that she is embroiled in an investigation. I was compelled to attend an unveiling ceremony at the Museum in the rather elegant park across the other side of town. This was for the stuffed squid that Maude's sisters had spent day and night stitching back into some semblance of life. When we arrived for the sherry cocktail reception this evening in that rather musty, dusty municipal establishment, the squid was suspended in a delicate cat's cradle of silver threads, which gave it the appearance of swimming through the cavernous room. All of the guests – Whitby's great and good in their finery – stood milling underneath, gazing up at the frozen tentacles and the shiny carapace of its purple skin.

I nodded politely and smiled as my sister gabbled away at Maude's sisters, who were attired in suitably witchy – and rather scandalous – gowns for the evening. They smiled demurely and seemed to be the toast of the town. I wandered about the other display cabinets, finding a bewildering selection of mouldering dolls' houses and ragged bears. There were Valentine's cards from the previous century; tiny gloves and shoes; stuffed woodland beasts and seabirds. It was a shabby miscellany, I thought, with hardly any rhyme or reason.

Anyhow, there was a proper ballyhoo when the Mayor of Whitby got up in all his robes and chains made his speech. He stood on a podium – this oleaginous Mr Danby, as they called him – and he chuntered on about their town and its glorious heritage. I was staring into the eyes of the monstrous beast, but its celestial orbs had been replaced, naturally enough, with something less potent. They looked rather like green glass plates and, indeed, Maude leaned in to me and hissed that that's what the squid's eyes were: two expensive serving platters she had brought back from a holiday on the island of Murano, near Venice. Oh, my heart leapt up at the mention of Venice, dear Doctor Watson. And then I shivered as I recalled some of the deadlier details of our adventure there, last autumn.

It was just as the Mayor was coming to the end of his windy speech that I noticed something rather odd happening to the suspended squid. One of its attenuated limbs seemed to flex and lash, of its own accord. There was a sharp cry as someone else noticed the same thing.

Then, all of a sudden, all its limbs were moving and screams rang out inside the stuffy museum. It was at this point that I noticed it was all due to the wires which suspended the beast: they were snapping, one by one, and then the thick, heavy body of the squid was swaying and then galloping about in mid-air. There was such a pandemonium at this, and I felt Nellie grab me by both arms and drag me backwards into the alcove where the ships-in-bottles were tidily arrayed.

With a tremendous crash of breaking cabinets and glass displays, the giant squid came toppling down. Some innocent bystanders had been transfixed with horror – including the Mayor – and they were soon pinned and wriggling under that giant, piscine form.

After a few moments there was silence, and billowing clouds of dust.

I heard Maude Sturgeon cry out, 'Sabotage..!'

And soon we were checking around, to see who was hurt. Maude's witchy sisters were shaken, but not injured. The squid itself had barely a scratch on it. The Mayor's ancient, wizened mother was hyperventilating and had to be taken home.

Nellie and I went straight to the nearest hotel, where we sat in the bar and took a fortifyingly stiff nip of brandy. 'Who would want to sabotage the unveiling of a squid?' I asked her.

She gave me a very dark look. 'Perhaps it's not the squid itself. Perhaps it is all about what was inside the squid.'

I raised my eyebrow at her as she downed her drink. 'What could be inside a squid?' I laughed.

'Whatever it was, it isn't there now,' she said cryptically. 'The squid was, as we know, rammed full of stuffing.'

She was mumbling rather drunkenly, I thought. And I also thought I could detect a touch of Raphael, her supposed spirit guide, in her eyes. 'Are you saying something was removed from the squid? By those who did the stuffing?'

She tapped her nose. 'I am, indeed.'

'Maude's sisters gutted the thing. What did they take out?'

'I don't know,' she said primly. 'I'm only surmising.' Then she was peering across the elegant lounge bar of the Miramar hotel at someone who had just stepped in, alone. 'Isn't that Denise?' she said. 'From Denise and Wheatley?'

And it was, Doctor Watson. Away from the stage and out of her finery, Denise was a rather shabby genteel figure, all bundled up in worsted and tweed.

'She's entering the bar on her own,' I observed.

'Oh, no one cares about that kind of propriety,' said Nellie. 'Not at the Miramar hotel, anyway. Look, I'm going to call her over.'

I wasn't sure I even wanted to be sociable with an exorcist, but voice my concerns about this I could not, for Nellie was on her feet and beckoning Denise by waving her skinny arms and winking at her with her one good eye.

'My life is in tatters,' Denise wept copiously, once my sister had started her talking.

'Why is that?' asked Nellie, agog at the spectacle of the blue-haired lady sobbing into her libation.

'He can be terrible, terrible,' she trembled. 'When he's in a fury.' Fear made her shiver and the brandy glass tinkled against her rotten stumps of teeth.

'Who, my dear?' Nellie pressed.

'Why, him. My husband. My terrible husband.' Then Denise clapped a hand over her mouth, as if she had said too much.

Nellie was intrigued and kept badgering the old dear, and I felt myself growing uneasy about this. What was Nellie doing, getting so close? Hadn't Denise been one of the reasons Nellie had been up all night on Tuesday? All gut-churning and collywobbly as she was?

'There, there,' Nellie kept saying, and the elderly Exorcist burst into more violent tears. She put her head on Nellie's hump and gave full vent to her feelings as Nellie patted her wispy blue hair. I didn't know where to look.

'He makes me do heinous things,' she said, through heaving breath and muffled by Nellie's hump.

'Where is he now?' asked Nellie.

'In our room, upstairs,' said Denise. 'He has gone to bed in fury and disgust. All because of that fracas at the museum.'

'The museum?' I asked. 'You mean, the cephalopod's unfortunate collapse?'

She sniffed. 'Yes, I saw you both there. But you left with the crowd, shortly afterwards. You never saw him, berating those sisters. Getting me to cut open the thing. Feeling around inside those slippery limbs... Looking for... looking for...'

Nellie was looking excited now. She had a fervid expression. Rather like Himself gets. You know, when the game's afoot, sort-of-thing. 'Looking for what, Denise?'

'Those blasted jewels,' cried the exorcist. 'The Eyes of Miimon. Smuggled here in the body of that behemoth. The rarest of jewels. Possessed of untold occult powers.'

Now, this was a surprise to Nellie. 'Jewels?' she said. 'Where from?'

'From the islands of Finland, far away,' said the old lady. 'And he has lost them forever, he fears.'

'But,' I broke in, trying to grasp the situation. 'The giant squid was stuffed, wasn't it? We saw Maude Sturgeon's sisters sewing it themselves in their backroom.

Rather like a shroud. Surely, if there were jewels inside the beast's body, then...'

Denise Wheatley was staring at me and her eyes were hard and glittering with excitement. 'Yes! Yes, you're right!'

I looked at Nellie and she was shaking her head at me fiercely. 'But, I just thought,' I began.

'We must go at once,' said Denise, slinging back the last of her brandy. 'Where do they live, these Sisters Sturgeon? Where are they hiding the Eyes of Miimon?'

And then, rather like your own dear self, Doctor Watson, I was left to straggle in the wake of the others as they dashed from the bar area, and out of the Hotel Miramar, into something of a balmy evening.

§

Dear Doctor Watson,

I am writing this on the back of a laundry list I have found in my coat pocket and using a nub of pencil that has worn almost to nothing. This is possibly the most futile and hopeless message demanding help that you will never receive. Still, it seems preferable to write it all down, rather than sit here in the dark, doing nothing. At least my hands aren't tied, I suppose. That is something. I can twiddle my fingers at least.

Nellie is with me, absolutely furious at our predicament, for which she blames me. At this present time my malformed sister is refusing to speak to me.

'You had to blunder in, didn't you?' was one of the last things she said. 'Everything was proceeding just as it ought, and you had to go opening your big fat trap.'

Never have I heard such coarseness from my sister's rather blubbery and unattractive lips. For a few moments I was convinced that the vile spook she claims to harbour in her soul was speaking through her, but alas, no: it was Nellie herself who was livid with me. It turns out that I had burst out with quite the wrong thing, and shouldn't have told Denise the exorcist about the Sturgeon sisters and their skills in the art of taxidermy. Everything, it seems, was already in hand, and Nellie was on the point of ensnaring the blue-haired woman in a trap. My sister and Maude Sturgeon had had everything worked out, and the idea was, apparently, to lure Denise Wheatley up to the ruined Abbey. There, to meet and greet her ultimate fate, as befitting a being as magically powerful as herself. She was to be lured there by the promise of having these magical Finnish crystals handed over to her by Maude, as the senior Sturgeon sister. Such had been the idea, anyhow.

But because of me, everything has gone to the bad. I never could hold my tongue, could I?

This house is silent now. The pair of us have been imprisoned in one of the attic rooms. We've tried to break out, smashing the few bits of old furniture against the solid door. We have shouted for help, but there is no one here. The Sturgeon house is quite empty. The lower rooms lie in messy chaos, following that terrible fight between the three Sturgeon sisters and Denise Wheatley. Shelves, jars, furniture and fittings – everything was smashed into smithereens by those... what would you call them? Lightning bolts? That they were all shooting out of their hands and eyes at each other. It was a terrible to-do. And all over a few bits of old jewellery that came out of a gutted fish.

LATER:

Maude Sturgeon eventually arrived to let us out. By then I was exhausted and in no mood for a long disquisition or inquisition about what had been going on. She was filling in her partner-in-crime, my sister Nellie, about the latest developments. How it turned out that Denise Wheatley was, in fact, a powerful sorceress, and the supernatural powers of all four Sturgeon sisters combined hadn't been enough to hold her back. She had stormed into their home and stolen away the jewels she was after.

Both Nellie and Maude gave me a hard stare at this point, for giving away their location. I merely tutted and set off down the stairs of the Sturgeon residence, eager to be out of that dusty deathtrap, filled with antiques and black magic paraphernalia.

I can tell you, Doctor, I wasn't at all impressed by this talk of sorceresses and so on, for all I had seen them shooting bolts of fire out of every which way.

Maude told us that the Finnish jewels had been discovered by her sisters during the stuffing process. They had been hidden inside the dead eyes of the giant squid. Maude had cleaned them up and popped them into the safe in her bedroom, which Denise Wheatley had no compunction about breaking into, blasting it apart with those queer bolts of lightning she manifested out of her limbs.

This was all rather too much for me. I didn't care who got hold of the jewels, and said so. What did Finland matter to me?

Maude glared at me angrily. By now we were in the smashed up herbalist shop downstairs. 'With the eyes of Miimon, a powerful sorceress like Denise could do untold damage to the world.'

Nellie was biting her lip. 'We were going to shove her in the Bitch's Maw, up at the Abbey. The idea was to dispatch her to hell.'

'But now she's on the alert,' said Maude. 'There's no way she'd let us lead her there. She knows full well now that we are set against her.'

I was seeing the extent to which I had scuppered their plans. 'Oh well, never mind. I'm very sorry and all that. I think my sister and I ought to be going, actually. It's terribly late and we've been through a great deal. Ah... where are your sisters now, Maude?'

It turns out they were out hunting Denise, who had gone to ground. They didn't come back until the early hours of the morning, apparently absolutely furious. By then, however, I was safely asleep in Nellie's spare bedroom. I was trying not to feel guilty for messing up their plans, and listening to the muffled voices of Nellie talking with her demon spirit guide, Raphael, in her bedroom. Really, it sounded just like Nellie talking to herself in a deeper, gruffer voice. I wasn't at all sure I believed in any of this occult stuff they were all talking about.

I went to sleep at last, and dreamed of those mesmerising squid eyes I had seen the other day.

§

Dear Doctor Watson,

Tonight we shall return to the Christmas Hotel for another night of Exorcisms. I'm really not sure it's a good idea at all.

Nellie demands (she's become rather forceful of late, and I'm not sure it's all down to her purported spirit demon) that we both don our finest gowns for the evening. I have told her that I prefer something I can run in easily, given the danger element inherent in these evenings out in Whitby. Nellie replied that it is possible to be mobile and ready for action, as well as maintaining an attractive and glamorous appearance. I did think this a bit rich coming from a hunchback with a clubfoot, one eye and permanently greasy hair, but I didn't say anything.

I did, in fact, wear my nicest gown – the emerald green silk – for our second Tuesday with the Exorcists and I think we made rather a splendid entrance into that festive foyer. Again the elves were serving their punch and taking coats, and again there was yuletide music and frivolity in abundance as we moved graciously through the crowd.

We saw the raddled Mrs Claus again, dolled up even more extravagantly and cackling madly. She drew Nellie closer and whispered something about the missing jewels and the stuffed squid. She seemed to find the whole thing hilarious. She is remarkably well-informed about goings-on in this town, it seemed.

Through the crowd we caught glimpses of folk we have met in recent weeks. I spied the Mayor and his tiny mother, both looking none the worse for being crushed beneath the collapsing sea monster. I noticed the witchy Sturgeon sisters moodily browsing the occult bazaar in the ballroom, but they took no heed of us. Clearly they were most vexed by my involvement in the Eyes of Miimon affair.

All of this fuss over some foreign jewels! It is ludicrous, is it not?

Then a crowd formed for the Exorcism part of the evening, and my sister and I stood near the back to observe the same species of shenanigans as we were forced to witness last Tuesday night. It was clear, upon second viewing, that it was all a piece of well-rehearsed melodrama. We watched volunteers expelling quantities of ectoplasmic Scotch broth. Even the spinning heads and the forked tongues didn't impress me much, now that I was becoming a regular at these soirees at the Christmas Hotel. I knew it was all fakery and quackery.

Then, however, there was a hush of expectation, and the lights were lowered, as if for a special act. Mrs Claus trundled onto the stage, helped by two of her heftiest elves, and she made a rambling introduction for the winners of the Christmas Hotel's 'Exorcist of the Year' competition. This was the first, actually, I'd heard of a competitive element to the proceedings. There was even a small trophy – in the shape of a disembodied and daemonic soul – which the proprietress presented to the winner.

Which turned out to be Denise and Wheatley. He – sweating and red-faced in his evening dress – shuffled onto the podium first in order to accept the award. He seemed especially pleased by the engraved plaque on the front of the thing. Denise was beatific in a lacy black gown, holding up her hands for applause. Her blue hair was teased out very glamorously, and she seemed so very different from the shambolic and distraught creature in the bar of the Miramar hotel, when she had hoodwinked information out of me.

I think you'll agree, Doctor Watson, that I am far too soft-hearted and ingenuous for these kinds of adventures and investigations.

The winning exorcists were persuaded to put on a little demonstration. A kind of jubilant, celebratory rite. The lights were lowered once again, and the husband fetched out his Bible while Denise turned to the audience and considered who could do with her attention.

And thus it was that my sister was called, once more, ineluctably, onto the stage at the Christmas Hotel.

There was something very odd about Denise's eyes as she called my sister forth, and a gap opened up in the audience. Nellie started walking through that channel to the stage and I grabbed hold of her stick-like arm. 'Nellie, no!' I cried. 'Can't you see? Her eyes... *her eyes are the Eyes of Miimon!*'

And it was true, though no one else seemed disturbed by the fact. Her human eyes were seemingly gone and Denise had glittering jewels in her cavities instead.

Maude Sturgeon appeared as if from nowhere at my side and held me back. 'There is nothing you can do. Poor Nellie is under the spell of the sorceress now.'

I stood helplessly by as my sister galumphed her way onto the stage. She was fighting the influence with every iota of her strength, I knew – but it was to no avail. Denise Wheatley had the upper hand.

'Raphael... Raphael...' cooed Denise, once she had Nellie where she wanted her. 'Come out of this broken body. Leave this pathetic form and manifest yourself for me. Raphael... come to me...'

Denise's crystal orbs lit up in her head and seemed to shot beams of blue light that bathed my sister in a spectral glow. The audience cheered at this. They obviously felt they were getting their money's worth this week.

Maude grunted and said, 'That's what she's after. She wants Raphael for herself, the scheming besom.'

My sister cried out, and writhed painfully as the demon struggled within her. She cried out, 'No! Raphael, beloved! Do not leave me...!'

But it was very plain that something drastic was going on inside of her. Under the baleful influence of the purloined Eyes of Miimon, my sister was being exorcised, even though – it turned out – that was the last thing she wanted.

But what could I do? Tell me, Doctor Watson, what would you have done? What *could* you have done? What could any ordinary, mortal being do in such circumstances?

Well, just then, something very unexpected happened.

Remember the gypsy? The woman we had seen on the previous Tuesday? The one who had seemed possessed of the true magical powers, who had first called my sister's demon hence?

All of a sudden, she was back on the stage. She darted forward, with her hooped skirts and her long black hair fanning out around her. The Romanish exorcist looked absolutely livid.

'What's this?' shouted out the jocular Mr Wheatley, as his wife continued her arcane ritual. 'The stage has been invaded! Hie thee hence, gypsy, and leave the exorcisms to your betters! Avaunt! I cast thee out, Romany witch!'

The gypsy woman snarled at this. She was well nigh feral, I thought. Maude and I exchanged a glance at this sudden turn in events. Denise's concentration had lapsed, and my poor sister sagged back onto the stage floor.

'You are dabbling in things you do not understand,' said the gypsy, in rather screeching tones. She thrust a finger in the face of Denise Wheatley, who was out of breath and venomously cross.

'Get off the stage, Romany whore!' the prize-winning Denise thundered, and took a swing at her.

The gypsy dodged the blow and swung back with a rather swift upper cut to the jaw. Denise staggered backwards and put her hands up to her face. She shrieked and called the gypsy something I will not write down nor send through the Royal Mail. Soon, both female exorcists were engaged in a hand-to-hand catfight while the audience roared their approval.

'Someone should stop them,' I said nervously to Maude.

She tossed her head. 'Nothing wrong with a good grapple to sort things out. I just hope Nellie doesn't get hurt in the crossfire...'

Mr Wheatley was hovering anxiously as he watched his wife fighting the gypsy. He clutched his Old Testament to his chest and looked worriedly at Mrs Claus. 'Fight! Fight! Fight!' cried the owner of the Christmas Hotel.

It seemed that all her magical powers couldn't help Denise Wheatley in a fair fight. Soon the gypsy had her pinned to the floor and was clawing at her face.

'Oh my god!' Mr Wheatley bleated. 'She's pulling out her eyes...!'

But that wasn't happening at all. The gypsy was, in fact, removing the Eyes of Miimon, which Denise had affixed into her sockets in front of her already rather deepset eyes using rather a lot of eyelash glue. We all cheered as the gypsy held up the two glittering jewels. We watched her clamber to her feet and keep the so-called champion exorcist on the ground by standing on her blue hair. Behind them, Mr Wheatley noticed that his prized trophy had been smashed in the kerfuffle.

'The Eyes of Miimon!' cried the gypsy, in a rather grand voice. Then she tossed them into the crowd, which

I thought was a rather cavalier gesture. But the gypsy's aim was good and true. Maude Sturgeon plucked them out of the air and stowed them swiftly in her handbag. 'Take good care of them,' warned the gypsy.

And then she basked in a warm round of applause from the crowd.

Mrs Claus took the stage again, and declared the evening's bizarre entertainments over. She told us all to fetch ourselves another drink and to have fun. The dancing would recommence, just as soon as the band could set up.

We saw her in earnest conversation with the gypsy, and I hurried over to help Nellie, who seemed rather woozy after her ordeal.

'Are you all right, my dear?'

'I am... fine,' Nellie struggled to hear feet. 'Raphael is still inside of me, which is the main thing.'

'Oh good,' I said, though I still felt very dismayed by the thought of my sister actually wanting to be possessed by this being, whatever he was.

Maude slapped her shiny leather handbag triumphantly. 'And thanks to the gypsy, I've got the Eyes of Miimon! Safe, where no one can make mischief with them!'

Nellie looked rather pleased by that.

But we all had one remaining question, and it was to do with the gypsy woman. Why had that beaky-nosed creature helped us like that, in our moment of direst need?

It was some time later, in a quiet corner of the public rooms, near the roaring fire in the lounge, when we caught up with her.

'Look here, gypsy woman,' said Maude Sturgeon, with her usual bluff heartiness. 'I suppose we owe you our thanks for your intercession tonight. If that dreadful woman Denise had been allowed to keep these jewels, who knows what terrible sorceries she might have unleashed.'

'Where is she now?' asked the gypsy sharply, glaring at the three of us in turn.

'That's a good point,' said Nellie. 'She vanished into the crowd, once you let her go. And so has her husband.'

'They live to fight another day,' shrugged the gypsy. 'Ah well.'

She was pulling a shawl around her, clearly ready for the off.

'Look here,' I said, stepping forward. 'You still haven't explained anything...'

The gypsy laughed. 'I trust Maude Sturgeon to do the correct thing with the crystals. They were stolen from the Finnish people and they must be returned. Miss Sturgeon will act in accordance with the law.'

I looked at Maude and she seemed determined – on the contrary – to dispatch the things straight into the Bitch's Maw, as planned.

'Well, yes,' Maude said. 'Quite right. I will contact the authorities tomorrow.'

'Excellent,' the gypsy nodded. 'Then my work here is finished.'

Nellie was frowning and her single eye was blazing. 'Hang on a moment!' she cried. She had to yell over the noise of the band playing Christmas tunes. They were getting louder by the minute. 'Contact the authorities? Return the Eyes of Miimon to the Finnish people?' She sounded scornful. 'What kind of gypsy exorcist are you, woman?'

The gypsy started laughing at us then. It was a harsh, gasping, somewhat sarcastic laughter that came bubbling out from under the shawl and her dark ringlets.

It was a laughter I took only a second or two to recognise.

The Romany woman reached up and dragged off her shawl and her wig and gave us one of those quicksilver grins I was so used to seeing.

A grin I was in no way expecting to see in a hotel on a cliff above the dark North Sea.

'Good Goddess!' cried Maude Sturgeon.

'I don't believe it,' Nellie gasped. 'Hettie,' she turned to me. 'Did you know about this?'

I stared at her and then back at Mr Sherlock Holmes. I couldn't help but laugh out loud. 'I most certainly did not!'

And then, still half-garbed as a gypsy, our mutual friend Himself gave a theatrical bow and turned on his heel. Would you believe it, Doctor Watson? He flew out of that Christmas Hotel without a single further word.

And I suppose he will be back with you now, Doctor. You will be reading this over breakfast. Perhaps reading this final missive aloud to him, as you scratch together your bachelors' breakfast and use the last of the damson jam I left out for you. Never fear, I will be back in Baker Street by tomorrow evening, to clear up the mess you have both undoubtedly made of the place.

Tell Mr Holmes that my sister and her partner in supernatural investigations both thank him profusely for his help in the case of the Eyes of Miimon and the Giant Finnish Squid and the Exorcists at the Christmas Hotel. Tell him from me that I will resist, in future, the temptation of ever again taking a relaxing fortnight by the sea.

Yours,
Mrs Hudson.

§

*From the Journal of Dr John Watson.*
  *November, 1925.*

That is the end of those letters which, now that I am reminded of them, strike as queer a chord in me as they did back then, some thirty years ago.

We were all so young in those days! Mrs Hudson included. Now she lives at the home of Professor Challenger in Norfolk, where she acts as his housekeeper and occasional companion on his bizarre adventures. All of a sudden I find myself keen to take a train journey to a reunion with Mrs H and a meeting with the formidable Professor. Perhaps there really will be something in this business of the Finnish stones, found hidden in the eyes of a giant squid all those years ago.

Won't Mrs Hudson be surprised!

Yes, in fact, since I've nothing planned for the rest of the week – whyever not? My beloved wife surely won't mind if I go gallivanting in search of new adventures.

I shall make the journey at once and report back fully, later on.

*NOTE, LATER ON:*

*What followed is, of course, a tale for another day.*

*A ghastly tale for which I don't feel the world is yet ready.*

# 6

# The Arabian Nighties

Effie is right, of course. Things are clearly in decline when Pound Shops start opening up on your high street. Now, you know me and I'm no snob, but it was such a shame to see the old fishmongers go. And then the fancy frock shop, Hildred's, on Silver Street – which catered for, as Effie always puts it – the more select end of the market (i.e., her). All these nice, family-run businesses are vanishing forever from our town centre and they're being replaced by establishments that Effie says she wouldn't be seen undead in.

I don't mind them as much, however, even though I do know that Pound Shops and Bargain Emporiums and the like are shabby replacements for proper shops. I find myself keen on the little bargains you can sometimes pick up in there. Me with my penchant for foolish geegaws and unusual ornaments – I'm quite happy browsing my way round the cut-price shelves.

Effie despairs. Today she rolled her eyes at me when I produced the jumbo polyester nighties that I picked up in 'SAVE SAVE SAVE!' One pink, one yellow and one in baby blue. She sneered at the labels, the stitching, the material – which she said was scratchy and nasty and bound to make me sweat like pig all night. 'I don't care if they're in just your size, Brenda, and I don't care about the miraculous price. They're vulgar, nasty and cheap. And don't stand too close to your gas hob while wearing one of the horrid articles, either, or you'll go up in a sheet of flame.'

We were sitting in our favourite café at the time and I started to stuff my nighties back into my shopping bag. I was feeling rather embarrassed, to tell the truth. She'd made me feel I'd wasted my money on rubbish.

Effie has impeccable taste, did I ever tell you that? Actually, I shouldn't be sarcastic because, really, she does have rather good taste when it comes to couture, her with her turbans and capes and snugly-fitting suits. I go galumphing round in rags, compared with her. I always look like nothing next to Effie, is how I always feel.

'You should splash out a bit more and buy yourself nice things,' Effie tells me, sipping her highly-sugared Assam and glaring at me over the rim of her china cup. 'Spoil yourself. Don't buy cheap things.'

I sigh because, to be quite frank, money's a bit tight just now. The same wave of economic depression that has sent the fortunes of some of the older, specialist shops in town tumbling has affected my guest house, too. Bookings are down for the coming months – even into the summer season – and I've been forced to advertise all kinds of special offers and knock-down rates just to keep my head above water. I haven't explained any of this to Effie. The two of us never talk about money, as it happens. No doubt she'd find such talk just as vulgar as my polyester nighties. Not for the first time I wonder where she gets all her money from. That dusty old antiques emporium can't be making much. She never seems to sell any of that precious, chipped and shop-soiled tat she's got heaped up in there. Perhaps she simply magicks herself wads of cash when she needs it? Perhaps somewhere in her old aunties' books of spells there's arcane instructions for the spontaneous generation of endless wealth?

I'm obviously looking at her speculatively because she gets annoyed. 'Don't you go into a sulk with me, lady!' she croaks. 'Sometimes you need telling these things. If you want to be a lady like I am – and I trust that you do – then you must listen to my advice.'

I'm really not sure that I've ever said I wanted to be a lady like Effie is. All I've ever said is that I'd like to fit in, here in the town of Whitby, where Effie has been a resident all her life and where I came, after a long and busy life, in order to retire.

I can't promise the snooty old witch that I'll give up shopping in the cheap shops. I find that I can't give up rummaging in those places at all.

Especially that particular one. SAVE SAVE SAVE. It's exerting a special kind of fascination on me. They get deliveries almost every day and there's always something novel and new and unexpected popping up on their shelves.

I don't try to explain things to Effie. When she's already made up her mind it's all in one ear and out the other.

It's my turn to pay the bill and I wince slightly at its size. They've recently done up our favourite café on Church Street. Out went the faded chintz and the gingham tablecloths. Now it's all upcycled Victoriana and twisted driftwood nailed to the walls and tasteful white fairy lights. And they've doubled the cost of their comestibles. No wonder I'm having to economise!

On our walk home to Harbour Street we discuss our pending cases. There have been sightings of a ghostly ice cream van on the West Cliff again and that can only mean one thing. Hans Macabre is up to his old tricks, possibly. And there is a poltergeist – by all accounts – on the Sandsend Funicular, several miles up the coast, which Effie has offered to investigate (I'm not keen. I can't abide poltergeists. They're so rough!) Also, there's a very curious case in the offing to do with a hotel that prides itself as the place that the Reverend Charles Dodgson used to stay, back when he was writing 'Alice's Adventures.' I haven't had all the details yet, but the little I've heard from my partner in creepy investigations seems to beggar belief. Anyhow, we're past mistresses by now at handling and organising several cases at once, and a vague timetable is drawn up between us even before we reach the street where my B&B and Effie's ramshackle house stand cheek by jowl in the long shadows of the late afternoon.

§

The next morning I'm in SAVE SAVE SAVE without even thinking about it. I've got a trolley and I'm cruising up and down the aisles, full of purpose, my head jangling with the pleasant, tinkly music they play in order to put you at your ease. The place is packed. Word is spreading, it seems, about the strange and unusual bargains to be had in this the newest of Whitby's bargain stores.

Already I've picked up some lovely new bathmats in multi-coloured wool. And some toilet pedestal rugs. And a two-thousand piece jigsaw with a lovely picture of all the rooftops of this very town. I like a good jigsaw to while away a quiet evening at home. I've snagged three bottles of Romanian sherry at an astonishingly low price (what's a couple of years out of date between friends?) And I've got a few tins of cocktail fruit (at least that's what

I think it is). The writing on the label is some language I've never seen before.) Then I'm in my favourite aisle, which is devoted to luxury household items. Today I'm looking at incense and oil burners and all those things that give your home a special, aromatic ambience.

I'm opening little bottles of oils and sniffing the contents. Sandalwood and musk, jasmine and lavender. All of them are lovely. I could have a different scent in each room of my B&B, how about that? I could theme the rooms around the scents, perhaps, and give them all a bit of exotic allure, summoning up the atmosphere of faraway places...

Which to have in my own little hideaway at the top of my house? Vanilla and cocoa bean? It would make me crave chocolate bars all day long. Strawberries and cream? I'd be wanting to eat cheesecake in the middle of the night. What about this one..?

I inhale deeply from a stoppered bottle I've found right at the back of the shelf. Unlike the others it's dusty and bright green in hue. It doesn't seem to belong to the rest of this consignment of aromatic oils. What is it...?

I freeze in my tracks as the strange scent makes its way up my hooter.

It's the most gorgeous smell I've ever experienced.

It's like... yes, it's like those faraway places I was only just thinking of. It's like the spices in a Moroccan bazaar, or the tang of the fanciest bottle of vintage wine from the deepest cellar in the world, and there are hints of an oasis in a desert and ice caverns deep underground... It's very strange, but there's a bursting of all these images in my mind as I take in a great lungful of the scent. I realise that my tired old heart is going like the clappers and I can see black circles ahead of me when I look up and for a terrible moment I believe I'm about to pass out. Whew. I pop the stopper back on quickly and look for a price.

£1001.00

Surely that has to be a mistake?

I grasp hold of the arm of a young lad who's stacking the shelves in the next aisle with last year's Christmas Selection Boxes. When I drag him round to see the green glass bottle of aromatic oil he's as perplexed as I am by its label. 'One thousand and one pounds?' I scoff. 'I thought this was the shop where nothing cost more than a pound?' I can hear a note of concern in my own voice, as if I'm worried that I'm not going to be able to purchase the oil and leave this shop empty-handed.

The lad fetches his manageress. Miss Timperley, her name badge says, and she frowns at the bottle and its label. 'I've no idea what it is,' she says briskly. 'But of course it doesn't really cost that much.' There's a whiff of the glorious scent lingering on the air and she pulls a face as if it's disgusting to her. 'Here, take it. It doesn't belong here. It's not something we sell. I don't know how it ended up on our shelves. Take it for 99p with my compliments.' Miss Timperley just about throws it back at me.

Well, there's a good result, I think, hurrying back to choose just the right oil burner and some night lights.

That evening I light the candle in the burner and I open the green bottle and savour the smell all over again as I tip a couple of spoons' worth into the ceramic dish above the flame. As the oil warms the aroma grows even stronger and sweeter, and more complex and subtle... It ensnares me and I feel as if I'm on the brink of some tremendous new thought or revelation. I feel exactly like I do when some cobwebby chunk of memory is restored to me and I slip into one of my immersive flashbacks from my lurid past. But this time I don't. I just stand there, swaying in front of my wall unit, high as a kite on my burning incense.

Effie's loud banging at the side passage door brings me back to my senses. I hurry down to let her in.

She takes several long, disapproving sniffs as she follows me up the stairs. I don't have to look at her to know she'd be wearing an expression that could curdle milk. It's exactly the look she gets when someone's trodden in dog mess and tracked it onto the carpet.

'Eurggh, ducky,' she grimaces as we enter my attic rooms. 'What the devil's that infernal pong? Ooh, dear me. That's turning my stomach, that. It'll bring on my migraine. Whatever is it? You haven't been smoking drug-flavoured cigarettes, have you?'

I roll my eyes at her and pop the kettle on. I'm in a more mellow mood than usual and not even Effie's snide remarks can put my back up tonight.

'Your pupils are dilated,' she tells me. 'And you're wearing a very slack expression, Brenda. Whatever have you done to yourself?'

I shrug and look at her. She's unloading a sheaf of notes and newspaper clippings from her handbag. Now here's a funny thing. There's a shimmering purple glow all around her. There are silver lightning bolts shooting out of her head. All of that bristling irritability of hers. Effie's endless irascibility. For some reason I can see it all, in gaudy multi-coloured emanations all around her skinny body. I gasp out loud. 'Effie! I can see your aura!'

She looks extremely startled by this.

And that's when I flomp backwards onto my green bobbly armchair and, according to her, I've fainted.

§

My dream doesn't last very long, but it's very colourful and rather hectic.

First of all I feel I'm floating high above the rooftops of Whitby, staring down at the glittering expanse of the North Sea. I'm noting with interest all the delicate pleats and folds of the coastline and the welcoming maw of the harbour, where ships of all sizes are vying and jostling on the choppy waters.

I appear to be floating on a magic carpet of some description. A quick, panicked glance reveals to me that it's one of the rag rugs I bought for the bathroom floor. It seems to have developed amazing powers and has no problem transporting me through the turbulent skies. Ooh, the clouds are bonny tonight. Thick magenta and Prussian blue with golden trim. We're flying into the last of the sunlight.

The bath mat is a bit larger than the one I splashed out on today. It's large enough to contain not only me, but a somewhat oversized duck, too. It's an exotic-looking bird, with tufted feathers of orange and gold. It's staring at me beadily and doesn't seem at all perturbed to be perched here on a mat with me.

'Hello,' I say.

The duck quacks solemnly.

And it's at this point that Effie slaps me hard about the chops in order to bring me round.

She brings me a steaming mug of spicy tea as I struggle to sit upright in my armchair.

'Well, you went peculiar,' she says crossly. 'Mucking about with funny scenty things. It was probably narcotics, I shouldn't wonder.'

I sip my tea and realise she's opened all the attic windows to let the fresh sea breeze seep through.

'Where have you put my oil burner?' I ask, sounding shrill. 'And the little green bottle?'

She narrows her eyes at me, and plonks her skinny bottom on my settee. 'The oil burner's in the dishwasher. And don't worry. I didn't throw out the bottle, even though I felt I ought to. It made you pass out, Brenda! It must be something a bit funny...'

'It... It has magical properties, certainly... but not wicked ones. They're benign, I'm sure...'

She starts flicking through her clippings and her investigation ring binder and simply tuts at me in a sort of 'we'll see, won't we?' fashion. 'The thing is, ducky. We can't be too careful... with the likes of Mr Danby still at large, and Mrs Claus up to her old tricks, and these reports of Hans Macabre... Lots of our old enemies are still out and about and intending us harm, Brenda. Brenda? Do you hear me..?'

It was her calling me 'ducky' that broke my dream. Suddenly I could see that exotic-looking duck again, sitting on the bathroom mat and glinting its clever eye at me.

'Y-yes, yes, I'm fine. I'll be more careful.'

But as we go through her notes and newspaper articles again, I'm thinking about that strange oil and the hypnotic properties it seems to possess...

§

Much later, when Effie totters off home, tipsy on several Romanian sherry nightcaps, I hurriedly get myself ready for bed, flinging on my night-things and slathering on face cream and then fetching out the burner from the dishwasher and starting to burn the midnight oil.

I sit by the window that overlooks the whole town and the gorgeous dark that hangs above the stark headland and old Whitby Abbey. I sit with my journal open but I don't write a word. I breathe in the queer incense and let my mind relax... wondering where it will wander this time?

I don't even hear the crashing and banging of all the bins from down in the alley. This, I learn later, is all to do with Effie and an untoward encounter that had everything to do with the Romanian sherry she had consumed. Its specific and not altogether unpleasant tang on her breath had summoned attention from an utterly unexpected quarter. But more of that later.

For now, let me present a picture of myself in my attic at night, wreathed in that heady scent.

Amongst my many bargains from SAVE SAVE SAVE were several bottles of cleaning agents, much cheaper than I'd ever had them from my usual supplier. One of them was one of those bottles shaped in such as way as to allow you to squirt detergent up inside the rim of your lavatory: very useful. A Toilet Duck, I believe they are called.

Before I know it I'm in the kitchen – feeling a bit woozy – rummaging through my still-unpacked shopping bag and fetching out that toilet duck. Why hadn't I noticed this before? All the writing is funny and foreign. This isn't any old Toilet Duck after all.

It's a magic Toilet Duck.

I unscrew the cap and give it a little squeeze.

There is a whoosh of green, pine-scented smoke. It churns and plumes before me, and smells ever so fresh.

And then the duck is standing on the kitchen table, squinting shrewdly and looking just like he did in my little reverie earlier.

'I knew you were real!' I cry. 'So it wasn't just a dream?' The duck shakes his head and clacks his beak impatiently. 'Of course I'm real. You're Brenda, right?'

I nod, marvelling at his beauty. His fire-hued feathers are shining and beautiful. His eyes, now I look, are a deep and fabulous gold. He's a creature out of legend and he's decided to manifest himself here in my tiny kitchen. 'But why are you here?' I ask. I hug myself. I'm shivering with pleasure but also because my new polyester nightie is somewhat – I realise it now – too thin.

Are we going to take to the skies again? Should I get the new bathmats out?

But the magic duck makes no mention of flying carpets. He just looks me up and down and coughs grandly, announcing: 'You have been granted three wishes, Brenda, dear. You must use them wisely. And you mustn't muck it up.'

I simply boggle at him, for I can hardly believe my luck.

Of course, I don't rush in and start using them right away. I know enough about the old stories and myths not to be too rash. This needs thinking about carefully and with great consideration. I tell the magic Toilet Duck that I am extremely grateful, and I hope that he will allow me to sleep on the matter and make my wishes in due course.

'Naturally,' he agrees, and starts waddling back towards the green plastic bottle that is apparently his home. He ruffles his feathers and yawns, declaring himself too worn out just now anyway to be granting anyone's wishes at this time of night. 'Till we meet again, Brenda, dear,' he squawks, and vanishes in a sudden rush of jade green smoke.

I'm sat there looking at a Toilet Duck and an incense burner and other, sundry, less magical items from the Pound Shop, hardly daring to breathe.

With all the world to wish for, what should I choose?

Just what is it I want more than anything?

§

The next day, I don't know if it's my imagination or what, but Effie seems subdued to me. Almost shifty perhaps. When she looks directly at me it's as if there's something on the tip of her tongue she wants to tell me, but then she changes her mind.

We catch the bus that rolls along the coastal road, right beside the cliff edge and we head out of town. We're such old friends now that we hardly need to exchange a word, but all the same, I know there's something troubling her.

It's a lovely journey, I must say. The roads are narrow and the bends are tight and there are some stomach jolting rises and plummets up and down the verdantly wooded hills. We roll through the fishing town of Staithes and then advance northwards a little further until we arrive at the Victorian spa town of Sandsend. Here there are hotels similar to the ones we have in Whitby, but they are fewer in number and even closer to the cliff edge and it feels somehow as if the whole town might suddenly be pitched into the sea. Everything is very steep and, on a stormy day like today is turning out to be, the place can make you feel a bit queasy.

I'll tell you what else can make me feel queasy – and that's the terribly vertiginous railway track belonging to the Sandsend Funicular. It's not very long, just a couple of hundred yards, but it rises straight from the beach far below up to the level of the hotels on the cliff edge. It's a feat of Victorian engineering that is extremely impressive when you think about it, but usually I'm too busy feeling vomitous to marvel much. Strange, I know, for a woman who dreams of flying through the night air on magic rag rugs, to be scared of travelling on a Funicular that has been bolted safely in place for over a hundred years, but there you go. I never said my fears were rational, did I?

Effie is businesslike, professional. She straightens her jacket and cape and sets her trim little hat to a determined angle. We are here to make an investigation.

'Could you explain the nature of these occurrences to us?'

A matter of minutes later we are sitting in the tiny office of the conductor of the Funicular. He's a swarthy-looking fellow from South Shields, wearing sunglasses and seeming ill at ease as he makes us a brew. His office is cluttered and bordering on the claustrophobic, what with his gas fire switched to full. All the walls are covered with signed photos of all the celebrities of the past 150 years who have mounted the cliff face aboard the miniature railway.

'We-eee-ell,' he says, and hands us both tiny golden cups of coffee. He's left the grounds in, and so we chew our way through our espressos, feeling quite dizzy as he tells us his tale. 'Let me see where it began. First of all it was just noises, you see. We had passengers telling us that there were untoward noises inside the carriage.

Mechanical noises, we thought at first, and so we took turns to sit aboard and listen to the clanking and whirring of the machinery. But everything is tuned up and cleaned and repaired during the winter season. The funicular runs as smoothly as it did when it first opened!'

'I'm sure it does,' Effie says smoothly. She grimaces because she's getting coffee grounds under her false teeth, I can tell. 'Do go on.'

'I spent hours going up the cliff and down the cliff, listening hard. I even took a tape recorder at one point. And it was true. There was a noise. But it wasn't to do with the workings...'

All at once the gloomy afternoon draws in around us. Rain starts to patter on the roof of his office. We hunch forward to listen to him.

'It was when we played back the recordings I had made that we heard the voice...' he said.

'The voice?'

'Clear as anything, once you knew it was there.'

'What did it say?'

'Nothing out of the ordinary. It was a child's voice, gabbling on about the seaside. Excited. Pleased. A happy child's voice.'

'So?' snaps Effie. 'Wasn't it just one of your passengers?'

The funicular railway man shakes his head. 'There was no child aboard that day. Not the whole time I was there with my equipment. I am quite meticulous. Sometimes I was recording and the voice came out on the tape, even on the journeys up the cliff when there was no one else aboard...'

'Hmmm,' says Effie, looking frankly sceptical. 'Could we hear these recordings, please?'

He's only too keen to fetch out his ancient, clunky, twin-spooled device from his cupboard. We spent a fruitless hour hunched over the primitive speaker, trying to make out a ghostly voice.

He seems very disappointed that we can't hear a thing.

The afternoon's gloom seems to be generated directly by his despondent mood as he lets us out into the fresh air again.

'I'm afraid I didn't hear any evidence of any kind of paranormal activity,' Effie tells him crisply. 'And neither did my colleague, did you, Brenda?'

I concur and the railway man lets out a groan. 'Oh, please... just spend a bit longer. You've been kind enough to come all this way on the bus... Why don't you ride on the train itself, hm? Just up and down a few times? And then... then, I think you'll see?'

Dark clouds are rolling into town, along with a cloying sea mist. All at once I want to back away and tell him to take a run and jump. I want to dash back to our bus stop and hurry us home. There's nothing I want to do less than ride up and down on his peculiar vertical train set.

But Effie nods brusquely. 'Very well. It can't hurt, I'm sure.'

Delightedly he leads us down the wooden steps from his office to the start of the track, down on the beach. 'You'll see! You'll hear it! And it's not even the voice, so much... it's the feeling... the terrible sensations that you get...'

I can't say that I'm crazy about the idea of having terrible sensations. But, as Effie reminds me, we are investigators and we must put aside our own fears and scepticism at times.

'Mind,' she tells me, sotto voce. 'Part of me thinks this fella is just chiming in. That's what it's like in the little towns around Whitby. They're all jealous of our paranormal activity and are craving some of their own!'

'Really..?!' I can't imagine anyone being so silly.

'Ladies, please,' our conductor calls us, holding open the door to the single carriage of the haunted train. 'In you go,' he commands, his tones all dulcet from that dark, dark coffee.

And then we're shut aboard the carriage and choosing a seat and he's dashing off back to his control room thingy. I'm reminded briefly of that old story by Dickens about the signalman and I'm trying to remember just what it was that was so spooky about that. At least that train stayed on the level, I'm thinking, as the machinery jolts into life.

§

Thirteen times we go up and down that blummin' cliff face. It takes up much of the afternoon and by the time we're just about finished it's completely dark outside and we can hardly see two inches through the dense and dripping fog.

I'm peering out the windows and wondering why no one else has got aboard the funicular with us. Wasn't it open to the public today?

'Who'd want to go up and down the cliffs on a day like this?' Effie shrugs, as the rain starts to lash at the sides of the carriage.

I've lost my bearings. Are we halfway up or halfway down?

'What's that fella playing at?' I grumble. 'He's had us going up and down for hours... Can't we tell him to let us out?'

'We've miscalculated,' says Effie. 'We don't have any way of communicating with him, I'm afraid.'

Whenever we've reached the top or bottom the doors have stayed shut. Engrossed until now by trying to listen for poltergeists, we hadn't really considered ourselves trapped aboard...

And now we seem to have stopped, but we're not at the top or the bottom. I get up and advance gingerly to the door, Effie following, and we realise that there's nothing but empty air outside.

I already feel nauseous and I've been hiding it well. But the thought of being stuck halfway up the cliff in stormy climes is something I'm fully expecting to have a funny turn about.

'Is this it, do you think?' Effie asks in a low voice. 'Is this part of the haunting, do you think, Brenda?' She sounds spooked and thrilled in equal measure.

§

A mutual friend once described Effie as a 'fun vampire.' I found this a bit cruel at the time, but I did partly know what they meant. She finds it hard to join in sometimes, and she can look disapproving when others start letting their hair down. But I would never say – as Robert, our mutual spook-hunting friend did on that occasion – that her very presence could suck all of the fun out of the room with one sharp in-breath. I always knew that Effie was quite good company in her own way, with a dry and laconic sense of humour. Plus, she was warm-hearted, deep-down, under her frosty layers of resentment and snootiness, and she was always endlessly brave.

Like today – or rather, this evening – when she decides to take matters into her own hands re our being trapped in the fog halfway up the cliff in this poltergeist-haunted funicular .

The man in charge of the diagonal railway has seemingly vanished. We haven't heard a peep out of him for ages. We have been abandoned here, with night moving in across the vast bay.

'The only thing is to break open those doors and climb our way to safety,' Effie decides. She takes off her cape and jacket and rolls up her sleeves. 'I'm not hanging around here all night. It's liable to get freezing up here.'

'Do you think we should?' I ask her. 'I mean, it's pretty steep and perilous out there...'

She gives me an appraising look. 'What's the matter with you today? You're all dithery. You sound like a right wet nelly. What's got into you, Brenda? You're usually tougher than this!'

She is right, of course.

But I can't explain. All the while we're having this irksome adventure, my mind is partly elsewhere. I'm wondering about my three wishes, granted to me by the Toilet Duck.

'Never mind,' she mutters. 'We all have off days, don't we?' She smiles tightly and turns her attention to the roof of the carriage. 'Now, if I'm not mistaken, there really ought to be a hatchway or an access point, somewhere up there...'

It dawns on me, just as she's clambering on top of one of the seats, what she's planning to do.

'You can't, Effie! You can't go climbing out onto the roof!'

'I think I have to. Unless you want to sit in here all night long!'

'But we're halfway up the cliff! And it's even higher and steeper than all the cliffs in Whitby! You'll come off and break your scraggy old neck!'

'Scraggy!' she bursts out. 'I like that!'

From somewhere deep inside her handbag she's produced a couple of heavy-duty tools. Some kind of wrench and a crowbar. Immediately she starts to clatter and bang at the ceiling of the carriage. It sounds tinny and insubstantial as it takes the brunt of her frustration. Effie hates to be locked up anywhere.

Outside there's a gale howling by now, and the water that lashes against the wide window panes could be rain or it could be waves as far as I can tell. All of a sudden I realise just how dangerous it's going to be out there for my spindly and elderly friend.

'No, Effie! You must let me go! I'm stronger than you! I'm bigger than you!'

She glances down, just as she's making progress with opening the emergency hatchway. Her expression is ironic as ever. 'You're certainly less svelte and stylish than me, ducky. But you're also a bit bloody clumsy. Do you think I'd let you stagger about out there, clinging to the roof of this thing? No, really, I'll be back in a jiffy. It isn't far too climb, I'm sure. I'll find out why we're stuck and be back in no time. Honestly!'

And, quick as a whistle, she crawls up through the gap in the ceiling and I gasp. She can be ever so nimble and acrobatic at times, can Effie. She's right: I'm a huge, galumphing ninny compared to her.

Once she's vanished into the stormy night I call after her: 'Are you all right out there..? Effie?!' And straight away I imagine that the wind has dragged her away into the night and dashed her against the jagged cliffs. 'Effie...!'

After a few seconds her voice comes shrieking back to me out of the darkness. 'I'm all right, ducky! It's... just a bit... further than... I thought... to climb!'

I'm relieved to hear she's still hanging on. But now I start picturing terrible things. What if that silly man in the control room suddenly remembers us and sets the funicular in motion? What if the horrible thing starts moving while Effie's still hanging on the wires? Will she be electrocuted? Will she be sliced and diced like vegetables in that crudité slicer I bought for a pound in SAVE SAVE SAVE..?

'Effie! Effie, I've just had a terrible thought...! Perhaps you'd better come back down...?'

But the only reply is the tremendous noise of the sea crashing on the rocks below and the whipped-up frenzy of the storm.

Really, I think: BUGGER Sandsend. And BUGGER that man with his horrible coffee and his suspected poltergeist. Effie was right: it was all a load of hooey.

The creepy old windbag just wanted us at his mercy and trapped on his model railway set. Really. Just BUGGER him.

I'm quite livid.

'Tut tut tut,' comes a disapproving noise from the seat behind me. 'Such language, Brenda!'

My first thought is: it's the Poltergeist! But since when did Poltergeists ever complain about swearing? In my experience they're all potty-mouths themselves. All that showing off they do. So juvenile.

But it isn't anything ghostly in the seat behind. When I turn around it turns out to be my Toilet Duck, preening his feathers and looking very pleased with himself. 'Could you close that hatchway, do you think, dear?' he quacks. 'Contrary to popular belief, we don't actually relish wet weather.'

'I can't close it,' I tell him. 'What if Effie wants to get back in?'

He tuts again. 'Silly old moo. Whatever does she want to go shinning up power lines for? If they come back on she'll be fried alive.'

'Fried alive!' I gasp. 'She's on a power line?! Effie..!' I started to panic all over again.

'Don't fret,' he tells me. 'They won't come back on. She won't be fried.'

'What's going on?' I ask the duck. 'Why's that man done this to us? He lured us here, didn't he?'

'How should I know? Why would I have all the answers?'

'Because... because you're like a sort of genie, aren't you? You're the genie of the Toilet Duck. You can grant wishes and... you know everything...'

'Not quite everything,' he concedes modestly. He ruffles up his wings as if he's quietly very satisfied by my flattery. 'But I do know quite a lot. And yes, I do believe that man has called you here today in order to capture you both. Why that is, I don't quite know. But the pair of you must be quite used to such affairs by now.'

'I suppose we are...' I agree. 'Look here, can I use one of my wishes to rescue her?'

The duck boggles at my request. 'What?' he gasps. 'You'd waste one whole once-in-a-lifetime magic wish in order to save that waspish old witch you knock about with? When you could have anything? Absolutely anything at all...?'

Something about his gleaming little eyes stops my panicky flow of thought. 'W-what? What do you think I s-should ask for...?'

The duck chuckles at me. 'Effie will be all right. She'll be quite safe. What's climbing up a seventy degree incline on electrical wires on a stormy night compared with some of the terrible things you two have faced over the years? It's nothing! She'll make it. You don't have to worry about her.'

The duck's eyes are mesmerising. They're spiralling. Orange and purple swirls and golden stars. They're drawing me in...

'Why don't you think about yourself for once, Brenda? Why don't you think about what you really and truly want...more than anything in the world...?'

'No... no...' I protest – but rather weakly. 'Must... save... Effie... mustn't fall... under your... spell... mustn't think... of selfish things...'

'Yes! Yes! Think selfish thoughts! Have selfish dreams! Have selfish fantasies, Brenda! This is your time – if any time ever was – to think only of yourself and your secret desires! Tell me, Brenda... what is your first magic wish?'

And I waver for a second. The wish is crystal clear in my addled mind. I think it for only the tiniest of moments. But the duck glimpses what it is and SHAZAM.

The next moment, I am elsewhere.

§

It's a pleasant little town somewhere on the continent. I can tell at once that it's abroad because all the people are talking what sounds like German, or maybe French. It's a quaint little snowy place, where all the buildings have gingerbread rooftops and all the streets are cobbled. Carriages go running past, pulled by horses, and I get shouted at a couple of times – good-naturedly, mind you

– because I have suddenly materialised in the middle of the road.

As I stagger backwards into the doorway of a chocolatier's bijou shop it hits me that I have been precipitated into the past.

Now, as you may know, I'm no stranger to time travel – either physical, mental or on the astral plane – and I pride myself on taking such things in my stride. But I can't help marvelling at the wonderful crispness of the alpine air (Yes, alpine – that's exactly what it is!) and the clarity of the colours and the detail around me. The puffing breath issuing from my lungs and the beaming, rubicund faces of the foreigners all about me. It's all so clear. I'm right here in the moment, many years ago. Now I start to wonder why it is my subconscious chose this place and time to expend a magical wish. Am I secretly very fond of skiing, I wonder?

Maybe that intrusive duck is here somewhere, and he can let me know? But there's no sign of him. And remembering him makes me think of Effie, still clambering about on the cliffs of Sandsend somewhere far in the future. I feel like I've abandoned her in the pursuit of my deepest, most heartfelt desire.

The man in charge of the confectioners comes bustling out. 'Entschuldigen sie.' Brusquely he wafts me away from his display window, which I'm blocking from view of potential customers. As I move away I get a glimpse of the wonderfully intricate castle made all of chocolate inside the bay windows. I bend closer, drawing in my breath, and see that he has built an entire model of a snowy town, with perfect little buildings just like those around me, huddling round the base of the castle. The towers stretch tall as I am. That's a hell of a lot of chocolate.

It takes only a couple of seconds for me to realise exactly which castle has been lovingly rendered in the very darkest chocolate.

It's not a castle I have ever been to, but still it is somehow scorched into my memory.

In a curious way, my deepest wish and desire has brought me home. Or rather, to my ancestral home.

But this little epiphany means bugger all to the Chocolatier: he shoos me away busily. He treats me as if I'm a vagrant or a potential thief or trouble maker. I look down at myself and realise that I am attired in an utterly inappropriate fashion for the era or the weather. I'm in one of those polyester nighties from the cheapy shop. It seems that journeys into one's deepest wishes can be made only when you're swathed in man-made fibres and ruffles. I'm in the pink one from my set of three and as I wander through town I'm attracting funny looks from the burghers and good people of this little town high in the mountains.

I keep my head down and bustle along, suddenly feeling the cold. I pick up speed as I hear murmurs starting up all around me. I stand out. I am grotesque. I am virtually nude as my pink nightie stretches and the machined stitches of its seams threaten to burst, as if embarrassment was making me swell up and flush with shame.

I know where I am going. All these winding, snowy-packed streets slope upwards to the same destination: to that patriarchal edifice at the very top of the hill. I look up between the chintzy rooftops and there it is: the castle that sometimes haunts my dreams with its unfathomably tall and embarrassingly phallic towers.

The whisperings at my back as I pass through the streets get louder. The locals sound less friendly. I get catcalls. Someone throws a snowball. I hear someone shout something in guttural German and it doesn't sound very nice at all.

I have to get to the castle. I have to go banging on those huge, protected doors and gain admittance to the courtyard and meet the master of the place. He has to let me in. This is what I am here for. My heart has led me to this place, whether I willed it to or not.

I am here to get some answers.

§

Queer thing is, there's no fuss when I go hammering on the fortress doors. A curious eye surveys me from an aperture above, blinks once and, shortly afterwards, the grand door creeps open wide enough to let me in.

The courtyard is vast and chockablock with snow. No one has cleared it. No one has walked through it. It's like a vast empty page walled around with black stone. Only a few windows are lit. They pulse with torchlight. The castle encircles me and it's an uncanny embrace: it fills up my whole horizon. It's like being thrust into the coliseum, onto the floor of some grisly gladiatorial arena. I've banged hard on the entrance to be allowed inside and I can see that I won't be getting out quickly.

At the main door I am met by a meek serving boy. A footman, then an obsequious butler. When I'm shown inside there's a kind of baronial hall with maids flitting to and fro. Tapestries. The heads of wild beasts mounted on plaques. A terrible whiff of must tickles my nose and makes me sneeze. There's a worse smell underlying it: a stench of fetid corruption and – bizarrely – the vinegary aroma of pickled eggs.

I am brought towels and warmer clothes by the quick, compliant servants. They're very helpful, but unsmiling. I am brought before a huge fire and urged to sit and bask in its warmth. I am given a silver tankard of some kind of dreamy, frothing, honeyed wine. It's delightful and I'm slurping it like nobody's business before I hear Effie's voice inside my head urging caution on me. 'Never drink or eat a single thing when you're inside the enemy's home.'

But this isn't the home of my enemy, is it?

The fire roars and its heat seeps into me quite wonderfully. I hadn't realised how chilled I was. Not only since I arrived in this snowy land, but previously, too. Sitting in that funicular carriage for hours on end, going up and down. And before that as well. A cold that was in me for quite some time, that I never could quite thaw. The warmth of this hearth is such that it could even melt the sliver of ice in my heart.

I doze off.

And when I wake, there is a worried-looking young man standing in front of me, splendid in green velvet and a grey cravat.

'Good evening,' he says, and his voice is mellifluous, cultivated. He sounds a bit soft.

'Is it evening? How long have I slept?' I'm so parched. I hunt around for the rest of that delicious wine. But it's gone, and someone has wheeled a gleaming hostess trolley into the hall. It stands before the fire, freighted with delicious cakes and fancies.

The elegant man with the sideburns and fair hair swept so elegantly away from his forehead bends over the tea things, being mother.

'Welcome to my home,' he smiles, proffering a china cup and saucer. They look tiny in my hands as I take them from him. 'And who are you, my dear? Why were you so keen to be admitted, hm?' His look is questioning, but not hostile in anyway. He is studying me with a keen eye. His face is alive with interest.

And I am studying him back. I drink him up with my avid eyes.

He is..! He is who I think he is. Yes, I am sure of that.

'My name is Brenda,' I tell him. 'Hello.'

'Enchanted,' he nods. 'I am Baron...'

But I hold up a hand to stop him before he can say the name. The hated name. The name that makes me shiver and feel nauseous whenever it is spoken aloud. 'I know... sir. I know who you are. Please, don't...'

He frowns at me, bemused. Even, perhaps, amused by me. He sits on the tall-backed armchair across from the one where I'm sitting slumped in borrowed clothes under a hairy blanket trimmed with... is it wolf pelt?

'A mysterious stranger, blown in with the snows,' smiles the Baron, sipping his tea. 'How very intriguing.' Then his pale eyebrows do a little quirking thing. 'And yet, there is something about you. Something rather familiar, perhaps...' His voice drains away, and for a moment a shadowy thought flits across his face, but he bats it away and resumes his smiling good manners. 'You must recover here. I cannot send you out into that terrible night again. Consider yourself a guest here and Castle F...'

'Please!' I burst out, sounding crazy, I know. 'Please, don't say the name. I beg you.'

'My dear,' he chuckles, and looks concerned now. Perhaps he thinks he has allowed a lunatic to step foot over his threshold.

Oh, but if only he knew who I was. What would his reaction be then, I wonder? But how could he ever suspect such a thing? It would be impossible for him to guess, wouldn't it?

'I am sorry,' I tell him, slurping the rest of my tea. 'You must think me strange. But I have travelled a long way... my wits are scattered...'

He nods, smiling, and calls out to his servants. I must be given the Purple Room. His very best guest apartment, in the northern tower. They must make me comfortable. He studies me even as I am led away by his housekeeper. What does he see? An ungainly old woman, spouting nonsense. One who arrived babbling, sodden and frozen in her night things. Why on Earth would a Baron – however kind – waste his time and kindness on such a person?

I don't know. But I'm grateful.

§

I sleep in the Purple Room for what seems like several days on end.

My dreams are deep and profound, and sometimes very silly. Sometimes I dream about my real life, my every day life in Whitby and my B&B and the friends I have known there in that adopted town of mine. Sometimes memories of my previous adventures and escapades flit before me and these seem highly improbable. A part of my dreaming self starts wondering: are these the dream itself, and I'm only fancying myself as a woman who does battle with monsters and demons on a weekly basis?

I wake up muddled and all topsy-turvy and dash to the turret's windows and survey the wintry landscape outside. Mountains and more mountains and basically not very much for hundreds of miles around. That piddly little town filled with cross German people down there. And endless snowy woods.

I am told by the housekeeper that I may go almost anywhere in the castle. Certain areas are out of bounds, of course. The Baron's private wing is a place only his most trusted servants may visit. But apart from that, I must consider myself at home.

Days pass, it seems, and I am fed good, stodgy, reviving foods. Lots of steamed puddings and custard. Great hanks of dripping meat. Venison, on several occasions. I am informed that the venison and the boar I'm eating hail from the woods hereabouts. The Baron is a keen hunter, I am told.

I don't see anything of the kindly Baron for several days. He leaves me to my recovery and my own devices. I hadn't known I was quite so tired or in need of a delicious rest like this, but it seems I was. Perhaps this is all part of my wish from the genie of the Toilet Duck? Perhaps this is what I was really hankering after? A luxurious sojourn outside of real time?

Sometimes I get a stab of guilt, remembering how I left things in my own world, with Effie clinging to the wires on the Sandsend cliff-face, and so on. And yet that world is seeming muzzier and fuzzier to me, day by day. It's as if I am looking at my real world through a frozen window pane as a blizzard rages outside, slowly blotting out the view that I was so sure was there...

I wander the castle courtyard and snowy gardens. I discover the library and find that most of the books are in languages I don't even recognize. I find fascinating and alarming diagrams in some of the harder-to-reach volumes at the top of the library ladders. There are etchings of fabulous creatures, exotic flora and fauna. Cross-sections of bodies and organs and brains. Some of these delicate drawings are so beautiful I could stare at them for hours. I still wouldn't be sure if I was looking at something animal, vegetable or mineral, and perhaps that's just as well.

Then, several days in, I meet the Baron again. He joins me, quite unexpectedly, for dinner down in that splendid hall again, at the long table before the fire. He beams at me, all charming, once more. But as he smiles and makes idle chitchat, keen to know if I've been enjoying my stay at Castle F... there is a tenseness about him. A strained look about his eyes and in the sharp line of his mouth as he tries to smile and converse with me. I gradually realise that he is putting on a tremendous act and trying to seem like he hasn't got a care in the world.

I am much too polite a guest to ask if something's bothering him.

Instead I ask questions of a more innocuous kind. I ask about his childhood and his family, and I learn all kinds of interesting things about his early days in a small, remote town, hidden away in the alps. An idyllic childhood, a loving family who doted on him. They were all very proud of him. He was a child genius. A prodigy. He stood out so conspicuously amongst the others of his age. Neighbours and aunties and cousins all muttered: where did he come from? He was almost like a changeling. His articulacy from an early age. His brilliant scores at every test the schoolmaster could muster. The other children were wary of him, and some were jealous. And yet it was never in his nature to be boastful or sneering about his intellectual inferiors. It would never have occurred to him to look down upon his school fellows or the members of his family... He read and read and read and immersed himself in all the knowledge that the library of his small home town could supply. He outgrew the place, and the environs. It became obvious that he was going to have to go away from everyone. His destiny clearly lay elsewhere. He was itching and pining for the wider world and, when he came of age, he set off for the nearest city he could find that boasted a university and a library and a host of professors who might between them furnish him with some of the answers his restless intellect desired...

Well!

I listened to all of this with great interest. We drank quite a lot of blood red wine that night – the butler hovered at our elbows with a carafe, then a second. I listened as the Baron dug into his past and smiled at the long ago memories and wept as he recalled how he had to move away from his people. When he talked about his mother and how proud she had been of him he looked into my face and beamed at me. His expression was soft and his cheeks were wet with tears.

'You remind me of her, Brenda,' he told me then, towards the end of that long evening of storytelling. 'Quite a lot, in fact. Why, it's almost uncanny. I saw it at once. That first night you stumbled into my home and I met you here in the hall. The resemblance is remarkable... I think it is, anyhow. It is such a long time since I saw her.'

How long could it have been, really? 'You're still quite a young man. It can't have been so long ago... And it isn't too late to travel home, surely? And then you could tell her... you could tell her how much you miss her?'

I meant it kindly. I really did. But I saw at once that I had made a mistake. The Baron sat bolt upright and his face went puce. His eyes boggled at me. 'Of course it's too late. She is long dead.'

'Oh...' I said.

'Long ago. They are all dead. All of them.'

We'd both had too much too drink that night. He started sobbing, unashamedly, sitting there before me. His shoulders shook. Great fat tears dripped down onto dark polished wood.

I got up and made my way steadily down the length of the table and, awkwardly, took him in my arms for a hug.

I found myself murmuring to him. 'There, there, ducky. There, there.'

And I called the housekeeper and the butler over so they could manhandle the Baron and take him off to his private quarters and see that he was safely put to bed.

Then I stumbled off to the Purple Room, where I lay drunk, awake, with the ceiling spinning slowly above me and the snow blatting hard at the window.

What are you doing, Brenda? I asked myself roughly. Why on earth are you giving succour to that man? When you know what he did? What he will do in future years?

When you know what he is actually responsible for? How could you take him in your silly old arms and rock him like that, doing your best to reassure him that everything would be all right?

Because it won't, will it? Because you come from the future – so far in the future – and you know how the bloody awful story ends...

Eventually, berating myself like this, I fell into a deep and mercifully dreamless sleep.

I was astonished, the next morning, to find him bright and awake and eating breakfast. I must have looked like hell. I felt as though we had drunk the entire contents of his wine cellar dry the night before.

'Nonsense,' he chuckled, forking up his scrambled eggs. 'Just a couple of bottles of very nice wine. And what a very convivial evening we had. I am very sorry that I became so emotional towards the end, though, Brenda. Red wine always gets me like that. I get so terribly mawkish.'

'There's nothing to forgive...' I assure him, and pick up my coffee and sip it while it's too hot. And I think: actually, there's an awful lot to forgive. But you don't know it yet. And I can't tell you. You will do terrible things in your life to come and I will live with the consequences of those acts for decades and centuries yet...

I stare at his fresh complexion and his bright, clever eyes and his brisk, eager movements. You're to blame for everything, Buster. And I find I can't tell you. I can't accuse you. I can't stop you, either.

And I have wasted this magic wish, haven't I?

I've travelled all this way and I find that I actually quite like him. More than that. I love him. I can feel a warmth spreading in my chest when he smiles back at me.

'Will you forgive me, Brenda?' he says, getting up from the table. His words chime so closely with my reverie that I'm startled at first.

'What for?'

'I must go away from here. I must go on a journey. It is our conversation of last night that has provoked this resolve in me.'

'Oh, yes?'

'Though it is true, as I told you last night, that most of my family is now deceased, I find that I have a hankering to return to my old home. It is many leagues north of here...'

'This castle isn't your ancestral home?'

'This?' he gives a bleak laugh. 'No, that's just my pretension. My silly, jumped-up, godawful pretentiousness. I am a very shallow, vain and venal fellow, Brenda. And you... it's you, somehow... you've reminded me... of what is important. What I need to remember. And what I have left behind. My childhood sweetheart, Elizabeth. Only she is left alive of all those people I knew then. She writes every month, begging me to return and I have been caught up for too long in my work to take any notice of her at all...'

'Your w-work..?'

He nods and waves a dismissive hand. 'Foolish work. Dirty work. Hubristic nonsense that flies in the face of God and all mankind. I have been living in a dream for too long... I have been living in a nightmare. But thanks to you, Brenda... I have been made to remember more vital things. I have remembered what it is like... to be alive. To know love.'

I gasp at this. I have taught him all this? Just by chatting nicely with him? Just by lending a friendly ear?

I watch him as he whirls about, giving instructions to his servants about the horses, his carriage, his belongings. I even laugh at his excitement. It's infectious.

'Brenda,' he asks me, just before he leaves. 'Will you remain here in my castle while I'm away? Will you stay and hold the fort for the weeks while I travel home? I intend to find my darling Elizabeth and bring her back here as soon as I can. I want you to be here when I return with her. So you can meet her. So that, perhaps, you can be here at our wedding?'

He is almost shy and boyish, as if he is making a very onerous request.

'Of course, I tell him,' and once again I have pushed the pressing concerns about my real life to the back of my mind. 'Of course I will, Victor.'

He salutes me and grins. 'You know, you really do remind me of my beloved mother,' he tells me, just before he leaps into his carriage and the horses are stamping and steaming in the frozen air. 'It's so strange. It is almost as if you are an apparition. You have come to make my life better.'

I bow my head as he kisses me. 'I am so pleased to hear that,' I tell him. 'That's so good to hear.'

Then he is gone.

And I am left alone in his place.

I find myself mistress of Castle Frankenstein.

§

It isn't for very long, though.

It's me who spoils things. Me and my infernal curiosity, of course.

I've been told several times that I may wander freely anywhere in the castle. But where I must not venture is into my host's private chambers. The butler, the housekeeper, the maids: they've all told me this several times since I arrived in this place.

Now I feel that my relationship with Victor has changed. We are on first name terms. He has entrusted his home to my stewardship until he returns with his intended bride. He wants my approval.

Why shouldn't I wander where I will?

And so this is what I do, very late at night, when I find I can't sleep.

Secretly, I love the idea of being mistress of such a grand and mysterious place. I flit from landing to landing, always discovering new nooks and hidey holes. I even feel like I could be at home, here.

Some times I hear voices. Disembodied cries and moans. They hail from the attic, or from the cellars. The servants assure me they are nothing. Echoes and memories. My ears playing tricks. The wild eastern wind playing fast and loose round the turrets and the ancient tiles. I am to pay these worryingly animalistic cries no heed.

But still I wander through the darkest hours before dawn, wearing my polyester nightdress, carrying a candle like Wee Willy Winky. I try to block out the noises of the wind and the cries that I still feel sure come from within these walls...

And so it is that I, almost inadvertently, find myself straying into a part of the castle I don't recognise. The wall-hangings are unfamiliar. The twists and turns are new to me. And that queer aroma I noticed upon arriving here is much stronger. A reek of something rotting overlaid with that vinegary smell.

At first I don't understand that I've found myself in the forbidden chambers. And then it is too late. I decide that now I'm here I might as well have a good poke around.

Victor's rooms are terribly messy. Even dirty. The remains of meals and worn clothes lay strewn about his apartments, along with papers and opened books. Ink is splashed liberally across his pages of notes, spilled in his haste to scribble things down in his indecipherable hand. Strange, for one so fastidious – even dandyish – in his dress, to live like such a pig in private.

Then I come across a door that needs a hefty shove.

And within a find a roomful of treasure.

Ladies' clothes. Two whole wardrobes filled with sumptuous gowns and dresses. A cupboard stiff with old-fashioned wigs, suitable for every occasion. There's a cabinet teeming with paints and powders and a dressing table with a mirror as tall as I am.

For a while I am bewildered. Is Victor a dresser-up, I wonder? Is he one of those boys who likes to go about as a lady?

With greedy fingers and envious eyes I go through all the cupboards and drawers. What a lucky lady – or lady-boy – to have all this stuff belonging to them. And I thought I had a lot of make-up!

It hits me then. His mother. These are things belonging to his mother. Did she live here, at one time, then? Victor never mentioned her living here. He just said he left his family far away. He left them in the mountains and now they are all dead. He never said anything about hoarding all of these ladies' things for his mother.

All of the clothes are pristine, I realise. All the cosmetics and the wigs – everything here is new and never been used. It's as if everything is still waiting for the mother that never came here to visit. It is like standing in an empty tomb...

My heart goes out to him. The poor boy. No wonder he's been glad of my attention these past few nights. He's nervy and sweet. He needs mothering, of course he does.

I am so nosey. And I love all these fripperies and necklaces and jewels. I should realise that this is heading towards disaster, but daft old Brenda can't help herself, can she?

I open every single cupboard there is.

Even the last one.

It's up a little ladder and it's hidden by a stiff, brocaded curtain. My stomach does a little flip of alarm, warning me even as I snap the flimsy padlock between my fingers.

And I open the cupboard and gasp at the sharp scent of vinegar. Formaldehyde, rather.

I hold aloft my guttering candle and I'm almost gagging.

The flame is reflected off smooth, rounded glass. It's a jar as big as my head I'm looking at.

At first I think it's my own pale reflection I can see.

But the eyes in this woman's face are closed. Her lashes are long. Her mouth is a perfect cupid's bow, pursed as if she's dreaming an old and complicated dream.

I stare for a few long moments.

It's a woman's head in a jar of soupy liquid.

It's his mother's head.

*And she looks exactly like me.*

§

I reel backwards on the stepladder and lose my footing and the candleholder in the same instant. I glimpse a flashing arc of fire and, seconds later, feel a nasty bump on the back of my head.

But I find that I'm not lying on the plush carpet of the dressing room of Victor's mother.

I'm lying on something much harder and unforgiving... and cold.

And right now I'm toggled up in my heaviest coat and scarf and I'm lying flat out on the floor of the funicular .

I'm back home!

And the carriage is in motion. The whole machine lurches and descends and my heart and lights and offal go with it. I feel sick to the pit of my stomach. Sick with dread and relief all at the same time. Home! Home again at last! And I must only have been away for a matter of hours, or even minutes, perhaps. The fog is still cloying at the windows. It's no brighter out there in Sandsend.

More alarming, there's no sign of Effie. Is she still on the wires as the carriage clunks its way down the cliff face once more?

I sit up and drag myself onto the nearest seat.

I sneeze away the last vestiges of that horrible smell of pickled eggs. Did I really see what I saw? Victor's mother's severed head looking back at me? Looking back through the ages through these very same eyeballs?

It was all a fever dream, I tell myself. I was all a lot of nonsense. I'm having a nervous breakdown, or something similar. Or I've fallen under the spell of a wicked enchanter. That flaming duck! I gasp out loud. Yes! The magic duck is evil, quite definitely. And he led me to dream about terrible and impossible things... Yes! That's what happened here tonight...!

There's no sign of him anyhow, and I'm relieved. I'm on my feet and ready to dive out of the carriage door when it sets down – rather heavily – at the bottom of the track.

The door flies open and Effie is standing there, wreathed in luminous fog!

She's battered and exhausted and she's lost her hat and her face is smeared with oil and dirt – but she's alive!

She holds out her arms and we embrace with relief.

'I did it!' she cries. 'I worked the controls by myself! Aren't I marvellous?'

I hug her so hard it's like her skinny little body is going to snap. It seems like weeks since I last saw this irritating old woman. 'Effie, you've no idea how marvellous you are!'

It was the jolting of the carriage – knocking me to the floor – that brought me rudely out of my horrible fantasy. I know it now.

But there's no time to explain this to Effie now. We've a more terrible truth on our hands to deal with.

She shows me what's what in the funicular control room.

'I had to work the controls myself,' she says, gesturing to the far end of this room filled with complicated switches and levers and dials.

The man who ran the funicular has skedaddled.

She's shivering. She's about to have a funny turn. 'He was gone when I came in here. I shinned all the way up to the top and then I ran down the steps and I found the place abandoned.'

'Let's get out of here,' I tell her.

We sneak away into the night, and find ourselves a taxi. We ask the driver to get us back to Whitby, to Harbour Street toot de sweet. And we tip him heavily to keep his trap shut. He never saw two old ladies, one oily and bloody, the other still ravaged by nightmares about castles and mothers and sons.

And soon we are both back in our own beds.

§

The next day I really want a quiet time of it.

But I get an urge, first thing in the morning, to build a bonfire in my back yard.

I notice Effie watching me from her back window, alarmed by my manic energy and determination.

I'm piling up a lot of old rubbish that needs torching anyway. Some useless furniture, old papers, other bits and bobs I'm not wanting. But also, onto the heap goes everything – and I mean, absolutely everything – that I have ever bought from SAVE SAVE SAVE. Even the Magic Toilet Duck and the strange bottle of aromatic oil. Even the three polyester nighties in three different colours. All of it goes on, and it all burns quite satisfyingly when I put a match to it.

There's a bit of an explosion at one point, which makes a lot of noise and scorches my eyebrows and brings Effie running out of her back door.

'Whatever are you up to, ducky?' she shouts, over the roar of the flames, which for some reason are bright green. 'It doesn't matter,' I tell her. 'Cup of tea?'

She suddenly looks thirsty. I'm parched, too. 'Do you have any of that Romanian vodka left?'

It's the one thing from the cheap shop I haven't bunged on the bonfire yet. I know Effie's developed quite a taste for it.

'Dare we have some this early in the day, do you think..?'

I nod firmly. 'If you wish, Effie. I reckon we deserve it, don't you?'

# 7

# The Woolworth Horror

The dust settles gradually.

It takes a few days to get my breath back after all that. I try not to think about it too much and, when Effie comes round for her supper on Friday night, we don't talk a great deal about the debacle on the so-called haunted funicular .

I shrug, and bend to take my casserole out of the oven. I shoot her a glance through the steam, meaning 'let's not talk about it now.' And now, as we tuck into the beef stew and dumplings, and tear into the crusty loaf, Effie's moved determinedly onto the next thing. She's got that look in her eye again. Zeal, is what it is.

'Not another poltergeist,' I break in, sounding dismayed as I bisect a rather claggy dumpling.

'No no no,' she says impatiently. 'Nothing so mundane as that. This is something of quite a different order, Brenda. Something much more peculiar and deadly.'

'Oh, good,' I say, meaning to be ironic – which is wasted on my fellow investigator.

But still, as she starts to burble on, I find I don't mind so much, after all. Anything to take my mind off the curious astral journey I made last week to another time and another place. Though I wrote about all those appalling events in my secret journal, I haven't gone back and reread those pages. I've tried not to think about any of those occurrences at all. They were far too shocking and unsettling. I'm happy to be taken out of myself by whatever it is Effie is suggesting.

'Woolworths,' she says.

'Pardon?'

'Woollies. In the town. Right on the harbour.'

'Yes, it's been shut for years. Ever since the whole company went bust...' I sigh a little then, thinking of how I used to like nothing more than getting a quarter or sometimes even a full half pound of fancy sweets from their Pick-n-Mix. Shovelling all the sweeties into a paper bag and queuing to get them weighed.

Effie's shaking her head. 'No, if you think back, we had a pretty unusual Woollies here in Whitby. Every single branch in the country closed down. Every single branch in the world closed down. But our Woollies here in Whitby refused to die, remember? It stayed open for a full year after it was meant to have gone.' She gives me a significant look and in the candlelight it's quite ferocious. 'It was like a Zombie Woolworths.'

Actually, she's right. It was a most peculiar thing. The staff members were bewildered, but grateful to keep their jobs. But the sweeties gradually became rather tasteless, and the toys became dismal and phantasmal on the shelves. If you bought a record or a cassette tape it played ever so quietly, even with your stereo turned right up loud. Eventually, everything they had in stock simply faded away. After a year, there was nothing left and the doors were locked up for the last time.

'And nothing has ever taken over those premises,' says Effie. 'Not even one of your precious cheapy Pound Shops, Brenda. The windows have stayed dark. Darker than dark. If you peer in, right up close, there is simply nothing to be seen inside the old Woolworths. It's like the whole of the inside has simply ceased to exist...'

'Don't be daft,' I say. 'How could that be?'

'I don't know. But I've heard some very alarming things about it recently. Noises heard from within, late at night. Screams and so on, from deep within the building. Kids, teenagers broke into an upper window one night and barely escaped with their lives, they reckon. One kid's hair turned white as a result of what he said he underwent in Woollies that night.'

I roll my eyes at her. 'That's just daft kids. What are they coming to you, telling you stuff like that for?'

'They didn't. I overheard them. They weren't bragging or trying to convince anyone. There were three of them, and they were in my shop. Good kids. But I overheard them talking about Woollies and a night of terror they had endured when they broke into the old shop.'

'Hmmm.' I'm still sceptical, watching Effie slurping up the last of her stew. She's been so caught up in telling this tale that she's not been appreciating her supper at all. 'Well, I suppose we could look into it,' I tell her. 'But between this and the Carroll Hotel and Hans Macabre, we've got a lot going on...'

'We can handle it,' she says.

'Well, maybe we could talk to these kids,' I muse.

'It's already organised,' says Effie, smacking her lips. 'Ten o'clock tonight, at the amusement arcade on the front. That's where the young people enjoy hanging out. I've arranged for them to meet up with us and tell all.'

I nod, and think sadly of the quiet night I had planned. Friday night post supper was reserved for a marathon of 'Die Hard' movies. Effie seemed keen on the plan earlier. She's very partial to that kind of picture. But instead we're donning our coats and hats and setting off down the front, where all the lights of Whitby are quivering in the dark harbour tonight. A chill breeze comes rolling in from the North Sea and I'm trying my hardest not to think of it as foreboding.

§

Only one of the teenagers turns up to meet us. It's the boy who reckons his lank, colourless hair was jet black last week, before he and his friends ventured into the abandoned Woolworth building. It's true, the whiteness of his hair doesn't look like it was caused by a bad bleach job. It really looks as if it was caused by a terrible shock. I have seen such things before.

'The other two cried off at the last minute,' says Devlin. We're sitting in a grimy café by the arcades and he's drinking a can of Fanta Effie's bought. We've all got cans of pop with straws. He looks shifty and malnourished, as well as supernaturally blond. She's bought him chips as well. 'They were too scared,' he adds. 'They just don't want to talk about it. About the... things... we saw in Woolworths.'

As he sucks up the last of his orange pop Effie and I exchange a glance. Gut instinct tells me that this boy has been truly spooked and that he isn't faking this or stringing us along. It's taking a great deal of courage for him to meet us like this. I wonder if Effie is paying him cold hard cash for this information. She must be. He looks like he wants to run a mile.

He even seems unnerved by me. He won't look me in the eye and directs most of his utterances at the melamine tabletop.

'Tell us in your own words what happened to you and your friends, Devlin,' I urge him, in my most reassuring and maternal tone.

§

Much later that night.

'Here, you hold the bag.'

'Urggh.'

'I know it's heavy. It's got the rope in it, hasn't it? And all the other stuff you made us bring.'

'Sssh.'

'What now?'

'Keep your voice down, Brenda. We don't want anyone seeing us...'

'Good point. But I can't promise that this is going to be quiet, when I...'

Crash. Tinkle.

But, mercifully, the racket is short, sharp and soon over as I smash open the back public entrance of Woolworths. I tried messing on with pliers and a crowbar, but it was no use. Hefty brute force sometimes suits me better.

Effie is wincing all over at the noise. She's shrank back into the shadows, clutching our bag of tools. 'Sssshh!'

'All done now,' I tell her.